# SOUTH AFRI

*Dedicated to all of my South African friends who made a five year stay in the country an absolute pleasure for Pauline and myself...*

# PART 1 – SOUTH AFRICA

**ONE**

Sitting on the terrace of the Beverly Hills Hotel in Umhlanga Rocks, Durban, Tim Broad would never have believed he was in South Africa. On television, South Africa was about poverty and crime, and sitting where he was right now, looking over the Indian Ocean and following the course of a school of dolphins, he didn't feel threatened or poor at all, not like in some countries in sub-Saharan Africa. In fact he felt extremely spoilt.

The view was picture-perfect, beautiful blue skies, crystal-clear ocean, the umbrella shading him from the midday heat. The sandy beach stretched out of sight to the north and beauties with little clothing on walked the promenade. Down by the hotel pool, people stretched out in the African sun, and flowers in red, blue and white seemed to be everywhere.

He reached for his glass of Simonsig Methode Cap Classique – they were not permitted to use the name Champagne here, as it was patented to the French region it originated from – and sipped it carefully. He was trying to taste the difference between this drop of bubbly and an equivalent drop of Moet. So far he'd failed miserably.

He stabbed an olive with a cocktail stick and pushed it in to his mouth.

"So you feel we could sell the stuff down here," he asked his host. "I mean with your margins, and with me still making a decent profit?"

"I'm telling you man, it will sell. I have the contacts."

The host was one Victor Madlala, a wheeler-dealer of note, who could sell anything from houses to underwear at a profit. It certainly was a case of 'who you know' rather than 'what you know' here. If it was 'what you know', the guy would be begging on the street, Tim thought.

"So, Victor, I leave it to you. If you make a sale, I ship in a fire truck within a month. I'll include your commission and once I'm paid in full, I pay you."

"A fire truck Mr Broad! I don't do single items, my friend. Let's say ten to start."

"You bring the orders, I'll bring the trucks."

"I think I am going to keep you busy."

Let's wait and see, thought Broad.

Ten weeks later and with fourteen fire trucks on order, Tim Broad was wondering where all the trucks could even be going to. This Madlala guy was doing magic. And now he was also asking about road-making machinery, a subject Tim knew nothing about, but he had just completed a quick course on Google to learn about it. This could be a gold mine. OK, the commission was ridiculous, but still, if he made a profit…

Maybe on the traffic stuff he'd add another half percent for himself, he thought. Not too greedy, but a couple more bucks in his pocket.

Victor was sitting in a government office sharing a coffee with a friend from 'The Struggle' days. The old boy had been one of the underground leaders during the Apartheid years, a senior man in the African National Congress's executive committee. He had spent a little time in jail – nowhere famous like Robben Island or anything, just a jail in what was now Kwa-Zulu Natal – but for this he was owed favours. One of the gifts to him from the ruling party had been the position of Mayor of Empangeni in Zululand.

Victor had been a boy when all this was going on, but his father had died in the struggle for freedom, and Victor had been a runner for messages, so when government contracts came about, he was in a strong position to win them. The fire engines were a good example, these being supplied to the new King Shaka International Airport. They had only needed ten, but with his connections and knowledge of the funds available, he had managed to take the number up to fourteen.

Andile, the old man, sipped some more coffee.

"So what's in it for me?"

"One percent of total contract value," said Victor. "You know the budget, if it all comes to me, one percent is coming straight back to you."

"But you know we have to tender."

"Sure, but we can be 'inventive' with that, can't we? Maybe I supply the price after the tender is open, but all other documents at the right time? Or maybe we just state that you take the tender with the best technical solution and not the cheapest price."

"Hehehe!" laughed the old man. "You are just the same as your father."

"You mean a good friend?"

"No, I mean a bad old man."

"And now I make you a rich old man."

"And yourself my boy," he said. "A great mind, just like your dad."

"Siyabonga!" Victor replied, thanking the old man in his own tongue.

"We will do much business together my son."

"Holding thumbs," said Victor, using the local expression for good luck.

Victor phoned Tim on his cell after the meeting.

"Tim, Sawabona! I need to build a two lane road in Zululand to link some villages to the main N4 road from Durban. It will need some mobile equipment to crush down the chippings and lay the top layer of tarmac. I know nothing about these things, but could you look into it for me?"

"No problem Victor. How long do we have?"

"I need to start the project in three months. I think the road will stretch around fifty miles."

"Plenty of time," said Tim, wondering what sort of equipment he needed and what the lead time was on it. "No problems."

"I leave it all with you."

"Take it easy Victor."

After another hour on the web and previous research he had completed with the Google search engine, Tim had a list of equipment he thought should be enough to build a road. The price was well over ten million pounds and he was going into selling on a scale he had never experienced before. He had to admit he was getting nervous, but also excited. This was a freelance venture, and every penny profit would be his. The higher he drove that price, the better things were for him. And Victor had already admitted he knew nothing about this business. How greedy should he be?

He decided to go mid-range: instead of the usual one to one-and-a-half percent he took for himself, he would go for five. He'd probably lose some of it in negotiation, so it wasn't too greedy he consoled himself.

He started calling the European companies he'd found on the internet who supplied road-making gear. He started with Wirtgen for milling-machines and slip-form pavers, moved on to Hamm for rolling, then to Vogele for the asphalt, and Kleeman for the crushers. His shopping list was going well, and he began to envisage the fun he could have holidaying with half a million pounds.

Or maybe another percentage point would make negotiating easier, he told himself. Why not?

The deal went through without a hitch. Everyone was smiling as far as Tim could tell. The European suppliers had made a good margin as they dealt with someone not knowing the market, allowing them to off-load stock that would have stood around for months the way the market was. Tim had made his cut. And Victor seemed more than happy, so he also seemed to be getting something.

To make sure that no-one was changing their minds at the last minute, the suppliers insisted on a quick delivery, with everything backed up by a letter of credit from a major South African bank. With the short lead time given by Victor, this was fine with Tim.

A small niggle at the back of Tim's mind asked who was eventually footing the bill, but he soon pushed this aside as he thought about the holiday in the Seychelles.


Victor was with the Mayor again in his office, having just organised a first payment of a hundred thousand South African Rand to the man's account. They were drinking a shot of Johnny Walker Red Label to celebrate the occasion.

"If your father could see you now boy, eish, he would laugh, I'm telling you!"

"And if your doctor could see you now, Sir, he would tell you what a bad man you are!" Victor responded, laughing. "This stuff is a killer!"

"But what a way to die, eh?"

"We cannot die yet Mr Mayor. We have too much business to organise."

"Phuza!" the Mayor toasted Victor. "We have another tranche of money coming our way to build houses out at Mtubatuba," he told him. "Maybe you can start looking at that one."

"A pleasure Sir. How many houses would that be?"


'When you're on a wave, ride it,' Tim's father had always told him. And right now he was on a damned big wave.

Victor had been on the phone again, this time with a housing project – RDP Housing they called it in South Africa, but he really had no clue what the RDP stood for. Not that it mattered. He needed cement mixers – fixed and mobile – cranes – tower and mobile – and bricks, roofing material, electrical fittings and wiring, wood – the list was endless.

He mentally pinched himself – could this be true? It was only a year ago he'd been asked to visit South Africa by his then employer to chase up a project for a few fire engines, and now he was supplying enough equipment to keep him busy for years. As he worked for himself, deciding on the margins, he was becoming rich at a rate he could never have imagined.

Where was it all going? When would it end?

His own theory was that as long as he supplied what the Africans wanted, when they wanted it, he would remain the man to supply them. His invoicing was legal, his profits good but not obscene, and what happened after he supplied the stuff was really not his concern. It's not like he could change that side of it anyway. Africa was Africa. If he didn't do it, someone else would.

He got back on his computer and started looking at people supplying the building trade in the UK, and as he got to know the jargon, started looking at other sources, always trying to find a route to the original equipment manufacturer to ensure he got the unit at cost price, leaving more room for him to line his own pockets.

Half a bottle of whisky later, Victor left the Mayor's office and got in his BMW 8 Series, a beautiful sleek black number only three months old. He was too drunk to drive the hour-and-a-half back to his five-bedroom house in La Lucia north of Durban, but he didn't really care. If he was stopped he could soon drop a thousand Rand in the policeman's pocket and be on his way again.

He put on his D & G shades and had a long slug of cold water. There. That was better. He put the car into drive position and pulled away, over-steering at first but gradually getting things balanced. It would be a long hour or so on the road to Durban.

Tembe Mkize watched the car pulling away from the Mayor's office. He didn't look for long – there was no point dreaming about what would never be. He had on a pair of oversize jeans that had once belonged to someone else, held up by a length of rope he'd found on the road one day. His T-shirt was full of holes and faded from black to a whitish-grey colour and torn on the back. His hair was curled tight and short and hadn't been washed in a week. The training shoes he'd found in a skip had holes in and had been thrown out by a rich white guy. Nothing was new.

With the car gone, he went back to what he'd been doing before the driver had got in – digging in the rubbish bin for scraps of food, or a cigarette butt. He found a pizza box with the crusts still in, so he wolfed them down.

This was the other side of the track in Africa.

**TWO**

The Anglo-American mine in Rustenberg, in South Africa's North West Province, employed around 15,000 people from the local area and probably provided for more than five times that number. Pay and conditions were not good, and it was quite normal to read in the national newspapers or to see on the TV news that another person had died in the mine. It was quite normal to show dead bodies on TV in South Africa. Politicians talked endlessly about raising safety standards in the industry, but little or nothing seemed to alter, especially for the men working the product underground.

They mined platinum. South Africa was the second largest producer of platinum in the world, second only to the Russian Federation. Mining forms a large part of South Africa's Gross Domestic Product, or the country's worth. When the mine didn't work, the country lost money. Big money. And right now it wasn't working. The miners were on strike.

The strike had only lasted three weeks, but already the company had lost production worth approximately 700 million Rand, equating to about 70 million Euros. This was as a result of around 40 thousand ounces of lost platinum production.

Money was the reason behind the walk out. And support of miners from other areas, especially in Johannesburg, where over forty miners had died when police opened fire on them. It was said to be worse than the days of Apartheid. Dead bodies and wounded people everywhere. Screaming, frightened people. And only because they were striking about wages.

The miners earned about seven thousand Rand a month, or seven hundred Euro. They wanted twelve thousand Rand, not an incredibly large sum of money for working underground and risking life and limb daily. And this was pre-tax earnings.

The union negotiators tried to show the management what they were talking about, by showing them the extra cost, against the loss of earnings. The extra cost for all the workers would be in the order of seventy-five million Rand per month. The extrapolated cost of lost earnings per month was more than 900 million Rand. It wasn't too hard to work out that having the men back underground was a good thing for the company.

But nothing in South Africa was so easy and straight forward. The mine was already paying twelve thousand Rand per month per man. So where was the problem?

The problem was that the money the mine paid was paid to a senior party figure, a man who was strong with the unions. It was believed he could stop industrial actions like the strike from ever happening. In the end, he was causing the strike. He was receiving the full money from the mines to pay the men, but then only paying them the seven thousand Rand. The rest was disappearing off in to a bank account in Lichtenstein.

The day was hot, and the striking miners were getting restless. The unions promised daily that the strike would be resolved 'soon' and that they would be returning to work with the new higher wage. Many didn't believe it but going back to work was also a dangerous thing to do.

Some of the men went back to work. They had no money, and whilst on strike, would get none. They had families at home: hungry mouths to feed.

One of these men was Mikey Morwe. He was forty years of age and had worked the mines in the area since he was fifteen. He had never finished school but had learned how to operate drilling equipment in the shaft by watching and copying other older workers. He had five children, the oldest sixteen and the youngest only three. His wife was pregnant with child number six. He also supported his wife's mother and father and their immediate 'family' as was customary in Africa, in a tradition known as 'ubuntu' where everyone was loosely related to one another. He needed food, and to get that he needed money. So he decided to go back to work.

He knew this to be a dangerous thing to do, because the strikers did not accept strike-breakers, fearing that enough of them would cause the action to fail. Mikey knew that if he was caught returning to work, they would certainly hurt, if not kill, him. But he needed food for his family, so he decided to take the chance.

The mine had one main entrance, but no shortage of other unofficial ways to get in. Mikey knew the strikers were camped out by the main entrance, as this was where the media were based and also where they could heckle the management when they came to work, stoning their cars.

He made his way to a break in the fence about a kilometre from the gate and passed through unobserved. He reported to his usual work station, only to find he was the only worker there.

"Hey Mikey, what you doing here?" asked his white supervisor.

"I need work boss," he replied. "Need food for the kids."

"Shame the rest of your boys don't think the same." The supervisor spat on the ground. "You know I can't let you work down there alone. Health and Safety Policy."

"But if you were with me boss…"

"No way Mikey! I can't do that."

"So what other jobs can I do?"

"There's no work today, and you can thank your friends out there for that. I'm afraid I have to send you home."

"But I need to work. I need money."

"I'll give you a lift up to the gate, and you can scoot off home. Try again tomorrow but bring some friends."

"I can't go out the gate boss, they'll see me."

"You know there's only one way in and one way out Mikey. I'll drive you there now."

"I can't do that boss."

"You will be breaking company rules if you go out any other way. Then you will lose your job."

"OK boss, but please take me out of the gate. They can't see me leaving the mine."

"I'll do that. Come on!"

They went to the supervisor's double cab station wagon, or 'Bakkie' in the local parley. The supervisor climbed in and indicated that Mickey should get in to the passenger seat.

"Please boss, I hide in the back."

"Whatever you prefer. I think you are exaggerating the situation though."

They drove to the gate, Mikey lying on the floor between the front and rear seats. He was sweating. This was not what he had had planned for today.

As they reached the gate, the crowd of more than two thousand strikers started shouting. The Bakkie was bombarded with stones, the sound of them loud as they bounced of the cabin of the vehicle. The crowd backed away slightly though as the Bakkie forced its way forward. A few hundred yards and it would be clear of the mob.

Suddenly a large stone hit the windscreen, turning it opaque as the shatterproof glass turned in to a thousand tiny gems of glass. Blinded, the white man hit the brakes and wound down the window.

"You stupid bastards. You're gonna pay for this," he yelled.

This only led to another round of intense shelling from the crowd, and the side window at the back also shattered, showering Mikey with window glass.

"Keep going boss," he shouted, his voice now rising an octave as the crowd bayed outside of the car. "Please don't stop."

But it was too late. The supervisor had already opened his door, shouting loudly at anyone willing to listen. Then a brick hit him on the back of the head and he went down, unconscious. The crowd stormed forward, pulling the wing mirrors off the car and lighting the tyres. Mikey couldn't move, hoping they would get bored and leave the vehicle, letting him have a chance to escape.

The front passengers door was pulled open and the glove compartment raided. The rear door came next, and Mikey was exposed.

"Strike breaker! Strike breaker!" the cry went up.

Mikey tried to get out and run, but the force of so many people pushing towards the vehicle meant he had absolutely no chance. He was grabbed by the legs from the other side of the Bakkie and dragged out in to the crowd, his eyes wide with fear.

"Strike breaker! Strike breaker! Strike breaker!" the chant was deafening. "Strike breaker!"

They tore off his shirt. His shoes went next and then his trousers and underwear. He was naked, scared out of his mind, and knew the probable end result of this nightmare.

"They made me go in," he shouted, not to be heard. "I was trying to steal mine equipment off the whites." Any lie was better than dying.

He was being carried to a central area. Passed from group to group, to where a senior union leader was waiting.

"Strike breaker!"

The leader waved his hands to silence the crowd.

"So we have someone who wants to go against us?" he asked the crowd. A roar of agreement came back to him.

"I was forced to go to the mine." Mikey tried arguing.

"Do you believe him?" The crowd roared back a negative verdict.

"So what do we do with the scum who go against us?"

The roar was louder than ever now and the answer was clear to all.

"Kill him! Kill him! Kill him! Kill him!"

"Please take care of our problem"

Four large men made a clearing in the centre of the crowd and pushed Mikey to the ground. He tried to get up, but one of them kicked him hard in the knee cap, making him fall. The four of them then began kicking him hard, his face, his chest, his stomach, his genitals, everywhere. After about three minutes of this he lay still, unconscious. The four backed off, and two women came forward, a car tyre in their hands. They hung it around his neck and doused it in petrol. Then they set it on fire.

Mikey came around as he burned, howling like an animal.

This was the African way. This was what they called a 'necklace.'

He died thinking of his kids and wife, and where they would find their next meal.

**THREE**

The leader of the ANC Youth League looked at his ten thousand pound white gold Omega watch and prepared for his speech to the masses assembled at the conference in Polokwane, the heart of Limpopo Province. He thought about the dinner he would be attending that night in Johannesburg, where tickets were costing fifteen thousand Rand a head. It would be a rush to escape here and get there on time, but it would be worth it. Twenty percent of all the takings tonight would be going to him and his campaign to nationalise the mining sector.

His name was Oliver Justice, a fitting name for one who was trying to bring 'justice' to the poor of his country. Not that it was really his country: he'd been born in Zimbabwe – or Rhodesia as it was back then – but his parents had moved to South Africa in search of work, so he had grown up and been educated there.

He checked the watch again, a little bit of a nervous reaction before every address, but something the masses never witnessed. Then he stepped out on the platform, moving quickly behind the dais, hands raised above his head, feeding off the screams, cheers and clapping of the audience. He breathed in deeply, taking control of his nerves, knowing that once he started it was easy.

"Comrades!" he yelled into the mike, driving the speakers to a point of distortion. "Fellow countrymen." He paused again, milking the feedback. "Brother South Africans."

They reached fever-pitch now, making even rational thinking all but impossible.

"I am here today to talk to you all about the huge imbalances in our great country. About the greed of the white man and the international corporations we are forced to host. About our poor brother Africans working from daylight to dusk. Underground. Not knowing the heat and beauty of the sun, not seeing the light of day. About earning almost nothing for their labours, while here on the surface, the white man is lining his pocket with our resources and our blood. Is this fair?"

He stopped letting the question and the message sink deep into their souls. He counted to ten slowly, not allowing the silence to rush him. As he hit ten, he hit a high note.

"WE ARE NOT HERE TO FEED THE WHITE MAN. WE ARE NOT HERE TO SERVE A FOREIGN COMPANY."

He paused again, a count of fifteen this time. Then he came back in a loud whisper.

"We deserve better things brothers. We deserve to live better. We deserve to benefit from the riches of our land." Then back to full volume. "BUT THIS CAN NEVER HAPPEN WHILE WE DO NOT CONTROL THOSE RESOURCES. IT'S OUR COAL."

He waited and a chant went through the crowd, started by his PR people and the crowd they had employed.

"Control our coal! Control our coal! Control our coal!"

He put his arms straight out from the shoulders, raising them above his head in a clap in time with the chant. He let it run a while longer. It would sound great on a CNN or BBC News channel, a clear message to the world.

"I will put my neck on the guillotine for you," he told the crowd, running a finger across his throat. "I will put myself against the white man, against the mega companies, AGAINST OUR OWN GOVERNMENT! I WILL GET US SOME OF THE MONEY THAT THEY ARE STEALING! I WILL GET US OUR SHARE!"

The crowd went wild. Justice knew that most of this was empty promise right now, but as long as people believed and supported him, all of that could change.

"Comrades. Brothers. I love you all. We will win."

He raised his arms above his head again, smiling broadly at the thousands of listeners, and basked in the noise made by the massed crowd. Turning, he walked off stage, waving a last goodbye.

His mind was already in Johannesburg, the evening meal and his next public address.

And whether he should wear the Yves Saint Laurent suit, or the Armani one…

**FOUR**

Khayelitsha was not a place anyone really wanted to live, but for the minority races there, it was a desperately bad place. The whole township – as it was described in official and media circles – was made of shacks. They were put together by their inhabitants, and made up of bits of wood, cardboard, road signs, and anything else that could be used to create a wall or a roof. The sanitation was a joke – people just found a clear area, often next to the main road, and relieved themselves there. Electricity was 'stolen' from anything that had local electrical power – transformers, street lights, traffic lights – and people often electrocuted themselves, or caused electrical fires in the huts that formed the town.

Theft in the township was uncontrollable. The bigger your gang, the more you could take, and the police didn't even bother trying to control the gangs. The police didn't even bother entering the township after dark, it was that dangerous.

When things went bad – which was fairly often – the groups would stick together and find someone to blame for the 'bad thing,' whether it was rain storms that washed out the shacks, a fire, no money, or because someone's daughter had been raped. There was a herd mentality. Anyone not in the 'herd' was therefore outside of it.

Outside of the main groups were immigrants who had left their countries to try and make it in South Africa, seen by many as the most advanced country in Africa, and a place where the poor man could make a life for himself and his family. They came from Somalia, Zimbabwe, Mozambique, Nigeria and Congo to name a few. Some of them did well: the stronger groups stuck together, and soon ended up running drug rings, prostitution outfits and other illegal activities. But the smaller groups had to be less overt, more peace-loving, some of them from their natural tribal characters. They were easy targets.

Mini Khafu's daughter had not been seen for three days now. She was a fourteen-year-old girl who thought she was twenty-one. Not a bad girl. Her name was Suzi, and many locals feared the worst.

"She didn't come home for two nights now," she cried to one of the township's elders. "She ain't never done this before. It's not her way."

"Have you spoken to her school friends?" Temba Gama asked softly. "Does she have a boyfriend?"

"I asked everybody, and even walked to her school and asked the teachers. No-one has seen her."

"Has anyone been hanging around your doors, watching the house?"

She thought about this a minute, tears rolling down her face from her big brown eyes, and her hand running through her long braided hair.

"Only the shop-keepers from next door, those bloody Zimbabweans," she said quietly. "They always try and buy my shack. They say it would be better for their business."

"But do they watch the house, watch your daughter?"

"I think they do, but I always thought it was my house they wanted, not my Suzi." The tears flowed again.

"Maybe we should go and talk to them," said Temba. "Maybe they can guide us."

"Thank you Temba," she said hugging him. "Thank you."

She left the hut and Temba called a couple of the men to him. He talked quietly to them for a few minutes and then they left to gather their followers to them. Soon twenty big black men were outside of Temba's shack, some armed with machetes, the rest with sticks.

"We are only going to ask some questions," Temba told them. "If the answers are not good, then we must look after our own people."

Just then, Mini ran back around the corner, wailing and crying and screaming all at once. She went directly to Temba.

"She's dead. The police found her by the road. She was raped and beaten, then strangled."

She screamed and the woman around her cried with her, the wailing building up in volume and the tensions in the gathering crowd reaching a tipping point where no control would be left. Temba looked at the woman and knew that things were getting out of his control. The men who had gathered were also getting restless now.

"Who did this?" one of them demanded.

"We think it was the Zimbabwean shopkeepers next door to us," wailed Mini. "They've been watching our house."

"The bloody foreigners again," said one man. "Come to our country, rape our children, steal our work."

"We must teach those bastards a lesson."

"Let's go!"

The men began walking around toward the house of Mini and the general dealer store run by the Zimbabweans. Mini led the way with five other women, all of them screeching and crying. The number of men was now over thirty, all brandishing a weapon of some sort. They were mad and shouting random remarks about the foreigners that were ruining their country. How they must put things right. Take the law in to their own hands.

As they past Mini's shack and reached the front of the store, one of the Zimbabwean men came out of the shop to see what the commotion was.

"He is one of them!" screamed Mini.

"Did you steal her daughter?" demanded one of the men, his machete held threateningly towards the Zim man.

"What do you talk about?" the man asked, confused.

"Was it you that raped her fourteen year old daughter?" asked another man.

"You killed my Suzi!" screamed Mini.

"I did nothing," the man tried to claim, defending himself. A second man had come out of the shop.

"Maybe it was him."

"Perhaps both of them were involved."

The two men looked at one another, fear in their eyes, not certain what was going on or why they were any part of it. They could feel the crowd's anger towards them; could sense the blood boiling in the men facing them. The second man to emerge turned and ran through the shop, not waiting to reason with the mob. Five of the crowd ran after him.

"They are guilty, or why would he run?" asked Mini, other women picking up the chant. "Guilty. guilty. guilty. guilty…"

The lone Zimbabwean tried to reason. "I don't know your daughter, I only run the shop."

"He spied on Suzi, I saw him."

The first swing of the machete sliced into his upper arm, leaving a three inch gash, blood pouring out of it. The second swing hit the side of his head, leaving a bloody wound and taking the top of his ear off. Too late, he realized how bad the situation had become. He tried to run, but it was now far too late.

The other men joined in, machetes chopping at his flesh and sticks hitting his body. Soon he was bleeding from over thirty wounds and he fell to the earth. The sticks continued their assault on him until he became unconscious.. The chopping continued. One blow to the side of his neck severed his carotid artery and within thirty seconds, the blood had left his body. He was dead.

His friend escaped the chasers and kept running until he reached the V & A Waterfront in the tourist centre of Cape Town. He knew he could never return to Khayelitsha. He knew he could not live in South Africa, knew his friend was most likely dead.

It was time to return to Harare. Things there were also bad, but at least he would be home.

## FIVE

The dinner was going well, well into the fourth course. The fillet steak was served with sweet potato, asparagus and creamed spinach, topped with a gravy: a reduction of the meat juices with a hint of cinnamon. All of the wines were South African, produced in the Western Cape, at some of the best wine farms in the country. Oliver Justice was sipping Chocolate Block – a red pinotage, selling at about two hundred Rand a bottle in a liquor store - and starting to think ahead to the speech he would make after the dessert course.

More than five hundred people were eating, and the caterers were doing a great job for such a vast gathering. All major African National Congress Youth League (ANCYL) members were present, along with their supporters – or people that needed their support for re-election – from the main ANC party. COSATU – the trades union organization – and the country's communist party (SACP) were also well represented.

The press had a strong contingent, knowing that Oliver had a habit of saying something controversial at these functions, especially when his lips were loosened slightly by the wine and spirits.

Surprisingly, a number of senior mine executives also paid the price to eat with their supposed enemy. Their view was an old one: stay close to your friends and closer still to your enemies. Better to hear the words first hand, not dressed up by the press corps.

The rest of the attendees were hangers on, wives, girlfriends – and it should be remembered that most rich black Africans had at least one of each – and bankers, who would win from the event no matter which way things went. If mines stayed private, they would continue to benefit from the companies operating now; if the mines were owned by the government, they would still need to bank the money, borrow money and get money out of the country.

The fifth course was now being served at the first tables, a crème caramel, with a blob of chocolate ice cream on the side. The speech was getting close now.

The lady next to Oliver was asking him a question about how he felt Bafana Bafana would get by in the upcoming African Cup of Nations. He didn't really care – he knew their performances on the football field of late had been woeful– but he gave the correct political answer, saying they would make the African nation proud. She smiled at this. Maybe he should consider her for a bit of fun later…

The dessert finished and the plates were cleared. It was time to earn his money.

"Fellow Africans," he began. "I thank you all for being here tonight and supporting what I believe is a very worthy cause. We all need to pull together to ensure it moves forward and moves forward swiftly." He paused, his eyes drifting around the room, feigning eye contact with the whole audience.

"South Africa's mineral resources belong to South Africa," he continued. "Why do we allow others to benefit from them, when we have indigenous people living here with nothing to their name? Why do we allow them to rape our earth, digging the heart out of our land, and taking the profits to their home countries while South Africa receives just a pittance?"

Again, eye-contact, a count to ten.

"Because our government is weak," he raged. "They are getting the back-handers, they are lining their offshore accounts, and they are selling the souls of the rest of our nation."

He looked down, again counting, this time to twenty. A few people started whispering, wondering if that was the end of the address.

"WE MUST CHANGE OUR LEADERS." he bawled. "WE MUST HAVE STRONG LEADERS WHO WILL TAKE BACK WHAT IS RIGHTFULLY OURS."

"Yeah!" shouted a number of the guests, mainly those belonging to the ANCYL. The cry grew as more joined. "Yes. Yes. Yes."

"But how can we do this?" he asked, silencing them again. "We can do it together. I can do it with your support. WE AS A TEAM ARE UNSTOPPABLE."

Thunderous applause around the room, almost everyone on their feet. He'd done it again, won the day.

The press secretary from the ANCYL took up his microphone. "Oliver will take three questions from the press, then we return to our celebrations and coffees. Then it's time for a dance."

Oliver looked to the back of the room where the press had been placed at a single table. They were holding a quick debate about how to best use the three questions they had just been granted.

"Are our learned friends from the newspapers ready to shoot?" asked the PR man.

The first press corps member stood up, clearing his throat and taking the microphone.

"Hi Oliver, I'm Larry Savage from CNN. Do you intend to negotiate a compensation package with the present mine operators when you put the mines under state control?"

"Why?" asked Oliver instantly. "Why? Did they not benefit from Africa's riches for the past hundred years? Have they not already been over-compensated by the profits they boast every year? Have they not killed thousands of our men is a constant search for more money and less safety?" He paused. "No, I have no intention in my plans to give them anything, except perhaps a plane ticket home for their Chief Executives."

The room erupted in laughter at the answer, the Youth League members loving the clear attack on the foreign owners.

"Question number two?"

"I'm Danny Walsh from the BBC, London. Running a mine profitably is a major enterprise," he started. "Does South Africa have people with the skills to do this?"

"YOU BASTARD," stormed Oliver. "DO YOU REALLY THINK WE ARE STUPID BLACKS WITH NO EDUCATION, NO BRAINS, NO COMMON SENSE? GET OUT OF THIS ROOM! I PAY HIS FLIGHT OUT OF MY COUNTRY TONIGHT. BASTARD."

He threw his wine glass in the direction of the press table, but it fell short and landed on the mine executives, hitting the CEO of one of the major players.

"GET HIM OUT!" he yelled again.

With questions prematurely over, the clapping began again. Two bouncers had grabbed Danny Walsh and were unceremoniously hauling him out of the dinner without letting him pick-up his sound and video equipment.

The party went on until late that night, but without the presence of the press or mining delegations. They had other things to sort out.

## SIX

It was strike season in South Africa. It started normally with the truckers, spread then to the unsupplied petrol stations, knocked on immediately to the ports and rail heads as these could not be cleared of cargo, then the whole country was effectively closed for business. It was always about wages, but many employers believed it was simply a wish to not work. Wage demands would begin at requests for 20% pay rises, and eventually settle on ten or twelve percent, but getting to those totally unrealistic figures would easily ensure a week away from business.

The strikes also led to interruptions in coal supplies, these knocking on to interruptions in power availability, causing the local governments to introduce power outages. These would normally come with no warning and affect whole districts. They would last from a couple of hours to a couple of days.

Trying to run a business in these circumstances was just about impossible, so most bosses just sent the workforce home. Others just let them stay at work, read books and drink coffee.

The unions would also be involved in this, jumping on the bandwagon and passing the effect on to metalworkers, electrical engineers, manufacturers and others. Pickets would be organized at the gates of business premises, cars stoned and windows smashed to stop people from trying to break the strike. Beatings would be handed down to anyone stupid enough to criticize the situation.

The effect on the South African economy was always devastating, costing billions of Rand each year. It wasn't only the direct cost of not producing coal and not delivering it to the port for example: there was also the additional costs such as demurrage, through ships being delayed in their loading and discharge, and the loss of vessels to ports in neighbouring countries, often never to return.

Sometimes even the people operating critical services also went on strike. Doctors and nurses, the army, the police – leaving not even a skeleton staff to cover emergencies.

"We cannot give in to the strikers, at least not for such ridiculous demands," said the senior politician for the opposition party, the Democratic Alliance. "We must negotiate something in line with the cost of inflation, otherwise everyone will look for a fifteen percent rise. We will cripple the economy."

"With no minerals leaving the country, the economy is already crippled," said the President. "We must let them have what they want to get some trade moving again."

"But we cannot give them such large rises EVERY year. We are becoming more expensive to produce products than even Europe. No-one will invest here."

"These people had nothing for so long," injected an old ANC minister. "They deserve to be treated better. You whites had a good life forever, we always had to live off your scraps."

"Thank God this isn't televised," the President said. "The Afrikaans would have us over the barrel for racism in reverse. You know we must be careful what is said in public."

"Oliver Justice doesn't seem to worry about it," said the old campaigner, more to himself.

"Oliver Justice is proving a pain in the arse for us when it comes to trying to attract foreign investment in to the mining sector," stormed the President. "I am black, I was also living through the Apartheid Era, but I still understand that we cannot run a country on fresh air. When will you?"

"You don't live in the gutter anymore," the old campaigner said, adding belatedly, "Sir."

"And neither do you Godfrey. Not for quite some time."

The DA leader came between the two. "We are meant to support one another. To work together. This is like a playground argument."

The President sighed. "You're right. If we all fall out, then our friend Justice is winning his game. The government will be weak and the Youth League will begin running us. We will cease to be the largest economy in Africa and end up being like Zimbabwe. Why can people not learn from what has happened just over their borders?"

"Sorry Mr President," apologized the old-timer. "Is Mandela willing to make a speech at the party conference? It would go a long way towards pulling people back together."

"I hope he will, but we must be fair on him: he is now an old man, and he is spending more time in the hospital now than he does in his home."

"This is sad but true. He saved the country from civil war back in 1994, but I think he would be out of his depth this time around."

"What about his children? Or another of the freedom fighters?"

"I think we must be honest and accept that the people from back then are all getting too old for modern politics. We need someone to identify with the youth, but also to have the age to demand their respect, a difficult mix to find."

"Why not his daughter?"

"Since he lost his granddaughter in the car crash, he has tried to keep the family out of the public eye. I'm not sure that she would agree."

"Then we have to think of an alternative."

"A good alternative."

"And we have to stop fighting with each other," the President added. "We have enough enemies without fighting among ourselves."

## SEVEN


Diane Kruger pulled up in her Avensis at the gate of her house in Pretoria and reached down behind her legs to locate her handbag. It had been a long and hard day in the office, with lots of talk about retrenchments and longer working hours for whoever survived the cull. It had been this way for months, everyone blaming the 'financial crisis' that threatened the United States and most of Europe. She – like many others in the office – put it down to bad management.

She found the bag and opened it, searching for the remote control that would open the large motor driven gate that guarded her home. Like most women, she had a good assortment of brushes, make-ups, jewellery, and other knick-knacks that made the search all the harder. Her hand closed over the remote.

CRASH!

Her driver's window imploded, showering her with small glass particles and momentarily stopping her from the natural task of breathing. She looked to her right where the window had been in time to see a man's arm coming through it, grabbing her by the throat.

"Out now bitch!" he ordered loudly, pulling the door open.

Another man reached in the opening door, allowing the first man to release her and fully open it. She thought about the pepper spray in the handbag, and how she was not going to get the chance to reach for it.

"Get out!" She was being dragged out anyway, but not from her wanting to. A third man had moved in to view, then a fourth.

"Get her to the back!" number three instructed.

She was literally carried off her feet to the trunk of the car, which number four was opening. There was a bag of shopping in there, but he just shoved it to the front and then turned to assist his colleagues, who were lifting her in there.

"You can have the car," she wailed. "Please take it! And the handbag. My wedding ring."

"Shut up bitch, we're having you first then we decide what to do."

She was in the boot now, smelling the spare wheel, the oil and petrol that made up the smells of a car. She was feeling sick: partly from the smell but mostly from fear.

"Please let me go," she pleaded. "I've got two kids to look after."

The boot was slammed shut, almost catching her fingers. It was pitch black in there, and her level of fear just shot up another two notches. She could hear them climbing into the car seats, feel the movement of the car as their bodies entered it. Reverse was selected, and the car re-entered the road with a screech of tyres.

She screamed trying to attract attention, but only frightened herself more by doing it in the enclosed space. She kicked the back of the seat, but just heard the men laughing about it, before one of them said to stop it or she'd be shot now.

She lay there, petrified now, having no idea where the car was going as it completed a number of turns.

After about fifteen minutes it stopped and the engine was shut down. She could hear the men talking quietly amongst themselves. Then doors opened. She couldn't hear them anymore. She wondered what they were doing.

The boot was opened after a five minute wait, during which time they had obviously come to some sort of agreement on how to move forward.

"You don't have much money lady," the first man she had seen told her. "Why should we let you go when you don't pay?"

"My ATM card is in there. We can get some more."

"We got your ATM card, but we don't have the number," he said. "Maybe you tell the number, and we let you go?"

She didn't trust him, but she had no choice. She knew from police advisory services that it was better not to fight, not to argue, just give them everything and live to fight another day. They would get things anyway, just using unpleasant methods.

"It's twenty-one ten, my date of birth. You can see that on my ID."

"You sure about that lady?"

"Twenty-one ten," she replied quickly, getting more frightened again. "We can go to an ATM and I'll show you,"

"Let's do that," number three said, heading for the front of the car again. The boot slammed once more, and she knew that the ATM might be a chance to draw attention to herself and the four blacks using her car.

The drive was short again, no more than ten minutes. A muffled piece of information came from the front of the car.

"We gonna try the number lady, so you better be right!"

She panicked realizing that they weren't going to let her out. There would be no chance to create a scene, no chance to attract attention. She started kicking the lid of the trunk and shouting as loudly as possible. She was in serious panic now, suffering from the effects of the cramped space she was confined in.

The boot popped open. The four men were looking down at her, smiles on their faces. There was no mall or ATM in sight.

"You thought you could get us all in trouble lady," said number one, now firmly evident as the leader. "You thought you could get some police to come and get us."

"No mister, I just got so scared in there," she whimpered. "You got to let me go."

"We'll let you go lady, but first we have to punish you for trying to get us in to trouble. Get her out," he told the others.

She was dragged from the car, struggling, but with no chance to escape four fit young black men. They moved her to the front bonnet, then forced her to lie on it, two holding her arms to either corner of the windscreen. The other two forced her legs open and then a hand went up the inside of her skirt.

"No!" she screamed.

The area was a piece of wasteland, with no civilization to be seen. There were no houses, not even shacks. No-one was there to hear her yells. No-one was around to help her out.

Her knickers were ripped away from her body and the skirt too. A black finger probed between her legs, trying to enter her body. She kicked at the man doing it and received a punch to the side of the head for her efforts. She continued fighting, getting another smash to the side of the skull, then another that knocked her out.

When she came to, one of the blacks was inside of her, raping her. She wasn't sure if he was the first, but she soon knew he was not to be the last, as they took their turns. She felt blood on her brow and blood between her legs. She thought about the high incidence of HIV in the black community and wondered if she was about to become a white statistic.

Eventually they finished and pushed her off the car so they could drive away.

A bad day in the office had ended as a dreadful day in the world.

**EIGHT**


Stuart Wellesley was relatively new to South Africa, having joined a local branch Coopers & Lybrand from the UK only three weeks earlier. He came from London and considered himself fairly street-wise, but he still had made a point of reading as much as he could about South Africa before going there. He knew about trying to keep the car moving by slowing down before a red traffic light, or robot as they called them here; he knew to hide the PIN on his debit card at ATMs and not to get distracted by others while using them; he avoided driving at night as much as possible, and also did not drive in areas deemed 'dodgy' by colleagues.

He was starting to feel quite at home in Johannesburg, especially when he was in the area of his Sandton hotel.

He was having an evening out with a lady colleague that he was seriously interested in. She was a local white South African called Tracy Jordaan and this was their first real date, after a couple of pleasant chats at lunchtimes when the office had all stopped for a bite out at the local coffee shops. She was blond, long legged, and gorgeous!

They went first to the bar in the Michelangelo Hotel, paying top dollar by South African standards, for a couple of drinks, but when he compared it to any boozer in London, deemed it cheap at half the price. She was enjoying it and really seemed to like his company.

"So there I was, sipping on my G & T, when in walks the boss, all lovey-dovey, with the secretary of the next door law firm. Not a bad thing you might think. But she was married to my best friend, and the boss was married too. That's London for you."

The two of them laughed at the story and Tracy set out on one of her own.

Finishing their drinks, they walked down to Nelson Mandela Square and pondered over which of the many restaurants to use. Pizza, pasta, seafood, steak... the choices were endless and none of them bad.

They eventually agreed on a steak – might as well break the bank, he thought – and were soon seated at a table and drifting through a never-ending menu.

"Have you ever eaten wildebeest?" he asked her.

"Of course. I was brought up here,"

"Always looks such a stupid animal," he said. "Can't imagine actually eating one."

"They are stupid, but I can tell you that when they are cooked right, they are great to eat. Try it!"

"I might just do that," he said. "Any idea what you want?"

They soon settled on sharing a calamari starter, wildebeest and a fillet steak, all washed down by a Beyerskloof Pinotage.

Starter gone, it was on to the main, all the time chatting and becoming closer to each other.

"Would you like to try a bit of my wildebeest?" he asked her, carving off a corner and dipping it in the gravy.

"Sure," she replied, leaning over and taking his fork, eating directly from it.

He could feel the wine was working and the chemistry between the two of them was unquestionable. She held his hand as she returned the fork, chewing the piece of game meat.

"Lovely," she acknowledged. "You like a piece of fillet?"

"I haven't had a bad piece of steak since I came to South Africa," he told her. "I'd love a bite."

He wondered if she would let him eat from her fork, and when she did, he felt his heart speeding up. Things were looking very good. He poured more wine in to both their glasses, finishing the bottle.

"Dessert?" asked the waiter, interrupting a silent look between them.

"Er, not for me," said Stuart, recovering his composure. "I'm full, but perhaps a coffee and a good brandy?"

"The same for me," Tracy said, smiling at his discomfort. "Your place or mine?" she said quietly, knowing where the evening was going now.

"I'm still in a hotel if that's OK for you," he said hurriedly.

"Then let's go to mine," she told him. "It's Sunday tomorrow, so no point us getting disturbed in the morning by room service."

Coffees and cognacs arrived, and he tried to be polite, but at the same time finish them as soon as humanly possible. She grinned, but was doing the same.

"Could I get the bill please?" he asked.

"Let's go Dutch!"

"No this one's on me," he said putting his card on the wallet containing the bill, not even checking it, not taking his eyes off this beauty in front of him.

"Would you like to leave a tip?" The waiter was not shy and was rewarded for his rudeness.

"Just add ten percent please," Stuart told him, eyes still firmly on Tracy's. "Then bring me the slip to sign."

The waiter looked at him, then left quickly with the card, not believing his luck. Within a minute he had copied the details with a small machine in his jacket pocket. He returned with the credit card slip and the card and Stuart signed off.

Arm in arm they went to the taxi rank, stopping to kiss twice on the way. They needed one another now, all other things far from their minds.

Stuart's cell phone beeped in the middle of their second kiss. "Be the bank telling me I used my card for dinner," he said, still lip to lip, distorting the words. "I'll check it's OK in the morning. More important things right now."

In the taxi, the smooching continued, getting heavier by the minute. Tracy felt Stuarts hand cup her right breast, and she knew it was going to be a long and sleepless night. In the darkness of the back of the taxi she ran her hand down his chest and on to his jeans, feeling a hot bulge down there.

"Oh my God," he whispered.

"That's forty-three Rands," the driver announced, bringing them back to the real world. Stuart stuffed a fifty in to his hands, as Tracy headed for her front door and took her keys out. He followed.

The phone beeped again, but he didn't notice it, or simply didn't care.

Tracy had the door open and he came in to the hall area of the flats and pushed her against the wall, kissing her hard.

"Not here, silly," she said. "This is a communal area."

She went up a flight of stairs Stuart following and looking half way up her legs as he followed.

She was amazing.

She opened the door marked with a number four and went inside. He followed and this time she grabbed him, opening his shirt and trying to get his jeans unbuttoned. Stuart was returning the favour, unfastening her blouse and lifting a breast from her brassier and kissing her nipple before even unhooking the rear clip.

As she lowered herself to her knees, the phone beeped again, but this time he definitely did not hear it and nor did she as she took him in to her mouth.


At nine o'clock the next morning, after another session in the bathroom, the two of them came through to the kitchen area of Tracy's flat, her in a white bath robe and

Stuart wrapped in a cream towel. They tried to keep a respectable distance from each other, as every time they touched, it led to something more.

Tracy put the kettle on and Stuart watched the way her blond locks fell around her face, and the impish grin she gave when she looked his way.

She seemed too innocent for the things they had got up to the previous night, but he was more than pleased she was not.

His and her clothes still littered the living space, but neither of them made a move yet to clear them. As Tracy had said the night before, today was Sunday, neither of them had to work, and neither was in a rush to end things.

Stuart moved through to the living room and plonked himself on the sofa, remembering what had taken place there. My God!

From the entrance way, he heard his phone beep where his jeans still lay. A missed call? The office with something for Monday? He decided to leave it as Tracy came through with a cup of coffee each.

"Can we do that again sometime?" she asked, smiling coyly.

"I think I could fit that in," he said, blushing. "No pun intended."

She smiled back and flicked on the television. His phone beeped again.

"I guess I should get that," he told her. "Could be important."

He got up, placing the coffee cup on a glass topped table. At least they hadn't done anything on that. He crossed the room and collected his jeans, moving back to his seat as he fumbled for the cell phone.

Typing in his security code, he first noted that he had twenty-six messages. Strange, he thought. Opening the first message, he noted it was from his personal bank, telling him he had spent five hundred and forty six Rand. Our meal, he decided.

He opened the next message. Again the bank, but this time two thousand one hundred and ninety nine Rand in Woolworths department store. Odd.

The next was also the bank, six hundred Rand at the MacDonald's in Kempton Park. Now panic was gripping him.

"Shit!" he said.

"What's up?" asked Tracy noticing his pale face.

"Someone's had a run on my bank account. I checked three messages and it's over three thousand Rand already."

"How many messages have you got?"

"Twenty-six," he said glumly.

"Shit!"

In the end they had a total of over fifty thousand Rand gone from his account, with purchases ranging from furniture to burgers.

An expensive night out. That's how quick a professional can fleece you.

They visited the restaurant with the police two hours later. The waiter who had served them was nowhere to be seen, and the management said they didn't keep records of who was working, most of them having no fixed abode.

No charges were pressed, as no proof was available.

**NINE**

Oliver Justice was at another rally with another speech at another mine, this time just outside of Brits. The crowd of about three thousand were having a great time – Oliver's backers had put on cheap food and free beer, and they were making the most of this along with the pleasant spring weather.

"Friends," he addressed the crowd. "When did you work less than a fifty hour week? When did you go home with more money than even the lowest paid white supervisor? When do you have paid holiday?" He paused. "I'll tell you when: NEVER!"

The crowd half cheered at this, but it wasn't enough to really stir them.

"When will our people get the riches they deserve? Riches from black African soil, not white man soil, soil WE were born on." Again, eye contact, the silence allowed to last until it almost became uncomfortable.

"I know the answer but do you?" he asked them.

There was a low rumble from the crowd, uncertain if they were really meant to find an answer, or if the question was purely rhetorical. They didn't have to wait too long.

"You will never work less than a fifty hour week. You will never get paid holiday. And most of all you will NEVER earn more than the white man." He stopped again, and this time the grumbles amongst the crowd became louder.

"That's not fair," came a cry from the front, probably one of his paid lackeys.

"You cannot leave it this way."

"These are the answers comrades, and they will remain the answers whether we like it or not, for as long as our weak politicians bow to the white mining giants."

The crowd was silent now.

"I AM VOLUNTEERING MY SERVICE TO YOU," he hollered. "WORKING TOGETHER, WE CAN FORCE THIS GOVERNMENT TO ADDRESS THESE ISSUES. MAYBE WE HAVE TO TOPPLE THEM, BUT WE TOGETHER CAN CHANGE THINGS."

The crowd was happy again, chanting his name.

"I WANT YOU, THE PEOPLE, TO HAVE WHAT YOU DESERVE. TO HAVE WHAT IS RIGHTFULLY YOURS."

The noise levels were increasing, the crowd jumping and shouting.

"IF YOU WANT ME TO LEAD YOU, YOU ONLY NEED TO TELL ME"

"OLIVER! OLIVER! OLIVER! OLIVER!" The crowd were getting feverish now. It was certainly not a place for the mine's white management to be.

"I WILL LEAD YOU PEOPLE. WE WILL FIGHT TOGETHER TO OVERCOME THIS NEW VERSION OF APARTHEID. WE WILL WIN."

The headlines in both the local and international press the next day, told the same story in different words: the South African government was losing control of the mining sector, with the leadership under threat.

Also, according to a 'source', all the international mining companies had put a stop on investment until the striking was fully resolved and the sector could promise them long-term safety in their investments.

The Herald and Tribune summarised with the headline –


SOUTH AFRICAN MINES CUT THEIR OWN THROATS!


While the Durban Mercury took another angle, stating –


JUSTICE SAYS THERE IS NO JUSTICE!


Both made their points…

**TEN**

Dumisani Silongo, the South African President sat with Graca Machel, the wife of deceased President of Mozambique, and now the wife of Nelson Mandela, ex-President of South Africa. He was really in need of help and he hoped she still had the political drive to give it. Though she claimed to be out of politics, neither she nor Mandela could entirely ignore how things were in her adopted country, and both had been through too many hard times in their pasts not to know that their assistance was needed now.

She crossed her legs, considering the discussion they had been through to this point.

"My husband is an old man Mister President," she started. "We can both see how difficult things are for you right now, but is it fair to pressure him to return to the media's attention?"

"Miss Machel, please call me Dumi. You know our shared country is on its knees right now, with strikes, violence, and the Youth League trying to stir up the emotions of the masses. If they keep going this way, our government will collapse, and I will be out of a job."

"If things keep going this way, you will have a civil war on your hands. I speak from bitter experience," she reminded him. "Do not ignore the facts!"

"I'm afraid I have to agree with you on both points," the President said. "I am misreading the facts to hide my own vulnerability, and I do not want a civil war.

"It's good that you at least appreciate the severity of the situation."

"But will you help?"

"I will always help to avoid the death of people who depend on us, but I am not happy to request my husband joins the fight. He's not young anymore."

"I believe that Nelson Mandela is the only person in this country who can stop things, and that is why I am talking to you now."

"I can promise nothing, but I will talk to him this evening over dinner, then I will let you know the answer." She uncrossed her legs, leaning in to the President. "I love him dearly, so please ensure that things go well for him should he speak," she said. "He is not young anymore and he has a large family to worry about."

"If the mines are producing, I can assist with anything he needs. If the mines stay shut, so do I."

"As said, I am promising nothing, but I will talk to him," she looked at the man opposite her. "He still loves his country more than you would know, but he is more than ninety years old now. Do not expect too much Dumi. I will come back to you."

The President released a deep breath that seemed to have been held forever.

"I understand and can only thank you for your help to date."

"Thank me if he agrees," she replied. "Then let us hope."

## ELEVEN

Captain Timothy Biko was in a quandary. He wanted to serve his country in line with his commission to the army, but he also wanted to have money to feed his family. He hadn't had a full pay packet for six weeks now, and things were getting desperate. His men were getting restless to say the least, and his superiors just kept telling him to pass on the message that things would be good soon, once the country's mines were back in action and South Africa had an income again.

Passing the message on wasn't working though. Some of the men were refusing to report for duty, and strike action for the whole of the military was being mooted. This was certainly one way of making a point, but it would still mean no money and no food.

Timothy drove from his home to the office, reaching the gates to the barracks in Port Elizabeth to find around two hundred soldiers with placards barring the way. What to do.

His first thought was to just drive through them and assert his authority. He had a good relationship with his men and thought he could pull this off. His second thought was that the men were right – no money should mean no work.

His anxiety deepened.

He halted his car about fifty metres from the crowd. Sitting there, he puzzled over what was the best course of action. He tried to consider not just the immediate situation, but also the various responses his actions might cause, as he had been taught to do in his military training. He found that neither option was a perfect answer: going through could turn nasty and turn his men against him; not going through could land him in trouble with his superiors.

One of his own troops saw his car and came over, snapping him a smart salute.

"Captain Biko," he said. "Do you wish to go through Sir?"

Timothy knew his future rested on the answer to this question. He hesitated. The soldier sensed it, wondering what to say.

"Sir, have you come to join us?"

Again, no answer was forthcoming, and the soldier started to turn away and re-join the crowd.

"I will leave you Sir. Sorry to ask so many questions."

"Who is the most senior officer in the crowd?" Timothy finally found his voice, an idea in his mind.

"There are no officers with us yet Sir."

"Then please let your men know that I am now their commander. We must get organised. If we really wish to make a point and get paid, we must have a coherent plan."

The man was facing him again. "Thank you Sir. I will let our people know you are with us." He snapped another textbook salute and left.

Timothy parked his battered VW at the side of the road. He got out of the car, put his beret on his head, and followed the young corporal.


The gathering in Port Elizabeth wasn't the only one made up of South African soldiers. Similar crowds had gathered at barracks in Johannesburg, Heidelberg, Pretoria and Nelspruit, to name but a few. They all had one constant bonding them together: non-payment for weeks on end, this leading to an inability to support their loved ones.

In Bloemfontein, the gathering was the largest of them all, with troops from the local parachute battalion, an infantry unit, an armoured unit, and the School of Armour all joining forces to make their message clear. This gathering moved from the various bases to the town centre, paralyzing the whole city. Police were ordered to control the masses, but most of them were suffering from the same lack of pay packets, so they actually sympathized with the protestors, some actually joining their ranks.

It was not a particularly peaceful protest, with a number of shops in the CBD looted and litter bins tipped over and thrown around the streets. The odd car was also set ablaze for good measure.

With no police to control the protesting soldiers, the city was their own.

The most senior officer in this crowd was a Major Stanley Nkosi. He had appointed himself the senior spokesman for them and was now standing in front of a South African Broadcasting Company (SABC) camera.

"I am Niki Ndebe from SABC 1, reporting from Bloemfontein in the Free State. Behind me you can see around one thousand soldiers, disillusioned with the government's promises to pay them soon, when for the last six to eight weeks it has failed to do so. We have also seen that some policemen have joined the protests, so law and order in this city is virtually non-existent, although I have to say, the people protesting are being exceptionally well behaved from what we have witnessed, but this may be a result of the discipline they must show in their normal line of work." She paused, the camera turning from her to Stanley. "This is Major Nkosi and the local Parachute unit, and he is the senior protester here, so we have asked him to say a few words."

Stanley was a strong and fit looking man, tall for a South African and looking every bit the leader of a group of rugged paratroopers. He smiled at the camera.

"Thank you Niki," he started. "We have requested that our men do behave today, and for as many days as we must protest." He swept his open arms around, taking in the crowd. "These people around us are soldiers. They are expected to give up their lives if this country is in danger. They will do this willingly, even though it will mean their families lose their breadwinner. This is what we all signed up for." He paused again, gathering his thoughts and thinking about what he had missed. "We are not greedy people. We will never become rich people whilst serving in the military. But we are people that deserve to be paid, and the government is failing us in this."

"Major Nkosi, you mentioned 'for as many days as we must protest.' Do you intend carrying this on after today?"

"We will carry this on Niki, as long as it takes for us to be paid. If we go back without pay, then nothing will change. We must force the issue."

"So tomorrow you will still be here in Bloem?" she said, using the usual South African abbreviation for the city.

"We will be here to make our mark, unless someone organises a major rally in Pretoria by the Union Buildings. Then we will join our other comrades to make our point directly with the President."

"Major Nkosi, thanks for your time and honesty. I am sure that the majority of the population will wish you and your brave soldiers their full support." She faced the camera, dismissing Timothy. "This is Niki Ndebe, SABC 1, signing off in the Free State. It's a wrap."


That evening the interview was broadcast to the nation on the seven o'clock news, and Oliver Justice watched it with gathering interest. Could this be another opportunity for him to raise his profile? Could he be the man to lead the military and possibly the South African Police Service (SAPS) through this crisis? What a voting base that would give him. He thought about the possibilities for a few minutes, weighing up the pros and cons.

He lifted his phone and put a call through to his PR manager.

"Did you see the news on SABC?" he asked on answer.

"It's my job to see the news, and I can probably guess your thoughts right now Oliver. I was waiting for your call," the PR man replied.

"And your thoughts?"

"I have already requested we have flights from O R Tambo tomorrow morning to Bloemfontein."

"So you can guess my thoughts."

They spoke for another ten minutes and agreed to meet at the airport in Johannesburg at seven o'clock the following morning. They would be in Bloem by nine.

During the night in Bloem, more shops were raided and cars set alight. With no police presence in the city anymore, the unpaid soldiers – and anyone else – helped themselves to food, drink and any other possessions they wanted from the unguarded department stores. Alcohol flowed freely and as people became drunk, they became ever braver, targeting rich black and white folks' homes, not discriminating on colour.

Houses joined the burning cars, and rape and murder were soon added to the list of atrocities that the crowds committed.

Rumours of the situation soon spread to other towns and cities, but the press could not confirm anything as the anarchy was too bad to safely send news crews to the region. Reports could only be passed by people calling friends and colleagues by their phones. These reports also reached the government, but with no control over the police or army, they were a toothless force, unable to react.

As day dawned, the hordes slept off the overindulgent night and smoke masked whole areas of beautiful Bloemfontein.


Oliver and his PR Manager met at O R Tambo International Airport at seven, as agreed, only to find all flights into Bloem had been cancelled. With no security for their assets, South African Airways had decided this was the only way forward.

"I have my Lexus in the car-park," said Oliver. "We could be there in about three to four hours. What do you say?"

"If SAA won't fly there and SABC won't send in TV crews, I say it's not too safe to do that."

"But what about the opportunity? We will never get a bigger chance than this. We will be in every headline and win a massive support base if we ever go to the vote."

"I heard they are robbing black people too, Oliver," the PR man said. "Just because they are rich. Imagine driving in to town in a Lexus."

"Then we take a cheap hire car."

They were quiet for a minute, thinking about the options. For the young politician, the gains outweighed the risks, but for the slightly older PR expert, it was the reverse. Dying for your beliefs was one thing, dying just to do your job, quite another.

"I have a better idea," said the PR man softly. "And we can take your Lexus and be there in one hour."

As they pulled up close to the Union Buildings in Pretoria, Oliver and his colleague noted that a good crowd was already gathered, many of the people in it wearing military uniform. On the way the PR Manager had called his connections in the South African Defence Force and suggested the rally could be 'interesting' and worth attending. It seemed that even without this promotion, the crowd was out for a great day.

Normally parking close to the seat of the government was not too difficult, but today the only place left was down past the memorial for police officers who had lost their lives in the course of their duties. Oliver thought it may be a fitting point to raise later.

Getting out of the Lexus, Oliver's PR Manager spotted a colonel he knew from a previous rally and headed over to him.

"Hi Julius," he greeted him, giving a high-five followed by a more traditional African handshake, having three parts to it: first the straight handshake as in Europe, then fingers gripping to fingers, then back to the normal shake.

"Hello Thabo," the colonel came back to him. "What brings you here, or needn't I ask? You can smell publicity."

"Have you met Oliver Justice?"

"No, but that really confirms to me that you are smelling the press coverage."

"After the problems in Bloem yesterday, we felt perhaps we could have Oliver talk to the men and try and help to keep a lid on things," said Thabo. "What do you think?"

"I think it could go the other way my friend, but I also think our case needs to be raised to a level where someone will take notice of our cause."

"Do you think the soldiers will approve me?" asked Oliver. "I am only the Youth League, so they may feel I am too young to be getting involved here."

"Most of them are also only youths, so you should fit in well. And if you can promise them some chance to get their money at last, then you have just won all of their votes."

They walked onwards, towards the Union Buildings.


The Union Buildings in Pretoria are made of beautiful yellow sandstone and sit on top of a hill overlooking the city. In front of them stretches a beautiful sloping hill, full of flower gardens and walks. At the top of the hill – known as Meintjieskop – and between the gardens and the Buildings, runs Fairview Avenue. When the clocks chime from the twin towers, the chimes are identical to those of Big Ben in London.

Just off Fairview, on the edge of the park, steps run down the hill and through the gardens. At the central stairs are a couple of old cannons, memories of South Africa's turbulent past – a little strange amongst all the beautiful architecture and fauna.

Today the gardens were hidden though, drowned out by a sea of bodies, mainly in brown camouflage, with some blue police shirts amongst them. The sun was pleasant but not too hot, so the attendance was up on the expected figures, and the calls circulated by Thabo´s friends had brought even more people to swell the ranks. Some people not in the military had also come along to enjoy the occasion, further boosting the figures.

Oliver leaned on one of the cannons, watching the proceedings begin. The status of the military present was increasing – the first speaker would be a general of about forty years of age, seeing this as a way to earn even faster promotion than he had already managed to date. He stepped up to the PA system, tapping the mike.

"Soldiers. Brother Officers Corps. Welcome," he started. He guessed about ten to fifteen thousand people were looking at him silently, and he knew his words had to count. "Thank you all for coming here today. We must all work together as a team that the military always is. We must all depend on each other."

He paused, again feeling slightly awed at the size of the crowd and the fact that he was standing up in front of it.

"I am here today, for the same reasons as you are all here today," he continued. "I need money for my family to live, same as you need money for your own families. And where better to make this message clear, than here in front of our own parliament."

A great cheer went up and the PA system was instantly overwhelmed. He waited, nerves getting to him a little.

"I want to hand you over now to a greater leader than myself, in fact probably the greatest one left in our country today." A pause. "I GIVE YOU OLIVER JUSTICE."

The crowd was roaring as he stood back from the mike, job done, turned smartly one hundred and eighty degrees and saluted Oliver, before moving clear. Oliver hung back a second, then walked to the microphone, raising his arms in the air in his own form of salute. He waited a few minutes while the applause carried on, lowered his arms, noting that the volume decreased as they came down.

"We seem to be meeting often brothers," he began. "I seem to be talking more than Mister President right now."

The crowd laughed, enjoying the dig.

"I just hope my words mean a little more than his," he added.

A further sound of laughter, some of the people clapping in appreciation.

"So brothers, what can we do? Here we all are gathered in front of our government 'leaders' and not one of them in sight. Have they not rushed out to talk to us? Have they brought us food and drink? HAVE THEY PAID US?" he bawled. "WHEN WILL THEY PAY US?"

The applause was now deafening, so he stopped talking, theatrically lowering his head and fixing his gaze on the ground.

"This crowd today is made up of heroes. Every day, you people risk your lives for the people of this land. Not just the soldiers, but the policemen too. Not a hundred yards from here is a place dedicated to the memory of our policemen who have died in the course of their duties." He stopped again, gathering his energy for the next outburst. "The dead are remembered and our politicians see their memorial every day. SO WHY DO THEY FORGET TO PAY THEM? DO THEY SIMPLY NOT CARE?"

He had to stop for a full minute before anyone stopped clapping, cheering and screaming high-pitched noises. For a full minute he sucked in the power of the crowd and wondered which way to take the day. He made his decision.

"Brothers, we all saw what happened in Bloem yesterday, and we do not want this to happen also in Tshwane. This only gives the powers that be an excuse to call us a rabble, a bunch of rioters, scum. We must not give them that. We must pose them a question, set them an ultimatum."

The crowd was calm now, some quietly discussing the words he'd spoken, most just waiting for him to guide them.

"We need our servicemen and women, our police, our emergency services to be paid. We need them to continue doing the difficult job that they do, making it safe for the rest of us to live our lives." His voice was low now, calm. "And we need this soon. Very soon." He looked around the quiet faces in front of him, feeling their support.

"We shall not be unreasonable people. We will be calm and peaceable, but we will make a line in the sand." With his right foot he made a show of drawing a line. "In forty-eight hours, we meet here again. If you have all been paid, we have a party. If you have not been paid, we request that the President steps down from his pedestal and someone else must have a chance."

He looked down again on the crowd, pleased with his choice of the word 'pedestal' that indicated to the crowd that the President thought he was above them all. It was strange, he thought, looking down on thousands of small black heads nodding in agreement. He turned half away from the crowd now and looked in to the TV camera, but still talking in to the mike.

"Mister President," he started, smiling. "I am sure you are watching this as we speak, so the message should be clear." The crowd were waking up again, laughing and jeering at the man who would be watching a TV screen not far away. "I invite you to join us and let us know your plans. If not today, then in two days."

He nodded to the crowd, getting their approval. He turned back to the lens.

"Because Sir, if we do not have good answers in two days, then I may not be in a position to control the military. What happened in Bloemfontein yesterday, may then just happen in Pretoria in two days. It is on your head."

He turned from the camera, saluted the crowd, and walked back towards Fairview Avenue.

## TWELVE

The great man, Nelson Mandela, was assisted on to the stage in his wheelchair, and positioned in front of a bank of microphones. It was hard to believe that this old man – a lawyer and a boxer in his youth – had potentially saved the lives of hundreds of thousands of good South African citizens at the death of Apartheid. He was thin and was in and out of hospital far too frequently, but he still held the attention of the entire nation.

He leaned forward in his chair towards the mikes, glancing at his prepared notes. Dumi sat close to him, ready to assist if necessary, but hoping not to be needed.

"Fellow South Africans," he began, his voice surprisingly strong. "I thought my days of talking on such a grand scale were done, but our President has requested I address you today, to try and bring us all together once again."

There was no audience, but the television crew and recording team clapped anyway. He waited for their hush.

"Some of our brothers and sisters in this great land are not happy. They accuse the government of selling them out, giving away our country's resources, and not looking after our people." He looked at the notes again, then put them to one side, not needing guidance from anyone but his heart.

"Please believe me. This ANC government is doing its best for all of us." Madiba coughed, struggling to catch his breath. His last words had been laboured and Dumi decided it was time to step in.

"Thank you Madiba. A nation will be happy to see you again." He put his hand on the old man's forearm.

"A country is like a business, and what it brings in must be paid for," he continued. "We sell our minerals, and we buy back food, televisions, clothes. We need foreign investment and export income to do this. Think of it on a smaller scale – you work, you earn money, then you spend the money on food and clothes for your family. Something must come in to allow the money to go out on those things. A country is exactly the same, but bigger."

He looked at Nelson Mandela, who nodded his support.

"Our country right now is looking darker than it did when Madiba won the battle over Apartheid. We are fighting our own brothers, killing fellow South Africans, whether they are black or white. Where is our famous 'Rainbow Nation?' Where is our belief in reconciliation?"

He paused, again glancing at the great man, but Mandela was looking tired now.

"This man gave up many years of his life for his beliefs. He sat in a prison cell for over twenty years. For us. For our country. For you and me." He pointed at the camera. "Please do not waste his efforts now."

A tear rolled down Mandela's cheek, as he looked into the camera lens.

"Let's make our nation great again. Make us the best and biggest mining power on the earth," he said, his voice now almost inaudible.

The recording crew signalled that time was running out.

Dumi stepped in again. "We can be great together, and together we will again show the world that South Africa is a world leader. I trust you, and you must trust me. Thank you all, but specially I thank Mister Mandela for his never ending support for South Africa."

The picture faded and the sound was cut. It was just in time. Madiba was out of energy, and that wasn't something the general public needed to know.

"Well done Nelson," Graca told him. "You will save South Africa once again, believe me."

The onlooking ANC hierarchy breathed a collective sigh of relief and hoped the broadcast would be enough to calm the people.


"That could be the end of our chances to make the top job," said Oliver. "He may be old, but the people still love him dearly. Me included."

"I know. The President has played his trump card. But is it enough?"

"The people are hungry, but so was Madiba for plenty of years. They know this."

"Tomorrow is the big day, Oliver. Either you get their support, or we go home empty-handed. No middle ground."


It was a strange thing, but even in the shanty towns, almost everyone had access to television. They were all glued to the address from the former President. He was like a God to the populace, a saviour from heaven. He was one of them, but he had achieved things that none of them could ever imagine. He had freed them from Apartheid and saved their nation from going the way of most African nations – to war with itself.

Many cried when they saw how frail the man looked.

He had been through so much hell, and now he was a shadow of the man from his youth who had stood up to the Apartheid regime and lived his years in captivity, coming out partially blinded by the hard labour enforced on him.

When he smiled in the middle of his speech, a cheer went up in many shacks. He was still strong.

In the eyes of the local South Africans, especially in the poorer townships, Nelson Mandela really was the father of their nation, in just the same way as George Washington was to the United States.


The President sat in a soft leather seat after Mandela and Machel had left. The rest of the politicians had also left soon afterwards, so at last he was alone. He had poured himself a large van Rhyn brandy, no ice, no mixer, and took a sip. It was the first time he had relaxed in days, but he now believed he was safe. The people would do what the old leader had requested, and that meant that he would stay in power, at least for now.

He had to think of a way to settle the mining crisis, and this in turn would solve the military crisis. The problem was he couldn't give the miners as much as they wanted, as he was already paying over the odds and the money was disappearing in to other people's pockets. And without getting an income from the mining sector, he couldn't pay the other sectors....

With the miners back at work, the international investors would start putting their money in to projects again too, further easing the crisis and creating jobs.

At least the Mandela speech had bought a little time he thought, but this was no time to rest on one's laurels.

He had to solve the mining problem the next day. It was a must.

## THIRTEEN

The next morning the sun rose as usual, beaming over the dry yellowed grass of the Highveld. Areas were so dry they would burn soon, some naturally and some in controlled burns. It would still be some months before it was green again in Gauteng.

People got out of bed, showered, had breakfast, prepared for work or school or nothing at all, the same as they did every weekday.

But this was no normal weekday.

The President picked up the desk phone on the second ring. It was only six thirty, but he had been signing off paperwork for almost an hour, one of the things he enjoyed doing before the hustle and bustle of the day began.

"Mister President, I have some terrible news," the voice at the other end of the phone said. He recognised his Press Secretary.

"Calm down Stanley," he said softly. "I'm sure it is nothing we haven't seen before."

"I'm afraid it is worse than anything we have ever seen before Mister President."

"Slowly Stanley, let me know what I need to," he said, worry starting to flood in.

"Nelson Mandela died in his sleep last night. He is gone."

The President said nothing, his breathing stopping at the shock of the announcement. This couldn't be. He was here last night.

"What do I do Mister President? The press will get wind of it anytime now. Ambulances were all over his house last night. And the police."

"Make a press announcement. We must let the people know before the press corps do."

"What do I say?"

"You say that he died peacefully in his sleep, and that a nation is mourning the loss of the greatest man ever to walk this earth."

The news was out. Every news channel worldwide covered it. Nelson Mandela had been an extraordinary man in life, and he was about to become a larger one in his death. He was the man who had saved a nation. Now his death would be used by some to try and destroy that same nation.

Oliver Justice was again in front of a television camera. He looked suitably shocked and sad, mainly from the use of stage make-up. Inside, his heart was singing.

"Madiba was an old man," he told the camera. "He was loved by every person in the world, not just South Africa, but he was ninety-four years old. He should never – never – have been used for a television interview yesterday evening."

The camera panned back a little, showing a girl leaning on Oliver's shoulder, crying her eyes out.

"My girlfriend will not be the last person crying today," he said. "I wouldn't be surprised if people drowned in tears today." He was being melodramatic, building up the tension, making people mad.

"Mandela died from the stress of yesterday's performance. He died from being forced to calm a nation, simply because our President couldn't control the country. When in doubt, call for Madiba," he raged. "He is dead because someone in Union Buildings didn't know how to manage our country."

He stormed away from the camera, turning briefly to yell a final, "We need a leader. NOW."

It was a great performance.


The soldiers were gathering again on the gardens in front of the Union Buildings. They were sad. They were angry. And they were restless.

No-one really wanted to speak, to lead, as no-one knew what to say.

This left the crowd rudderless.

The TV cameras panned around, but didn't really have a target, leaving the presenter to talk about the estimated size of the gathering, naming senior officers present when they recognized them, and generally filling air-time until something happened. The TV stations had a feeling something would happen, it was really just a question of what and when.

A commotion at the top of the steps off Fairview Avenue gave the cameras something to look at, though what they were looking at was at first uncertain. Then Oliver Justice stepped out of the melee and walked to the microphone.

"Please join me brothers, in a prayer for our angel, Mister Nelson Mandela."

He led them in the Lord's Prayer, every soldier out there saying the words from their hearts, tears rolling down their cheeks.

"The real leader of our country is dead," he told them. "I hope he has gone to a better place, because while he was here with us, he suffered for us in a mighty way." He gathered his breath and started on again. "He was like a Jesus for us. Everything bad that happened in his life didn't seem to make him want to take revenge. He was always forgiving."

He stopped, lowering his head and feigning tears, wiping his eyes with a white handkerchief.

"Can you be the same?" he asked the crowd. "Can you forgive the people that cost us our greatest asset in South Africa? I'm not certain I can."

"What can we do Oliver?" a voice in the crowd yelled, a plant from his party.

"What can we do? An excellent question brother." He pretended to be deep in his personal thoughts, mulling over the options he had. "We could all go home with our sadness, and our hunger, and sit with our sad, hungry families and mourn. That is an option," he told them. "Another option is to stay here together and support one another in this sad, sad time."

"There must be better things we can do. How can things get better?"

"Of course they are other things we can do," Oliver said. "We can try and make this country a better place, but we cannot do that while sitting on the lawn outside of the Union Buildings. The only people who can change the country are people that are inside the Union Buildings."

His voice box in the crowd didn't need to set things up anymore. The crowd had found their own voice, and the voice was loud.

"We need you inside those buildings."

"Please lead us out of these troubles Oliver!"

"We need you to save us, just like Mandela."

Oliver listened to the words, hardly believing he was hearing them, but knowing he had waited his whole life to be in this moment.

"Save us and feed us!"

"Make South Africa a place to live again!"

The shouts were washing over him, the hairs on the back of his neck felt like they were electric, and he could hear the blood pounding in his ears.

"If you want me to be your leader…" he started, pausing as if in thought. "Then it will be an honour to lead you all."

"OLIVER! OLIVER! OLIVER! OLIVER! OLIVER!"

He turned from the crowd and started walking over Fairview Avenue, and on up the next steps to the Union Buildings, the mob following him.

## FOURTEEN

President Silongo had left the Union Buildings with his staff when they guessed where things were going. In Africa, things were not like in Europe or America: the crowd would not have locked him up or simply thrown him out of office; death would have been the likely outcome, and not just to himself, and not in a pleasant way.

They had taken a private flight to Durban in Kwa-Zulu Natal, the home of the President and where his grass-roots support base was found. From the new King Shaka airport, his motorcade headed north towards the true land of the Zulus. Crossing the Tugela River, he began to feel more secure, and wondered how things had reached this crazy out of control situation. The nation was going mad, and he wasn't sure how to stop it.

Normally he had the police and military at his disposal to contain situations, but both were now against him. Normally he had money available to 'buy' people that he needed to control things, but with the mines on strike for over a month now, money was also a problem.

He had also spoken to the international mining community to try and calm their nerves and get them to continue with their infrastructure investments, but with all the talk of nationalization of resources, this had fallen on deaf ears. They had seen what could happen in Zimbabwe, and no-one was willing to take that chance in South Africa.

That was one of the main things that scared the President half to death. He had seen what had happened in Zimbabwe, and it had been horrible to watch. The country had imploded. There was a civil war that lasted years and took away much of the country's youth. The currency had devalued so much it was virtually worthless, people trading by bartering goods, like something out of the eighteenth century. At one stage the bank notes were so useless that they had a date on them, after which they were no longer valid. And we are not talking dates that were years off, but possibly 30 days off. A loaf of bread ended up being worth more than a million Zimbabwe dollars.

The next turning coming up on the motorway was for Empangeni and Richards Bay. Home was coming, and the safety of his own people.

Right now he needed that. He felt so tired out that he just wanted to sleep. He felt a failure. With a few days rest his batteries would be recharged and then he could focus on the problems at hand and try and fix his country.

But right now he just needed to feel safe.


Oliver Justice sat behind the desk of the President of South Africa. He put his feet on it, smiling to himself. In the surrounding rooms he could hear the crowd searching for trophies to take – money, food, water, ornaments, furniture – it didn't matter, they just wanted something for their hardships suffered over the last months. The fact that the item was useless to them and that stealing it made no sense did not matter.

A corporal opened the door to the office, barging in. He noticed Oliver.

"Oh, sorry," he said. "Must be the wrong room."

He hurried out. Was there a right room, wondered Oliver?

Getting up from the desk, he crossed the room to the window and looked out to see people scurrying in every direction, some leaving with arms full of curtains, some with a roll of carpet, a couple of men struggling with a sofa. A building that was the pride of the African nation was beginning to look like it had been visited by a plague of locusts. He should feel sickened, but he actually felt good – he had caused this plague, he had roused the crowd from their sorrows at the death of Mandela and led them on their destructive path.

Now the country was his. He could form his own government. The President couldn't run forever, and with the army on Oliver's side, he could find the President and remove him as a potential threat.


For the better off blacks and the white population of South Africa, this was now becoming a nightmare scenario. Security had gone out of the window with the police joining the army at the rallies, and their homes and families were now in danger.

The three South African international airports – Cape Town, King Shaka in Durban and O R Tambo in Johannesburg – were full to bursting point with people, mainly dual-nationality passport holders, trying to get out of the country. South Africans with origins in Italy were fleeing to mainland Europe; English flew to the UK; Germans to Germany. Anywhere. Before things could get worse.

Customs and Immigration were operating on a skeleton staff. Many of their people had joined the rallies, as their own pay had been cut, to get through the financial hard times. This led to delays and queues.

Flights were delayed and cancelled, some international carriers refusing to land in South Africa because of the political uncertainty, but also because fuel supplies were compromised, and getting a plane stuck in a war zone was not to be contemplated.

The border crossings were no better, with people fleeing in their cars over into Namibia, Botswana, Mozambique and even – believe it or not – Zimbabwe. Due to the high numbers of cars and the lack of Customs Officers, the tailbacks stretched back from the crossing points for miles and miles.

In the heat and with the delays, people became short tempered, so minor scuffles broke out between waiting groups.

Water ran out at the shops and kiosks near the border, despite some entrepreneurial attempts to exploit the situation. The price of a bottle of water at these places more than doubled in a day. Simply a case of supply and demand.

The police from the neighbouring countries tried to slow the exodus, not knowing where to put the crowds of people. The roads from the borders became blocked and the towns near the borders soon had no accommodation to offer. People who had trailer tents and campers started setting them up in lay-bys and parking areas.

The world, for so many people, had changed from good to very bad in a very short period. It was a very frightening time.


The country was splitting into groups, polarized around tribal regions.

In the north-east, the Zulus and the President grouped together. In the south, the region split in to three main groups – the whites the blacks and the Cape-coloureds. In the area around Gauteng and North West Province, the split was mainly the blacks and the white Afrikaans. Some of the groups could make uneasy alliances, but some were totally alienated.

South Africa has eleven official languages including English and Afrikaans. Others include, Zulu, Xhosa, Venda, Swazi, Tsonga, Sotho and Northern Sotho, Tswana and Ndebele. The languages originate from the various peoples that populated this part of the globe over the centuries. There are also nine unofficial South African languages, mostly derivatives of the main ones and others that come from the San and Khoikhoi people.

With all of these potential barriers to harmony, it was no wonder that the country could so easily become fragmented. It was probably a stranger thing that one man had successfully united it for so long.

As the groups crowded together like herds of frightened antelope, communications between them became worse. Each of the major groups had control of their own local television studios, and this allowed them to dictate and broadcast their own message to the local people. It was like a form of brainwashing: the result was having the populace believe the version of events that the broadcaster said was the right one.

The two main players in the 'blame game' were the President himself and Oliver Justice. From the outside it looked even more odd than it did from inside the country: the leader of the African National Congress, was locking horns with the leader of African National Congress Youth League. Surely the ANC shared the same ideology, whether it was the main stream party or the youth wing.

Sadly, this was nothing to do with ideologies and beliefs, this was about ego: the President didn't want to surrender what he felt he had earned, and the Youth League President wanted to further his career. The fact that one was a Zulu and one a Zimbabwean did nothing to improve the situation though – it only made things worse.

Both men were looking to increase their supporters, making pacts with other groups to push up their support base should things come down to a vote. More worrying was a situation where, if things didn't come to a vote, democracy failed. Then everything depended on who had the most people supporting them, and what resources those people had.

Oliver Justice had the military with him, at least in the Gauteng region. In Zululand, the President had a smaller local force. He also had the Zulus, warriors from the past, but were they up to a fight in the modern day sense?

As the days passed, smaller groups made their choices. The Western Cape stuck with the President, trying to keep democracy alive. The Eastern Cape, always a little more radical, sided with the Youth League, as did Limpopo and Mpumalanga. North West Province was mixed, with many blacks sticking with Oliver Justice and the whites deciding their safety lay with the President.

The country was split. On one side was a justly elected President. On the other a young man who had taken control of the country with rhetoric.

Who would be the eventual victor?

## FIFTEEN

Zeerust in North West Province was a small town of around six thousand. It was approximately 50% white Afrikaaners, and 50% from other races, mainly black and a few Indians.

A shanty town of Ikageleng stands on the edge of Zeerust, housing about one thousand poor people. This is where the trouble started.

With all of the divisions and mistrust between the various parties, coupled with a lack of fuel supplies and therefore a failure in distribution of basic necessities, Ikageleng was soon suffering from basic deficiencies. The water came from a central tap that served the whole town. This would occasionally fail, but the main town would then use water bowsers to fill the gap. With no fuel for distributing the water, when the supply failed, the township was left with nothing.

Also due to the distribution problems, food was running low. The more affluent white households bought what was available in the shops, stocking up their supplies. The poor people of the township didn't have this luxury and were soon unable to obtain either food or water.

At first the town's people approached the council and asked for support. But the council had nothing to hand out, so the people of Ikageleng decided to approach the white people directly.

The whites had only what they had been able to buy from the shops before they had all run out of supplies, so they were anything but happy at the thought of surrendering their food. They therefore turned the blacks away.

At the end of the second day of not eating a full meal, black people decided they had to feed themselves. At eleven o'clock that night, they raided the largest of the white-owned homes on the edge of the town. The intention was to simply take all the food and drink and distribute amongst their families. It wasn't to be.

When the first window shattered, Fanie Coetzee rolled out of his bed and picked up the shotgun that lay next to his bed. Most whites had their own weapons, some legally and some not. Living so far away from the large cities, many people had obtained weapons for defence from animals and humans alike.

Fanie came silently down his stairs. He shouldn't have bothered with his quiet approach though, the group of six blacks that were in his kitchen had been taking something stronger than water, swigging directly from a bottle of Fanie's Klipdrift Brandy.

"Put that stuff down and get out of my house," he ordered, lining the weapon up on the men. "Get back to where you belong!"

The men turned, laughing at him. "We need food man. You can't kill us for that."

Fanie's wife, Antje came down the stairs in her nightdress. "What is going on?"

"We need food Missus," said one of the men. "We're starving."

"You can stay starving," Fanie told him. "Now get out of my living room!"

One of the drunker youths started towards Fanie, arms outstretched in front of him. "We are not trying to be bad, man, but we need to eat."

A second one followed him, and Fanie panicked.

BAAM!!!

The shot was deafening in the small room and the first black man flew backwards into the far wall, blood spraying from a hole in his back and hitting the wall less than a second before he did.

BAAM!!!

A send shot took another man, removing most of his head. Fanie cocked the weapon.

BAAM!!!

Another fell to the floor, his right thigh in tatters, and screaming his heart out. The other three were already running out of the smashed French doors, Fanie firing after them. He hit no-one else.

His wife was screaming, and the kids had run down the stairs and joined in the uproar.

Two dead men lay on the floor, the third howling in agony, blood everywhere.

Lights flicked on around the neighbourhood as other families were awakened by the noise. The people from the next house were soon at the door.

"What happened?"

"They were breaking in to my house and wouldn't leave."

"Is anyone hurt?"

"Just these guys here."

"Shit! They're dead."

"I thought they were coming to get me."

"Calm down! We need to think about this. They may come back."

"You think so?"

More neighbours had come to the Coetzee house by now, and one of the women took Antje and the kids back to her house. The men moved the dead bodies out in to the garden, but no-one had any plans to take the wounded man to hospital. No-one wanted to go that far from home right now.

Two of the men picked the man up off the floor and put him on to a sofa. He screamed when they moved him, luckily passing out. Someone put a blanket over him, but no-one knew how to deal with such a leg-wound.

"Coot, you go around and wake up the other guys. I think we need to have a sentry system. These guys are hungry and thirsty, and now they're mad too."

"I don't think it will come to that Johan."

"There's a lot of crazy things happening in this country just lately. I think it is best we get prepared for the worst and wish for the best."


Back in Ikageleng the three survivors were recounting their story to most of the village. Almost no-one could sleep, through hunger pains, so they soon had an audience of over half the village, mainly the adults.

"So they will not give us food and water?" asked one of the women.

"They shot three of us, but I think Henry may still be alive. They don't want to give us nothing," said one of the survivors, still in shock.

"What about Mbuso?" asked a youngish woman. "We are dating."

The man looked down, ashamed. "I think he's dead. He was hit in the face."

She started crying, quietly at first, but becoming more hysterical.

"We need food and water."

"We will get food and water," said the older man.

"How? Do we all have to get shot?"

"We also have guns," said one of the younger men. Everyone knew he was involved in drug dealing, so this was not a great shock to them.

"What do we do?" a woman asked the older man. "We should not fight, but if we have no food and water, we will die anyway."

"I will go to the whites and ask for support. They are not bad people and they will help."

"They will shoot you old man, just like they shot the others. You will soon not be hungry, but you'll soon be dead," the young man stormed. "Sometimes you can only fight fire with fire. We must take the food and water we need."

"Do you not think the whites might be ready for us?" the old man tried reasoning. "We should wait until morning when people are less scared and the situation is calmer."

The young man pulled out a pistol. "See this? I have more of them, and so do others here in the village. Why must we wait? We must take what we need."

"I agree," said one of the girls. "I am starving and so are my kids."

"I'm going to get the others with guns."

"We must be calm."

"We must be fed old man."


Coetzee and the other whites were organised into groups, a small number of men at each fifth house to form a 'quick reaction team' and a two-men on all the main approaches. The reaction teams slept a fitful sleep while the other men and some women watched out for any movement from the township. Most felt nothing would happen.

The wounded man – Henry – still lay on the sofa, but this house had been abandoned until morning when it could be cleaned and boarded up. He was bleeding to death, but no-one was aware of it.

At three o'clock in the morning, just when the sentries thought the night was done and they were half asleep, the youths from Ikageleng reached the shelter of the trees, just off the street where the white district started. They watched a while, but seeing nothing, decided to go and get what they wanted. As they broke cover, a half-awake sentry saw them. He panicked and ran back to the nearest house, alerting the blacks to his presence. They watched where he went, then followed quietly behind, guessing the coast was clear.

The young sentry rushed in to the house where the reaction group was sleeping, waking them from their slumber. He was rushing his words, stuttering and not making much sense. One of the men tried to slow him down.

"What did you see Abraham?"

"The bl-bl-blacks are coming," he stammered, out of breath.

"How many and where from?" asked the older man.

"Not sure… a lot of them… from the township, I think."

"OK lads, let's get up and check this out."

People rolled off sofas and out of sleeping bags. Half asleep, they were not ready for what happened next...


Of the thirteen youths from the village, seven were armed with pistols, the rest carrying machetes. They watched things unfolding, in the living room of the house, from the garden, hiding behind a hut full of tools. They could see that the whites were older, almost awake and uncertain what to do.

It was time to strike before they got their acts together.

"We shoot them and grab all the food and water we can carry," the leader whispered. "Let's go!"

They charged into the house, pistols firing. None of them had any real training, but against a bunch of old men who were barely awake, it was a massacre. All seven of the Afrikaaners in the house were dead or mortally wounded within thirty seconds. Provisions and bottles of water were pushed into garbage bags, fruit, from bowls, following the rest into the large black bin liners.

Within sixty seconds they were on their way back to the township, screaming and shouting.

They had won the first battle.


The Afrikaans buried their dead in the morning.

The community met afterwards at the local school, all of the men in the assembly hall, the women watching the children in the playing area. About a dozen men with cell phones were at strategic points to monitor any approach by the people of the township.

"We have to defend ourselves. No-one will be coming to help us, not the police, not the army. It's us and it's them."

One of the town elders addressed the gathered men.

"We must pool our weapons, and every man and boy over sixteen, must be armed. If we have spare weapons, arm the ladies too. If they come again, we will destroy them, especially after what they did last night." He paused, noting a few tears amongst the men in front of him. "It reminds me of what our forefathers had to endure from the English during the Great Trek – we have to round up our wagons and protect ourselves, just the same as they did."

"Why don't we go down there and shoot the bastards right now?" asked the brother of Abraham, one of the dead and the man who had raised the alarm in the first place. "They did that to our folks."

The elder responded. "We have the food and water – they don't. That means they have to come to us. It's much easier to defend than to attack."

"He's right," said a large muscular man called Michael. "I fought on the border during the war with Angola. It takes less men to defend a position than it does to storm it."

"Thank you Michael. We have to pull together."

"So what do we do?"

"First we get armed up. Then we split into two teams. I'm afraid for a while we will have to abandon our homes and form a commune. Then while some rest, the others stand watch. The women cook and take care of the children. We can run small classes for the kids between us, I'm sure."

"Do you think they'll come back?"

"They're hungry, they're thirsty. They will be back."


The elder was right on the button. The villagers of Ikageleng were starving. People were already looking gaunt, even though the problem was only days old. And they were holding a council of war, just like the Afrikaans people.

"We should have approached them peacefully. I worked for one of them and they always looked after me," complained one of the women. "Now they will give us nothing."

"Stop crying lady! They killed three of our men. We were just revenging their deaths, and we brought the village food and water."

"And look how long that lasted," one of the elders complained. "It only fed you young folks, you never looked after the women and kids, or us old people."

"We will be doing the fighting old man. We will bring the next food."

"There must be a better way," a lady at the back said. "I also worked for the whites. Let me go and try and talk to them."

"You can do as you wish sissy, but the only thing they understand is force. We must TAKE the food off them."

Around two hundred youths, aged between sixteen and twenty-five, formed the nucleus of the meeting. They were armed. They were hungry. And they were in charge of their own destiny for the first time in their lives. It was an explosive concoction.

The black youths began their attack at midnight, after raiding the white homes and establishing that there was nothing there of sustenance for them. All foodstuffs and fluids were missing, as well as bedding and a fair amount of clothing. Stealing furniture at a time like this didn't excite them, so instead they simply burnt it. Some of the houses also went up in the flames.

The whites were pre-warned by the fires and raucous screams of the youths, so they knew what was coming. They didn't expect the numbers though.

The attack was head-on and on one front only. The whites were spread all around their makeshift compound, leaving them thin on the ground. Men were moved from the unaffected lines of defenders to where any attack was centred, but some had to be left at their posts to block any surprise pincer movements.

The ex-soldiers in the white ranks tried to calm the untrained. Some wanted to run, some wanted to fire as soon as the mob was in sight, but the veterans of the bush wars held their nerve and managed to get the rest to follow suit.

The attacking youths were the width of a two-lane street and about fifty deep. They were walking purposely towards the barricade of vehicles that the Afrikaaners had assembled. They were banging sticks together, clapping and shouting. Many were high on drugs. It was an intimidating sight.

Fifty metres from the barricade, the mob began running. The old soldiers ordered the defenders to fire, and the carnage began.


The next morning as the sun came up over Zeerust the town was quiet. Black smoke hung over the white housing area where the dwellings had been ransacked and torched and, to a lesser extent, over Ikageleng where people burnt wood to try and keep warm.

In the streets, flies buzzed noisily around the bodies of the dead black youths. A head-count had put the dead at one hundred and seventy nine, but more were still injured and dying out there, so this would increase.

The whites had also suffered horrendous losses but had held their ground. Seventy-four dead were accounted for, but their injured were being treated and would live to fight another day.

The two groups now stayed in their own territories in an uneasy stand-off. With most of the youths dead or injured, the chances of a repeat action were slim, but the Afrikaaners were not to know this, so carried on their defensive actions.

In Zeerust, the cost of not having food and water had been almost three hundred lives.

## SIXTEEN

The violence in Zeerust was not unique. It erupted in various forms all over South Africa, some small-scale and some large. In some places it was rich black households that were raided, especially in Sandton in Johannesburg, where the residents from the nearby township of Alexandra decided to take the law into their own hands. Here, people were living in properties worth millions of pounds, whilst just down the road people were living in shanty houses. Normally, even with the police presence, petty crime was common. With no police control, it raged out of hand.

Alexandra is rated as one of the poorest areas in all of South Africa. It consists of around twenty thousand shanties and a population of one hundred and sixty thousand poor people. All of their anger and hatred spilled over in one short night.

The first targets of the mobs were the hotels. Normally full of foreigners, the occupancy rates were way down since the flights in and out of the country had been cut. But they had food, water and money, so the mob stripped them bare of all these things. They stole the bedding, beds, chairs, sofas and anything else that wasn't nailed down. Some shacks in Alexandra displayed an unusual sight, the following day: walking from a street with open sewers, through a door made of corrugated metal into a living room with a sofa from the Hilton Hotel.

In the Protea Hotel close to Sandton, the mob took over the bar after one raid. It once had a beautiful wooden bar, old English style, but it soon looked like a shabeen. Decorative wooden pillars were broken, the furniture wrecked, and all of the liquor consumed. Drunks were lying half-asleep on the plush couches, others fought for the last bottles of whisky and attached their mouths directly to beer taps, and others had sex with the local prostitutes on the floor of the bar, with no intention of paying for the service.

The most extravagant hotel in the area – the Michelangelo – that had once looked like something out of a Batman movie, was torched after the locusts had stripped it out. It was considered an icon of the overpaid and underworked rich. It took years to build and hours to destroy.

The houses and flats in the area all had private security but, with no police, the security companies took the decision not to defend them. The risk to themselves was deemed too high. This led to many blacks and whites alike being robbed, then murdered or raped. In one household, the CEO of South Africa's state electricity supplier, Eskom, was tied to a chair and made to watch his wife and fourteen year old daughter being gang-raped by a group of five blacks. He offered the combination to his safe before anything bad had occurred, but the gang had already decided what they would do. The images of such barbarism did not live in the victims' minds too long though: they were all killed after the animals had finished. The gang then left in search of new targets.

Some of the locals managed to stop some of the looting. An ex-Rhodesian special forces officer was in his home when a gang of four youths broke down the door. He was on the other side of it with a Walther pistol in each hand. Four shots from each pistol left the youths with two holes in each of their heads. Owning the pistols was illegal – he never registered them with the authorities – but like many South Africans, he held them from the days when almost everyone owned a weapon. Today they had saved his life.

A young black woman living in a one bed apartment heard her door break down. Terrified, she hid in her bathroom, hoping the youths would take what they could see and leave. It was not to be, and when a single intruder came in to the loo, she confronted him with an illegally obtained Taser, downloading several thousand volts in to the intruder before running to the safety of a neighbour's apartment. He twitched on the floor for thirty minutes.

Some of the crime was more professional and organised. One group just went from ATM to ATM, tying the units to a truck and hauling them out of the walls they were mounted in. Even then, they didn't try and take the cash, just loaded the whole units onto the truck, using the small Hiab crane mounted on it.

Yet another gang focused on electrical goods. They amassed a collection of TVs, computers, laptops, tablets, iPhones and e-readers, with the aim of establishing a future black market for the goods while law and order were out-of-order. By the end of the evening they had a stock worth around half a million pounds.

Jewellery stores were another favourite target. Windows were smashed, and when the gangs found that the grills behind the windows were too strong for man-handling out of the way, then they were tied to cars and hauled off. Millions-worth of diamonds, tanzanite, pearls, opals and other precious stones were taken, along with other jewellery in gold, silver and platinum. Fortunes were made in merchandise that the robbers would find almost impossible to offload. None had money to buy it.

By morning, Sandton looked more like Beirut than an influential district of the most advanced society in sub-Saharan Africa.


The largest shanty settlement in Cape Town is Khayelitsha, meaning 'new home.' Some of it is brick-built basic government housing, but most of it is shacks built from corrugated iron, wood and bits of scrap that the residents find on their travels. It houses an estimated million people. Sanitation is worse than dreadful and the smells are unbelievable. It's like walking in to a bad motorway toilet and having your head stuffed down the loo. The police had no real hold on the place so, with the present situation, the place was controlled by the strongest gangs. Even before this, crime was king, and extortion, prostitution, murder, rape and child abuse were a day-to-day normality.

When the locals heard about the troubles in other parts of the country, they decided to go and 'take what's rightfully ours.'

Cape Town is a place of vast wealth, so the choices of where to get their illegal gains were unlimited, from shopping malls, to rich neighbourhoods, to the airport, or even the exclusive Blue Train, with its endless stock of alcohol and Cuban cigars.

As in Johannesburg, some of the crime was organised and structured, with ATMs and goods targeted. Some saw this as an excuse to 'go and live like the rich,' with gangs taking over pubs and restaurants and having a party to rival all parties. And some of it was just wanton violence.

Here in Cape Town, three dominant groups existed: the rich – whites and blacks – living in their exclusive developments such as Camps Bay and Table View; the Cape-coloured population – not accepted as blacks yet not included as whites – a sort of 'piggy in the middle' group; and the poor – black or white – who made up the whole population of Khayelitsha.

The various gangs targeted the easy hits first – the airport, the malls, the bars and restaurants. In Cape Town there is no shortage of malls, so there was plenty to go around for everyone. Even so, sometimes the coloureds and the poor chose the same mall, and this resulted in additional acts of violence against one another. Without law, they maimed and murdered at will.

Cape Town's wonderful mall down near the V & A Waterfront was a place built only to entertain tourists. For many of the Khayelitsha residents, it was their first outing at the V & A, normally a market far from their price range. For those that had been there, it was mainly to try their luck as pick-pockets or hookers. Even these people did not usually visit the Clock Tower Mall, with its choice of jewellery and diamond shops. These were soon looted, but not without inter-group fighting as the rewards were so great. Carrying a million pounds worth of diamonds is far easier than carrying a million pounds worth of stolen televisions.

The Ferryman public house in the V & A is usually full of relatively rich white tourists. Today it was full of blacks helping themselves to the outrageous range of beers the place stocked, drinking themselves silly after helping themselves to their choice of clothes, food and other goods from the nearby shops. No bar staff served them: it was a help-yourself day.

As people became drunk, they became rowdy and violent. One man would spot that another had a better haul than he had managed, so he would challenge him for it.

"Give me your bag!" a six foot black boy asked a smaller man drinking a Castle Lager.

"Go fuck yourself!" said the smaller man. A drunken scuffle broke out, the larger man getting the better of the other. It looked like he would get his bag, when the small man pulled out a revolver and shot him in the chest. Winner takes all.

The bar hardly stopped drinking. They weren't paying for it, so why waste time grieving over dead people?

Close by was a Protea Hotel named Breakwater Lodge. This had once been a prison, but of late it doubled as both a hotel and part of the Cape Town University Campus. Within the grounds was not only the hotel and university complex, but also some disturbing relics of the past that were fast becoming disturbing reminders of today. Part of the prison had once housed the 'death cells' but also an antique torture instrument to teach prisoners discipline. It looked like a mini-water wheel, and prisoners were chained to it and made to walk, the speed determined by the friction braking system. If they didn't walk fast enough, they fell off the stepped wheel, cracking their shins and bodies. It worked as well today as it had in the previous century.

On Camps Bay, residents had stocked up on food and drinks and barricaded themselves in to their homes. With such rich pickings in the city, they were not disturbed for the first few days and many became complacent, heading out to their local beaches. But once things started running out in the shops, the crowds needed new areas to get their fix and Camps Bay was as rich and good as any.

The story was an old one: homes were raided of possessions, money was taken, cars were taken, people were killed and women and men alike were raped. The beaches, once famous for their white sands and beautiful – but cold – sea, were now filled with all night parties, fed from the dozens of restaurants and cafes in the area. They were soon full of the remnants of the parties, bonfires, rubbish and bodies.

As the cities were emptied, the masses moved out to the surrounding towns. Places like Hout Bay, Muizenburg, Somerset West, Stellenbosch and Franschoek became victims of the anarchy that overtook the country. The wonderful, picturesque vineyards that had taken decades to cultivate, were drank dry and burned.

Industries stopped. There was no security, no supplies and no-one to sell the finished products to. Owners lost everything: factories were looted for stock and spares, and what the mob could not find a use for they burned. Hundreds of years of labour were destroyed within a matter of weeks.

South Africa had descended to its lowest level since history there had been written.

No-one was running the country.

## SEVENTEEN

As the situation worsened and international communication dried up, it was decided to move the President and his main cabinet members out of the country to the neighbouring Mozambique. Here he would run a government in exile and try to repair the country with any help sympathetic foreign powers would give. One of his final moves before the exit had been to ask Graca Machel to join him. Between them, he said, perhaps South Africa could be made great again. She said that she would think about it, but her mind was presently fully occupied with the loss of her beloved husband, Nelson Mandela. It would be a strange twist of fate for her: her previous husband had been the President of Mozambique before he met his untimely death in an aircraft accident on the border of Zululand and his country.

From the top floor swimming pool area of his hotel in Maputo, the President surveyed the city. It was still a poor place, and not really long enough from the ravages of civil war to have fully forgotten it, but the people were mainly happy. Not without problems – minor riots occurred from time to time when food was short – but they were expecting things to get better, especially with the massive coal finds in the Tete Province in the north. Oil was also expected to make an appearance soon.

Meanwhile, his own country seemed to be on a downward spiral with no bottom in sight.

How could he have missed the mood of his people? He knew how. Sitting in your silk-wrapped packaging in the Union Buildings, attending dinners each night that cost more than most of the population earned in a year, driving around in air-conditioned bullet-proof Mercedes cars, flying first-class to Europe... The list went on. You soon lost sight of what was really happening at grassroots level.

But how could he change it? He knew he didn't have the charm and charisma of Nelson Mandela. He knew youth was not on his side, neither in the voter's profile, nor in his years. Maybe it was just time to stand aside and let the pretenders in. Could he do that to his country?

He had spoken to the UK's David Cameron, Germany's Angela Merkel and US President Barak Obama, all of whom pledged temporary financial support if he could get the mines working again. The removal of South Africa from the markets had allowed other producers of mineral resources to push up pricing, as demand exceeded production. The sooner South Africa came back on line, the sooner the resource prices would return to normal levels. And high energy pricing affected every part of the supply chain.

With the collapse of the mining income streams, the Rand had suffered terribly. Only six weeks ago, seven Rand would buy a dollar. Now it was trading at fifteen Rand to the green-back, making the Rand less than half its pre-crisis value. Even with things running correctly again, it would take months to recover its former worth, and in the meantime imports would cost way above their true value for the country and the consumer.

It wasn't quite a Zimbabwe, but it wasn't a pretty picture that was being painted. He could already envisage the need to print even higher denomination bank notes.

He needed Graca to speak on his behalf. If she supported him, then the country might just unite under the magic of Mandela again. Even in his death, the man could still save his people from destroying themselves. It was his hope for the future, but it was a faint hope, and he knew that he was asking a lot from an elderly, grieving widow.


Oliver Justice was less worried about the state of the nation. He was just enjoying his elevated power and new way of living. With the President out of the country, even his power base in Zululand was weakening. Oliver could move around freely, with the Army controlling the country under his command.

As leader of the ANCs Youth League, he was used to living with privileges for years now, but the new situation was actually absurd. He could do what he wanted, and he did.

Every night he and his close political colleagues and the generals, ate and drank like no-one else on the planet. Living on the best cognacs, whiskies, wines and grappas, they ate kudu, steaks, lobsters, oysters, caviar and anything else they wished for. The costs for this type of eating were paid for using gold reserves held in the Central Bank: it couldn't last forever, but there was certainly plenty there.

Women were organised for every evening when the eating and drinking was over. He slept normally with at least two girls, but one night had been pampered by five, including three blacks, a white and an Indian girl who knew just how to handle him.

The generals were treated the same, so their support was secure. And while they were with him, he didn't have to worry about the rest of the population, whom he had basically abandoned when he seized control with the military.

His original support base had started out being the miners, but he had dropped them as swiftly as he could once the Army came to him. They were still out of work, still not being paid, and mine output had fallen to zero. The international players had pulled their people out of the country, and the mines were lying semi-dormant: some gold miners were still attending work, but only to raid the companies they previously worked for, selling the raw material on the black market.

The ports had closed, with all major carriers boycotting the country. This meant no goods in and no goods out, so the balance of trade was zero. Foreign governments were talking about trade sanctions, but with the private sector already ceasing to do business, there was no real reason to impose actual restrictions anyway.

The country's white population was at its lowest level ever: anyone with a passport to get out of there had gone. This caused a massive 'brain drain' on the business community. It would take years after everything was 'back to normal' before the lost business leaders would come back, and some simply never would.

Oliver knew all of this, but blatantly ignored it. Life was for now, and life was good.

He reached out with his right hand and picked up the Remy Martin from the bedside cabinet, sipping it and savouring it. He looked down his body and watched the Indian girl bobbing her head over his penis, sucking and licking him in a way only she seemed to know how.


The Avalon Cemetery in Soweto, Johannesburg, had seen many great people buried in its grounds, mainly from the days of the struggle against Apartheid. Joe Slovo, Helen Joseph, Lillian Ngoyi and Hector Pieterson, are among some of the famous deceased sleeping in this place of final rest, so it was fitting that Nelson Mandela joined their ranks there. He was without doubt the most famous of them all in the fight for freedom.

The cemetery was fairly much full now, its hundred and seventy odd hectares containing over 300,000 dead. Nowadays, people were usually buried in the newer Waterval Cemetery, but when one of the country's dearest sons dies, he must rest with his fellow comrades.

The police attended out of respect of Madiba, even though there was no real control over the force. They did it not for money, but for the great man. They estimated that twelve thousand people were in the graveyard and the surrounding area, all waiting to pay their respects to the great leader. It also took their minds off the suffering they were still enduring since the country had been 'freed' of the President.

Graca Machel, dressed in black, stood at the graveside with the children and grandchildren of Mandela. She'd had to do this once before in recent history, when one of his grand-daughters had died in a car crash. It was not easy then, and this time losing her soul mate made it even harder.

On the outside she didn't cry, even though her insides felt like they were being torn apart.

Her family needed her to be strong, and she had never let them down. Not now, not ever.


The violence that was ripping through the country was lessening, to some degree at least, as fewer and fewer places were left to rob. The total lack of law and order meant that communities had to police themselves. This led to vigilante movements springing up. People were sick of being robbed, raped and raided, so they set up their own protection groups for their towns and villages.

It wasn't the answer, but it did stop some of the crime and violence.

With nothing left in the stores and no supply chain, bartering for goods became the norm. People also turned to the land, growing crops and caring for livestock. It was better to live in the countryside than the city. Johannesburg was no longer viewed as being 'paved with gold.'

Along with the miners, the Army also, largely, went unpaid, many of them deserting and returning to their homes to try and find a better way to feed their families. They were not trained farmers, but they were strong and at least a little disciplined, so they were able to lend their muscle to the preparation of the farmlands, assist in laying down crops and harvesting the results. And probably more importantly, to defend what the locals were trying to achieve from roaming gangs.

Not all of the deserters took this route, and some – along with ex-police officers – formed mercenary groups. 'Soldiers for hire,' they called themselves. These were taken on by the rich for exorbitant fees. It stopped the problems for a while, but these people realized their worth and became greedy.

Putting South Africa back together again was not going to be an easy task...


Captain Ndile Mkwazi had been a patrolman in the South African Police Service. That was before things had changed, and now he had awarded himself a field promotion to give him the authority he needed over his men. Not that he needed much authority: at six foot two in the land of mainly five-foot-eight people, he was a strong and effective leader. He also always seemed to find the right places to rob so they were all well rewarded. Something to do with his 'local knowledge' as a serving officer before the troubles.

Today in Johannesburg, his plan was more than ambitious. He was going to raid the South African Gold Refinery. Depleted as it was by Oliver Justice, it was still a more than worthwhile target.

He had a friend working there from the old days. Mkwazi had helped provide the facility's security through his position as a police officer, but he had also provided a perfect route out for illegal gains. In the old days these were usually gold nuggets hidden in drilled out teeth and other orifices, but with today's restrictions they were generally more discreet: occasionally nuggets, but often petty cash and credit notes.

But today was intended to be a big one: Federal Reserve Ingots.

The plan was simple. They would cruise up to the gate in full police regalia, and hopefully gain unopposed access, otherwise they would force access. They had a flatbed lorry that would be loaded to full with ingots. Then they would flee to Zimbabwe as an easy border crossing point, then on to those African countries that would be happy to trade with them.

Gold was gold. Legality didn't matter.

His group was complete and at a final staging post – a deserted mine entrance, chained and locked by its owners before they had shut-up shop – ready to roll. Final briefings, a check on the cell phone communications and each man reciting his part in the task. Satisfied that they were as ready as they ever would be, he climbed in to the rear seat of his patrol car.

The flatbed lorry remained in the mine entrance with its driver and two other ex-cops riding shotgun. All three men were armed to stop other interested parties getting too interested. They would be called forward once access was gained.

Mkwazi's car rolled off, followed closely by a second police car. Four men in each unit meant a total of eight guns. Should work.

They turned in to Changi South Avenue in Germiston, a strange area to have the place that had produced approximately one third of the world's gold bar since its opening in 1920. Germiston was an industrial area and not a particularly pleasant place. Mkwazi was actually a little surprised no-one else had tried to turn the place over until now, but then again, it was well guarded and secure. He had two advantages over most people: he was known there by the security people from better times; and he had an insider to assist him.

The cars rolled up to the gates of the refinery and Mkwazi climbed out the back door of his car, walking over to the security office.

"Sawabona," he said to the two men inside. "Everything OK around here? No problems?"

"All's well here boss," said one of the men. Mkwazi recognized his face from before but did not know his name.

"You've been here some time now?" he asked.

"Be four years in June," the man said. "Time flies when you're having fun."

"We've been asked to come around by President Justice. He needs a top-up for his phone," Mkwazi joked. "If he carries on like this, we'll have to open the mines again to get some money back together. Things must be getting low."

"Can I just check if the Governor knows about it?" the guard asked. "Normally we get warned in advance, but nowadays…"

As the guard turned to use the phone, the inner door to the office opened and Mkwazi's 'inside man' came out.

"No need to phone Joseph," he told the guard. "I have the written authority here." He handed over a letter prepared earlier, complete with faked signature and stamps. "I'll see them in myself."

"OK Sir," the guard replied, recognizing the Deputy Governor. "I'll open the barriers to let their cars in."

"There'll be a small pick-up following in just a minute," Mkwazi said. "These cars aren't designed for heavy stuff!" He laughed and checked that a man in the second car was on his cell phone to the flatbed.

"Wouldn't want to damage a government vehicle," the guard joked.

He went out and unlocked a large Yale padlock and chain on the outer gates, swinging one of them open. The second security officer then pressed a button to slide back a second set of gates, and the way in was clear. Mkwazi's car rolled through the opening, the second holding outside until the flatbed arrived and drove through. The second car then followed and the gates were re-secured.

Vehicles parked, the 'policemen' followed the Deputy Governor in to the main building, leaving just three men to be ready with the vehicles.

Mkwazi hoped to get in and out without any requirement for armed force, but he was also more than ready to use it. So far all was going to plan, with no-one questioning their authenticity and doors and vaults being opened without question. It seemed that the plan would go off without hitch.

Opening an inner vault, full of ingots, everything fell to pieces.

"What are you men doing here?" demanded Governor Steed, one of the few whites employed in the whole facility. "There is no authorized collection due today. I would have seen the paperwork for anything like that."

A few of the security people turned to see what was going on, but the eight armed 'police officers' had already raised their weapons. Bullets thundered from the stubby barrels of eight assorted machine pistols, raking their way through the unprepared guards and the Governor. Blood spattered the walls and ran from their bodies once they fell to the ground.

Then only a deep silence, and the smell of cordite. It lasted about ten seconds until the first alarm sounded, this followed by others.

"We have around three minutes under normal circumstances to get out of here," the Deputy Governor shouted. "Right now, I guess five."

"Everyone take what they can carry and run back to the vehicles! This place will go in to lock down soon, and we need to be out of here," yelled the Captain.

Each man carried a small rucksack, and swiftly stuffed half a dozen ingots in to each one. They then headed swiftly for the vehicles.

With no Governor or Deputy, the security was a little disorganised and this assisted the raiders, as Mkwazi thought it would. They quickly made it back to the parked cars and truck before their luck ended. With the gates closed, the only way out was to seize the gatehouse, and the two men in there were prepared for trouble.

"Change of plan!" Mkwazi yelled to his men, swiftly telling them the new idea.

The eight packs were thrown in to the two car boots. Everyone jumped in the cars and lorry. Engines gunned up.

The flatbed led the way, ramming the first gate. It bent but didn't fail. Armed security guards were arriving at the parking area, alerted by the gatemen.

"Out of the cars! You two, cover the rear, you two the gate. Drivers stay ready to go."

The Captain ran to the flatbed. "Aim the vehicle at one gate only! And have a run up at it!"

The driver backed up and revved the diesel engine, then engaged the clutch, causing the lorry to burst forward. He aimed at one gate. It bent back, not enough to get through, but going that way.

A burst of rifle fire came from the gatehouse, shattering the windscreen. One round found its way in to the drivers chest, and screaming, he tried to reverse away from the gate. About ten metres back, he gave up trying, slumping over the wheel. He – like the truck – was expendable under the new plan, so Mkwazi didn't really mind.

"Sergeant get him out of there and someone else in! We need the barriers open or we're all dead."

The sergeant grabbed one of his men and ran to where the truck had now stalled, pulling open the driver's door. The men in the gatehouse had a limited arc of fire and couldn't do much about the change of drivers, only wait for the next assault on the gate. They kept below window level to ensure their own safety, only glancing up occasionally. With bullet-proof office windows they knew they were fairly safe, but no point taking chances. The driver was meanwhile hauled dead from the vehicle and a reluctant raider installed in his place.

By now a minor fire-fight was going on from the main building, as security people arrived and found firing points without coming into the courtyard area where the vehicles were. The raiders returned fire, but largely guessed where to send their rounds.

The new driver rammed the gate again, bending it more or less open. He quickly slammed the wagon in reverse, backed up and rammed again. There was now enough room to get the lorry through.

"Take the outer gate!"

The driver looked nervously at Mkwazi, knowing he would be in full view of the guardhouse doing this. The Captain noticed this and directed two of his men to lay down fire on the building, keeping the guards away from the window.

The driver took another run-up, doing about thirty miles an hour when he hit the padlocked gate. The chain sheared and the gate flew open, the lorry flying through as steam vacated a punctured radiator. The truck was goosed.

Mkwazi didn't waste time. "In the cars! Quickly!" he ordered.

The men fired a last long burst each at the security and started boarding up as they had practised.

"Which car am I in?" the Deputy Governor asked.

Mkwazi turned and fired a three-round burst at point blank range. No need to share the gold too many ways.

The two cars left with their ten live occupants and headed for the Zimbabwe border. They were almost half a tonne of gold richer.

Not a bad days work.

## EIGHTEEN

Then there was the wildlife, something that was once part and parcel of a visit to South Africa.

Pre-collapse, the wildlife parks accounted for a high percentage of tourist income: this formed a major part of the non-mineral wealth of the country. People flew from all over the world to experience the electric atmosphere of being in close proximity to a wild animal, whether it be a big cat, an elephant, or a zebra. This was something that you couldn't experience at home, even with the best Sky TV package showing National Geographical documentaries.

With the demise of the political system and law and order, the rangers in the parks received no protection or support from the dangers of the poachers, so poaching took on a whole new dimension. They also ceased to get paid, so some took to trading animals themselves.

The initial problem in the parks was the increase in poaching.

Previously most poaching was limited to high-return activities, initially for ivory from the tusks of elephants, and latterly from the sales of rhino horn to Far Eastern markets, mainly to the growing economy of China. The horn is basically made up of the same tissues that form human nails and hair, so why it should be considered an aphrodisiac is really a little bizarre.

A secondary poaching activity from the parks was the trade in wild animals. This increased more than tenfold, with precious animals such as lions, leopards, cheetahs and larger game being traded cross-border for peanut prices. Park populations fell drastically.

Within a six month period of the crisis, the black and white rhino population of South Africa ceased to exist.

A further problem was the lack of normal park maintenance.

Fences, electric or not, are no match for an animal such as an elephant. A bull elephant can weigh up to seven tonnes and run at speeds of around thirty miles an hour. Even a rhino can weigh-in at three to four tonnes and a water buffalo at one-and-a-half, so wire and wood have no chance at all. In the normal course of events, game rangers spot damage whilst out on drives with customers, but with no customers and no drives – vehicles all stolen by the gangs – controlled maintenance was not taking place.

Rivers blocked up and waterholes ran dry. Damage to dams meant that artificially formed lakes ceased to be lakes. This meant a forced migration of the hippo population and any other animals using the water source.

Breaches in the outer fences increased, allowing animals to leave and enter at their will. Africa was returning to its roots.

Some of the local villages tried to make their own repairs to the game park borders, but others saw how the disruptions caused by the dangerous animals could be used to fuel the anarchy that they were benefiting from.

They dismantled repaired areas, made holes of their own, and utilized the situation they had produced, either by shooting the animals for food, using them to destabilize areas, or offering their services to rid the village of the pests. Many villagers lost their lives to attacks from lions and other game. They no longer had the skills to defend themselves from what was once the norm.

Wild South Africa was on her knees.

A country of forty-five million people was disjointed, had no centrally organised governmental entity, and the populace lived in fear of one another.

It was the beginning of the end in no uncertain terms.


"And where the fuck is my caviar this morning?" Oliver Justice yelled. "What the hell is this place coming to? You'd think we are savages."

The black girl to his right rolled over, rubbing her eyes to remove tiredness after a bare three hours of sleep. The white teenager on his left slept on, oblivious. With the drugs, it would be hours before she re-joined the human race.

"The fish eggs do not come from our country, Sir," the butler replied. "And with the embargoes currently in place against us, we have simply exhausted our supplies of such luxuries. I am so sorry, Sir."

"Shit!" Justice swore. "Shit, shit and more shit!"

"Hey honey, why don't we have a little fun," the lady said, rolling a hand down his body under the sheets and trying to defuse the situation. "Now whitey is out of it, me and my man can get a little jiggey."

Justice looked at her, scowling. "Later I can do what I want with you bitch, but right now I need food." He paused a second, before continuing. "And I am not your man."

"I can offer a bacon and egg sandwich, Sir?" the butler enquired.

"I need food, so that will be fine," the great man replied. "And a champagne or something to wash it down with. And hurry!"

"Consider it done, Sir."

With no hospitals, and no doctors or nurses, traditional medicine was making a strong comeback in the country. African faith-healers known as Sangomas believe they have the powers to cure mental, physical and emotional health problems. In South Africa they have always been available in higher numbers than medical doctors, but normally a local would hedge their bets and consult both a Sangoma and make use of modern medicine. Now that there were no medical facilities, only traditional methods remained.

Most of the Sangomas used legal methods and were actually licensed to practice. Their treatments came from the plants and trees, but some turned to the dark arts that were illegal. They used Muti, the taking of body parts to cure or improve a person at the expense of another human. Sometimes the host was killed for the body parts, and other times only the required parts were taken.

The favourite human flesh to use came from the black albinos, known as the "invisible ones", or "white ghost people". Use of albino meat was almost sacred. Other flesh was acceptable, but a prized albino would be hunted down and slaughtered on the spot, men vying for the best body parts, with the genitals prized to improve sexual prowess.

With no law and order, South African albinos became extinct.


Alcohol was a great escape from the problems of reality, both before the country folded, but especially after the collapse. With no imports and local breweries out of business, the only way to obtain alcohol was to produce it locally. The knowledge to do this was around, as local shebeens had always made their own uncontrolled brews, but the scale of the local production needed to increase to meet demand.

Using yeast and sugar based mixes, basic alcohol was easily made, but the strength of the drink was quite low. Therefore shebeen owners found additives to beef it up. From the deserted factories they stole industrial alcohol. From the hospitals and chemists they took medical ethyl alcohol. They even took battery acid from garages.

The effect of drinking these concoctions on the body was disastrous, and people began suffering serious organ breakdowns, especially of the liver and kidneys.

Worse was to come as pregnant women used the liquor, the additives affecting the development of the foetus, causing deformities and brain damage. This led to a high level of child mortality, with stillborn numbers doubling on normal times.

The future hopes for South Africa were also in a mess.


Pre-crisis, South Africa had the highest recorded incidence of AIDS in the world. Protected sex was almost unheard of despite the government's campaigns to provide free condoms to the population in public conveniences. Multiple partners was the norm. Mother to child cross infection was high, but with the increasing use of antiretroviral drugs, this was being brought down.

Local production of ARVs also brought the price of the medication down and allowed larger sectors of the population to have access to it, slowing the reproduction of the Human Immunodeficiency Virus.

It couldn't be said that AIDS in South Africa was under control, but the message to the public was improving and the tools to combat it were in place. The old messages from government figures that it could be held off by eating garlic or sweet potato were finished, and the famous "shower after sex" idea was also gone.

In the poorer and remote areas, the belief that having sex with a virgin was still half believed, but the rape of young children to rid men of AIDS had fallen to the lowest levels. There was even hope that it could be totally eradicated.

With the collapse of the medical system, ARV drugs ceased to be available. Untreated, the effects of HIV on already weak bodies meant infection and disease wiped out hundreds of people every week. Children were left with no parents, having to fend for themselves in an environment with no social handouts and no services.

With the fallback to traditional medicine and beliefs, the rape of children increased and the virus spread quickly to the younger generation.

Whoever was going to put humpty-dumpty back together again was going to find it a tough task.


President Dumi Silongo sat in a dark leather wingback chair in the lounge of his suite in the Polana Serena Hotel. Opposite him sat Graca Machel, wearing a brightly coloured knee-length dress. It was probably the only thing that was bright about her, Dumi thought. Her face was gaunt, and it looked as though she had not slept well for months.

"So how are the children and grandchildren bearing up?" he asked her once formalities were out of the way.

"They are suffering. They miss South Africa but staying there now is impossible. London is fine and we have a nice place there, but it is not home. Cold and wet."

"Where is home right now?" Dumi asked. "The place we left behind is unrecognizable from when we left. I can't imagine when we can possibly go back."

"The stories coming out of the place are horrendous. Murder, rape, theft, all manner of hell. And the self-appointed President is living like a pig. He drinks, eats and has sex seven days a week. He is raping the country just as surely as the bandits in the cities are."

"I heard that the support for him is zero, but with the generals on his side, no-one is able to take him on."

"Perhaps one of the less senior military figures will try it. They are not being so well looked after, so we could see another coup-d'état."

They sat in silence for a minute.

"A source in the Union Buildings told me they burnt the original Constitution document last week," the President said in a grave voice. "The one put together and signed by Madiba himself."

"I heard the same but chose not to believe it. I just cannot believe that they could have sunk to those levels."

"The stories I have heard tells me that they could have. I despair at what has happened to my country."

An uncomfortable quiet came over the room, and Dumi knew it was time to ask the big question.

"Graca, before all of this got so out of hand, I asked if you or Madiba would give your active support. Basically come back in to politics." He was watching her reaction, but she was a long time in the public eye and knew how to hide her emotions. "What is your view on that now?"

"Dumi," she began, looking down at her thighs. "I have been through such a lot in my life. I have lost not one, but two great husbands, both true leaders. I am well over sixty years of age and I think my time for serving is over. I must devote the rest of my time on this earth my family, both from South Africa and Mozambique. I'm sorry."

"Thank you for such an honest answer. It is what I expected. You have given so much, and now is a time for you."

A pause as each thought about what had just been said. "What will you do now Dumi?"

He looked around the room, searching for a perfect answer. "I have been in Maputo for four months now, and I am making no progress. I need to be somewhere where I might make a difference. I also think London might be my next stop."

"You will form a government in exile there?"

"I have already sounded out Mr Cameron, and he is happy if I do. Perhaps we could call on you for support from time to time?"

"My heart will always be in Africa, no matter how bad things get. I will support you, but not full time."

"You are an angel Graca."

# PART 2 – THE UNITED KINGDOM

## NINETEEN

Jama Nomvula had been standing to attention on the parade ground for the last fifteen minutes. They were waiting for the General Officer Commanding (Southern Region) to finish his inspection of the troops, and he was taking his time. It was also pouring with rain, making Jama reflect on the meaning of his Zulu name: Jama, to wait and Nomvula, 'with the rain.' He felt he was living up to it quite well.

He was a bit of an oddity. At twenty seven years of age, he was a Captain in the British Army, and would hopefully pick-up his Major's crown at the next promotion board. For a black boy born in Durban, this was quite an achievement.

His mother Tobila was a nurse from Stanger, a town north of Durban. His father was a white English doctor who had been there as part of an exchange program from London. It had been love at first sight, and Jama had been the result. His father decided not to return to the UK and they married in Kwa-Zulu Natal, continuing to live in Stanger. Settling in Africa, they had decided between them to give Jama his mother's Zulu name rather than a British one.

Jama received dual citizenship because of this, but never went to England until he was twenty-one years old. On leaving school he had joined the South African Defence Force but found them totally unprofessional and left after a couple of years. He tried medicine at his parents insistence, but it wasn't really his cup of tea. He wanted to be a soldier, so he decided to apply for the British Army.

His father helped him pay for the ticket to England and he stayed initially with his grandparents in the ward of Walthamstow in north-east London. Here he learned to deal with the UK climate, and also discovered the evils of English beer in the quirky old Nags Head pub in the old village. It was a big change from where he'd been born. Here he needed to wear jumpers and waterproofs most of the year.

One night in the Nags, he got talking to one of the old boys at the bar. Jama had noticed he was a bit of a fixture in there: his own favourite position at the end of the bar and his own pewter beer mug. He had grey hair and looked to be early to mid-fifties. He was in reasonable shape, as though even now he still worked out.

Jama was getting himself a pint of London Pride with some money his grandfather had given him, when he heard the man's voice behind him.

"You're not from 'round 'ere are you?"

He turned to find the man looking directly at him, so no dodging the question.

"I'm from South Africa Sir," he replied politely. "Why do you ask?"

"Picked up on the accent, and couldn't quite place it," the man replied.

"Mam's South African and dad's from here, so I guess I have a bit of a mix."

"No 'arm in that son," the man replied. "By the way, I'm Pete." He stuck his hand out, and Jama shook it. "What do you do around 'ere?"

"I moved here from Durban a couple of weeks back. Stay with my grandparents."

"What work do you do?"

"I was in the South African Defence Force, but right now nothing."

Pete started laughing, slapping the bar with his open hand.

"What's wrong?"

"Nothin' at all! South African Defence Force. What sort of unit's that?" He continued laughing to himself.

"A crap unit, that's why I left. I had hoped to get in to the British Army, but no idea where to start."

The laughter stopped. "Now we're talking. A real Army."

"But how do you get in? Do you know something about it?"

"Somethin' about it? I was in it."

For the next two hours and four beers, Pete recounted tale after tale about his exploits in the military, from London to Londonderry, and Brixton to Baghdad. He told of all night parties, of fire fights with Iraqi terrorists, training courses in the Brecon Beacons and leading soldiers on the streets of Belfast. By the end of it, Jama was well and truly hooked.

"But how do I join?" he asked.

"That bit's easy." said Pete. "Just go down the recruiting office on the High Street in the morning. Do some exams and they'll tell ya if you have a chance."

Jama finished his beer, thanked Pete for the evening and walked home.

He finally had a goal.


That had been six and a half years ago, and as they say, the rest was history.

He'd followed Pete's advice and gone to the local recruiting office, where a sergeant had taken down his details and had him complete some basic tests. The soldier had been more interested when he read the application form through and found that Jama was ex-SADF – at least he would have the basics he was told.

A medical with a local doctor told him he was fit enough to attempt the training, then ten days later he was on a train north to Yorkshire, to the Infantry Training Centre in Catterick. It was his first trip out of the capital, and the endless green fields and regular towns and cities fascinated him.

His choice of regiment had been the Grenadier Guards, mainly because they spent so much time in the City of London, the only place he knew. That meant a slightly longer basics course than other infantry trainees as they had to cover the ceremonial drill, as well as all the other soldiering skills. Twenty-eight weeks later, he passed out as a soldier.

After all the defence cuts of recent years, the Grenadiers had retained their own identity, but had been trimmed back to only one battalion. His first posting with them was what he wanted: back to the smoke, as the other lads called it.

London is a great place for a young soldier. Once your duties are out of the way, the city is your own. He lived it up.

On manoeuvres on Salisbury Plain, he proved himself a good soldier who had respect from the other troops and received his first promotion. He'd been a year out of Catterick and was getting noticed fast.

A short emergency tour in Northern Ireland gave him his first taste of decision-making under pressure. The Police Service of Northern Ireland had come under considerable pressure as Nationalist sympathizers tried to wreck the fragile peace process there. Jama found himself on the streets of the Bogside with bricks and petrol bombs raining down on him and lads. They held their line, not rising to the occasion and going after the thugs in the crowd.

Another night on the streets and things were getting a little ugly, with one of the troops from the other platoon getting a direct hit from a petrol bomb. With his clothing alight, his comrades dropped their guard to try and assist him.

The night was freezing and Jama was standing next to a water cannon. Pushing the uncertain operator out of the way, he took control and doused the burning soldier before turning it on the advancing crowd. The cold night air and the water did the rest, the crowd dispersing and the soldier getting the treatment he needed. Not a shot was fired.

On return to London he was ordered to report to the commanding officer, a Colonel McFarlane.

"You did a great job out there on the streets for a young soldier, Nomvula. I've recommended you for a Queens Commission from the ranks."

"Sir," he had replied, not sure what was going on, but maintaining military discipline.

"Don't worry lad," the CO said. "I've seen young officers with the same decisions you had to make freeze up. You'll make a good Grenadier Officer. Fall out!"

Jama about-turned and marched out of the office. He was met by the Company Sergeant Major. "Well done lad. The CO's already briefed me. We'll get the paperwork completed right now, then you can have a week's leave."

When Jama left the office, his head was in the clouds. Less than two years out of South Africa and he was in line to become a British Army Officer.


A couple of months later and he was in training again, this time at the Royal Military Academy in Sandhurst. This was much harder than the basics completed at Catterick, with a lot more tactics and military history. Some of it was boring, but the history of the Grenadiers enthralled him: it was his family now.

He learned that the Grenadier Guards had been around in one form or another since 1656 and had served in battle for ten Kings and three Queens during this period. They finally received the name 'Grenadiers' in July 1815 in honour of their heroics during the Battle of Waterloo.

Both the Irish Guards and the Welsh Guards were formed by the 'Grens' to show respect towards the men of these countries who had fought in their ranks.

During World War I, they were active in Loos, the Somme, Cambrai, Arras and the Hindenburg Line. The Guards won seven Victoria Crosses during WWI.

When World War II came along, they served with the British Expeditionary force and were part of the evacuation and slaughter at Dunkirk. Following the D-Day invasions, they served in Western Europe, North Africa and Italy, with two further Grenadiers being awarded Victoria Crosses.

Since the wars they had carried out peace keeping duties and served in the Gulf War and Northern Ireland.

And the Grenadier Guards traditionally are the pallbearers for all dead monarchs.

Jama knew he had a hard act to follow. Afghanistan was the campaign of the day, and he knew his turn to enter the cauldron would come soon enough. Though he had been cool and collected in Northern Ireland, he still wondered how he would react when on the receiving end of enemy rounds.

He passed out of Sandhurst with a good report, but not winning any honours. These went to younger men than him, but he didn't mind.

He had achieved something that his family would be proud of.


His first year as a new Lieutenant was served carrying out public duties in London, mainly at Buckingham Palace. Though proud as punch to be there at the heart of Britain, he really preferred to be soldiering. He was not a peacock. As a South African he loved the outdoors and living in a bush and surviving on army rations was where he liked to be.

He shouldn't have worried though, and at the end of about twelve months around the capital, the regiment received its orders to deploy to Afghanistan. They would train to be ready for Operation Herrick in Helmand Province for the next three months, sharpening up skills slightly dulled by the year on parade, then they would be heading south-east for the border of the Middle East and Asia.

The Army learnt about their enemy, a ragamuffin force of rebels that had beaten the British more than a century before and more recently kicked the Russians out of their home. Studying the methods used by Al-Qaeda, the Guards learned about their disregard for human life, including their own. Suicide bombings were common. Simultaneous attacks on a number of fronts were the norm. Civilian life loss was not a worry.

Al-Qaeda are Sunni Muslims, and any non-Sunnis are regarded as soft and not adhering to the teachings of the Koran. This means they are also legitimate targets.

Osama bin Laden originally set up training camps for what would become Al-Qaeda in Afghanistan in 1987. This was mainly funded by Saudi Arabia, but funds were also pouring in from the United States, as the Russians had invaded the country and the US saw this as a way to stop the spread of communism.

After the Russians withdrew, training in the country continued for operations elsewhere against the West. Bin Ladin eventually issued a Fatwa, or religious declaration of war against the US and its allies. He began using his fanatical beliefs to influence conflicts in Iran, Yemen, Somalia and Sudan. He also used his organisation's cell structure to carry out attacks within the West, such as the London and Madrid bombings, and of course the Twin Towers in the US, the infamous 9/11.

This triggered the West's War on Terrorism and, with Afghanistan a main training base, a war on the country.

Jama understood that he had to understand his enemy to beat him, so he studied hard. He read at night and trained hard by day.

After three months he knew he was as ready as he ever would be.

## TWENTY

Cathy McKeevy rolled over in her bed and, for a moment, wondered just where she was. It was hot and clammy and the ceiling didn't look right even in the half-light. Then she realized she was under canvas again in the Darfur region of Sudan.

She was twenty-five years old, and a little too thin from living in places where there was rarely enough food to go around for the aid workers or the locals. Her hair was blond, but often tucked up in to some sort of thatch on the top of her head like something Wilma out of the Flintstones would do. When you had no reliable washing facilities and no electricity for hair dryers and straighteners, this was the simplest solution. Make-up didn't feature here in the desert, but she didn't really need it.

Rolling out of bed still in her cargo pants and T-shirt, she put her feet on to the sand floor and looked for her Croc flip-flops. She didn't intend impressing the boys today.


Cathy had been born in Bangor, close to Belfast in Northern Ireland, the youngest of four sisters. The older girls had all gone to Belfast University and then married, fallen pregnant and had their own families. Cathy rebelled and went to Newcastle University in the UK, where she studied law. She also didn't meet the man of her dreams, didn't get pregnant and didn't get hitched. Her father worried about this, but her mother loved it.

She passed her degree with flying colours and joined a law firm in the north-east city. After a year of plodding through endless papers for high-flying male lawyers, she decided this wasn't for her. She didn't know what was, but it was not the paperwork jungle she found herself in.

Newcastle is renowned not only for its bridges, but also for the wild night-life it owns. After spending her university years there, Cathy knew where to have a good time, and where to get the cheap student nights out. After a day of piling and filing scripts she decided she needed a beer. Or two. It was Thursday, so the weekend was almost there.

Pulling on a pair of faded jeans and a woolly jumper, she headed for a pub called Bob Trollops down at the Quayside. Here they had real ale, and some good old bangers and mash.

A couple of people she knew were already there, so she latched onto the three girls and two boys at the table. She knew Kat, Angie and Tom from her university days, but Debs and Phil were new to her. They turned out to be a couple, but not married.

After a wholesome meal and beer or two, conversations turned to work. Cathy mentioned that she was looking for a change. All agreed that their own jobs were a grind, and all the promise of wonderful work opportunities post obtaining a degree, was just pie in the sky. It was a tough job market and not many great jobs were out there.

Debs and Phil said nothing all the way through this. Tom brought them in to the conversation.

"Hey Phil, why don't you tell the girls what you two do?"

Phil shifted in his seat, looking a little uncomfortable. He glanced at Debs for support.

"We're aid workers," she said.

"Aid workers?" asked Kat. "Like the people on telly in Africa?"

"Yeah, the same."

"Wow! Where have you been?"

"We got back yesterday from two months in Kenya, helping in the camp on the border with Somalia, but most of the last year has been in London and places organizing parcels and stuff. It's not all like the telly." Phil added.

"How was Kenya?" Cathy asked.

"To be honest, you live in some shit conditions and you see things that you wish you'd never had to see," Phil said. "I've seen three year old kids die of malnutrition, and people with gunshot wounds who'll never walk again, and people with really nothing. But when you help someone, you actually feel like you achieved something."

"You feel like you might have changed a life," Debs added.

"Then the next day you get another group come in at least as bad as the one you just helped, and you realize you won't change a country," added Phil sadly.

"That's why a few months at a time is enough," said Debs. "You need a time out."

"Bloody hell guys, you are doing something though," Cathy replied. "We do the same shit day in, day out and nothing changes! Your job sounds like it means something."

"Don't get me wrong, it does. But it is still hard to see so much evil."

A silence fell over the group for a few seconds.

"Can we leave it alone for now Cathy?" asked Phil. "Like Debs said we need a little down time, but nothing a few pints won't cure."

"This one's on me," said Tom.

The mood lightened and the night went well, but Cathy couldn't get the idea of working for something she cared about out of her mind.

To this day she wasn't really sure of the reason she finally snapped at work the next day. Was it the boss, the hope to do something meaningful, or just the hangover?

Looking back, she remembered vaguely that getting up had been hard, with a couple of snoozes needed from the alarm clock. A good shower had helped, then a strong coffee on the Metro train into the city. The cold winter air probably helped too.

In the office she had set about the normal organising of case files for the legal people who would be attending court or client meetings. It was mundane.

At eleven o'clock, the boss had summoned her to his office.

"As you know Cathy, the country is going through a bit of a rough time and we are too. Business is not great." He peered over the top of his black framed specs and adjusted his trouser belt to better accommodate his bulging gut. "We have decided not to make anyone redundant, but we are stopping all overtime payments and freezing pay levels. That means no pay rise for this year."

He reddened, trying to look stern, but not really knowing how to go on.

Cathy knew how. "So you're staying that despite my law degree, you are going to keep me on for another year basically as an office junior?"

"You would not be a junior, and you would still be learning your trade, but money is tight."

"Doesn't seem to have stopped you buying a new Land-rover." Cathy was losing it. "I'll tell you what. No pay rise and I'm off."

"Please calm down," he asked. "We are trying to retain our staff without extra expenditure so that…"

"I think you heard me Mr Beattie. I need more money, or I'm leaving."

"We have no cash to hand out…." he started.

"Then the answer's easy then. I'm off."

She got up from the seat and headed for the door. Lawrence Beattie had stood out of his chair to follow, but she wasn't waiting. "I'll work until the end of today, then if needed my notice period," she said turning back to him.

He was embarrassed. "You don't need to go, but if you must we will pay your notice period. Just tidy up your things and go when it suits. That's if you must."

"I must."

Cathy spent the rest of the day mulling over her actions and disrupting the company filing system. It would take ages for anyone to find where the report on Miss Wilkes road accident report was, or where Mr Barnard's injury claim lay. Served them right.

She wrote a short letter of resignation, again offering to work her notice, but knowing she had no intention of doing so.

At five o'clock she left the office, saying goodbye to the receptionist, the only person she really cared for there.

"Take care of yourself Cathy, and don't do anything I wouldn't do," said Isabelle. "That leaves you plenty."

She gave her a hug and left the office for the last time.

Walking from the Quayside office, she decided a drink in Trollops was a better idea than the Metro home. She had a month's money going in to the bank, so she wasn't too worried, but she knew she needed a new job or she would not be able to pay her rent on the flat in Jesmond. And a return home to mum and Ireland represented failure.

On entering, she was a bit surprised to see Phil and Debs in the same seats they'd occupied the previous evening. She bought a small cider and headed across to them.

"How's the 'down time' going?" she asked after the normal greetings were through.

"Better with every beer," said Phil. "You just finished work?"

"You could say that. I quit my job."

"That's a bit extreme," said Debs. "That bad?"

Cathy filled the gaps and explained why she'd quit. She knew she might have been a little hot-headed, but the decision had been taken and now it was time to move on.

"What will you do?"

"Something will come up. It always does."

"We head back down to London in a couple of days. Why not join us down there for a day or two? Give you a chance to recharge your batteries before you go job hunting."

A few drinks later and Cathy had agreed to join them for a night or two in London. Why not?

The two of them stayed in a small flat near Paddington and Cathy had a blow-up mattress and a sleeping bag. It was a break from Newcastle though, and put some distance between her and any job worries.

In the morning Phil had to go to the office, but Debs did a bit of sightseeing with Cathy. They had lunch out and came home late afternoon to find Phil already there.

"How was the day?" Debs asked him.

"Pretty busy," he replied. "We have a delivery due out to go to Kenya and nothing was ready. We also have a lot of our volunteers off sick with the damned flu, so a bit short staffed."

"I could have come in," said Debs.

"You've got Cathy here."

"I could have come in to. It's not like I've got loads to do, and it sounds quite interesting."

Phil looked at her and realized she was serious. "If you really don't mind, you could both come in tomorrow. We can show you what we do."

"OK."

"But tonight let's go for an Italian. There's great one around the corner."


Next morning the three of them took the Tube to the office. It was just a couple of stops and they were easily there before nine o'clock, so no-one else had reached the office. Phil unlocked the door and they went in, Debs going through the back to stick on the kettle.

"So this is where the universe is run from," said Phil. "We're an offshoot of the Red Cross, but you'll have noticed we have no signage out front. We mainly pack and send packages, rather than recruit and do the high profile stuff."

"No problem. Do you get paid?"

"Oh yeah, but not so much for a central London position. There again, we make a bit more when we're away, and then there's almost nowhere to spend it."

Cathy knew that aid agencies did pay most of their staff, but that they also had pure volunteers. She just had no idea how much they made. "But you can live on it?" she pursued the point.

"I make about twenty-eight thousand a year in this country, and Debs is getting about twenty-five, so it's OK."

"It's more than I was getting in that bloody legal joint."

"So why not give it a go? You're between jobs as they say."

Cathy thought a short while. "Let's see how today goes. But never say never."


The work wasn't more exciting than working in the legal office, but at least the people were less pretentious. Three more came in later, two female and a man. The girls were a mother and daughter, the mum a regular and the daughter just coming along as she had nothing to do during the holidays. The man was a sixty year old accountant who'd taken early retirement and wanted to give something back to the community. Cathy couldn't imagine Lawrence Beattie doing that.

Phil was checking the office emails when he suddenly said, "They're looking for volunteers to go to Sudan. Darfur region. Anybody up for it?"

They all laughed and carried on organizing boxes and paperwork to get the food away to Kenya.

At half four Phil said they should knock it on the head. They headed for the Tube and chatted about a Lebanese restaurant the two locals knew.

"Is there really a job in Sudan right now?" Cathy asked out of the blue.

"Yes, but it's a nasty place. Really."

"And how long do you go there for?"

"Are you serious?"

"Just researching the options Phil."

"We could send you down for anything between two and six months. Everyone's different. Some adapt, some need to get out. There's no shame if that's the case though. It is rough."

"Would you pay me?"

"Somewhere like that I'd give you thirty grand a year. Taken on a pro-rata basis of course."

"Give me tonight to sleep on it."

That had been two years ago, and she'd taken a three month stint there. It had been a shock awakening, but she had loved it.

Back to the present, and here she was again.

She stepped out of her tent at the aid workers end of the camp and looked at the rows of tents that made up the camp. It was estimated that 300,000 people had been killed since the beginning of the Darfur conflict, and more than three million displaced from their homes. Armed groups roamed the countryside and government forces had little control over them. They looted the aid agencies just as they robbed from the villages.

She went to the central water point with a small container and took some water back to the tent to have bird-bath wash. It didn't help much, but it was something.

Going to a larger tent used as a hospital clinic, vaccination centre and a million other things, she greeted her fellow workers. They all looked rough, they all needed proper baths and showers, but they all looked a million times better than the refugees that rolled in to the camp on a daily basis. Mothers carrying dehydrated and malnourished children, flies landing on their eyes and lips, but the kids and mums having no energy to bother to swat them away.

Everyone in Sudan seemed to have malaria. Everyone in the camp had diarrhoea and some had severe vomiting. Fever and infections were everywhere. But at least here they received some food and water, and medication if the NGOs had it.

More importantly, they received some sort of protection from the bands of robbers that roamed the surrounding desert. Here the mothers didn't get raped every week in front of their kids. Here the United Nations kept some sort of security.

It didn't stop robberies happening, and if things looked dangerous, the UN troops would simply disappear and let the rebels steal what they needed from the food and medical supplies. Cathy tried to reason with the men at first and got a punch in the mouth for her concerns. So she did the same as the rest and let them steal.

Another problem was the so called 'Arab Spring'. This had two effects. It gave the rebels another excuse to attack the government troops, and it also took the plight of those in Darfur out of the main news. It became a 'forgotten' crisis.

Cathy was assisting in the vaccination process of the kids being brought in to the camp. She'd become quite a proficient nurse in her time there.

"Pass me your young one over here," she told a mother of about seventeen. She was so skinny she couldn't have weighed more than six stone. Once it would have revolted Cathy, but now it was just the norm.

She took the child – a three year old according to the records, so mum had given birth at fourteen – and noticed its total lack of weight. "How are you sweetie?" she asked, sitting the child on her knee. She took a swab and rubbed the arm clean in the area she intended giving the injection, then took a prepared needle and syringe. She squirted out a little fluid to remove oxygen, the lined up on a child too knackered to even complain.

"Here you are," she said, passing the toddler back to mum. "Next please!"

Just then there was gunfire outside. This wasn't so unusual, but this seemed to be closer than normal and there seemed to be more of it.

One of the men went outside to see what was going on. He came running back thirty seconds later.

"The rebels are shooting up the soldiers. There's loads of them. We need to get away before it's too late."

"It can't be any worse than normal," one of the nurses said. She'd seen this plenty of times.

One of the UN troops from the Congo came in. "We have to get you out of here now."

"What about all these people?" asked Cathy.

"They must leave now too. Otherwise we'll all be killed."

Looking out of the open tent flap, Cathy could see people gathering what they could carry and leaving. This was no organized exodus. This was a charge. Something bad was scaring them. She knew it was time to leave.

Within an hour the camp was deserted of refugees, aid workers and soldiers. The rebels had won the day and the camp was raped of all usable materials.

The aid workers spent the next week and a half in the nearby town of El Fasher. When it was realized they were not getting the Kassab camp back, their agencies decided to get them out of Sudan and back to Europe.

Cathy was home again and a hot bath beckoned. She'd done six months this time.

## TWENTY-ONE

Afghanistan was a desolate country, or at least the part of it that Jama was living in was. He was a full Lieutenant now with two pips on his shoulders, not that they wore such things very often in Helmand Province. Desert camouflage was the order of the day, and rank was shown on the front of the combat clothing in a covert way. It didn't help to advertise who was calling the shots when standing in the middle of a battlefield.

The land around Camp Bastion was hard-packed sand desert. In the distance, rugged mountains could be seen, riddled with deep caves that the Taliban used to escape the West's air-raids. It was hot in summer, with temperatures sometimes reaching fifty degrees, whilst in winter it could drop to zero.

Construction of the camp had begun in 2006, and it housed the majority of the British Forces in theatre, while the nearby Camp Leatherneck accommodated the US troops. Bastion had its own airfield, a heliport that operated around six hundred sorties a day, a hospital with trauma unit and operating theatre, a gymnasium and believe it or not, a container containing a Pizza Hut restaurant. It had a mock-up Afghan village for training troops in close-quarter battle and to allow them to learn what to expect outside of the camp's walls.

The camp was bordered by a perimeter wall that totalled forty kilometres in length, encompassing an area the size of Reading. It contained 10,000 twenty-foot ISO containers, tented accommodation, a police and fire station. It had its own water source, and the imported food was stored in a warehouse said to be the second largest building in Afghanistan.

Jama was to be based here for six months, along with a military population that fluctuated between twenty and thirty thousand. The unit formed part of the on-going Op Herrick 16.

He and his men arrived at the end of the winter, so temperatures were a little milder. They were given a week to acclimatise and establish their routines, organise their equipment and complete a handover from the out-going Royal Regiment of Fusiliers.

The patrol of seven men had been dropped by Chinook helicopter on the edge of one of the villages about twenty-five kilometres from Bastion. Jama was in charge, he had a Corporal, two guardsmen and three Afghan troops with him. They were to basically 'show face and maintain a presence' for the villagers. No Taliban were known to be in the area.

The main reason for these patrols was to try and keep the Taliban away from the villages. When they took control of a village or town, they brought with them their own fundamentalist twist on Muslim law. This didn't allow schools, limited the rights of women and their movements, and imposed taxes to fund their cause. They also hanged anyone in the neighbourhood that they decided were spies.

It was the fifth patrol Jama had led like this, and they were being fed soft jobs as it was only their third week in the province. It was a sort of extended acclimatisation but without the walls of Bastion around them.

They were strung out at about five to ten metre intervals either side of a dirt road. They'd been walking in patrol formation for about thirty minutes, and the air was relatively warm after the UK. Jama was considering a water-stop soon.

Wearing desert combats and bulletproof vests, plus all of the other equipment they needed and their personal weapons, meant they were getting hot quickly. Jama could feel sweat trickling down the middle of his back. He looked around the rest of the patrol to try and gauge how they were faring up, but with all the equipment and helmets covering most of the head, it was hard to tell. One of the Afghans seemed be struggling a bit, but generally they all looked OK.

They could see the village about a kilometre ahead, but they were in no rush to get there. They would be on their feet until the planned pick-up on the far side of the houses in about four hours.

Looking around the barren surroundings, Jama was not too happy with a rocky outcrop about three hundred metres forward and right of them. It was the sort of place you could hide people, and those people could be hostile. He asked the guardsmen behind him to keep an eye on it as it drew closer.

After another hundred paces or so, they could see a dry wadi just ahead. The dirt track passed over it, but beneath it was a pipe tunnel for when the wadi was full. It was also a perfect place to position an Improvised Explosive Device, or IED in army jargon.

The front soldier went down on one knee and waved for the rest to follow suit. They pointed their weapons to the side of the road they were positioned on in an all-round defence. Jama strolled forward to the point man.

"I see it Burnsie," he told the guardsman. It was hard to be formal all the time when you had to live so closely. "I agree."

"You want me to go and have a look?"

Jama looked at the ground either side of the track. The Taliban had been known to plant mines just off the road, trying to out-guess the soldiers. The left side of the road was sandy, but the right was hard rock, leading up to the outcrop that still worried him. The sand meant it could be mined, but the rock meant there was little chance. Someone had to go to the right and look in the pipe.

"Corps," he called to his number two. "Get a couple rifles lined up on the outcrop over there. Burnsie is going to have a long range look-see in that pipe.

"Roger."

While the corporal readied the men, Jama briefed the point man.

"Get forward to a point where you can see into the tunnel, but don't get too near. If they have a remote facility, they could blow it as you approach."

"Understood Sir."

"And try and keep something between you and that rock pile over there. Somewhere where you can take cover."

"Already thought that too."

"OK Burnsie. Careful!"

Grenadier Burns moved off the right side of the track, his weapon pointing in the general direction of the rocks. His eyes scanned between the ground in front of him and the stones, with the occasional glance at the culvert. He saw no possibility of the Taliban mining the area as everything this side of the road was boulders, which would also afford him some cover if the shit hit the fan he thought.

A minute later, he had a good view in to the drain and could see it was clear. He signalled this back to Jama and headed directly to the road. The rest of the patrol moved up to join him.

"All clear," he told them.

BANG! A rifle shot cracked out of the silence and the Afghan with the radio span around and fell to the ground screaming. The rest dived to the ground as they'd been conditioned to do, crawling to the nearest piece of cover. It was the first time under fire for all of them except the Corporal and the other Afghan soldier, but training took over and they all did the right thing. The wounded Afghan lay where he was, still yelling out.

"Burnsie," shouted Jama. "Give me a hand! We have to get him to cover."

The two of them grabbed the soldier by his web straps and hauled him to the nearest rocks, not worrying about whether the action worsened the wound. As they did so, a hail of bullets came their way, but somehow they all missed.

"Can anyone see exactly where they're shooting from?"

"Not really," said Corporal Dawes. "It's that bloody pile of rocks, but I've seen at least three different muzzle flashes, so there's a few of them."

Just then a burst of machine-gun fire raked up the ground close to their cover, the stone splintering with the impacts and spraying fragments in all directions.

"Return some fire," yelled Jama, holding his SA80 above the boulders and firing blindly. The men followed suit, but the fire from the enemy didn't let up.

"One-eight Delta, contact, wait out!" Jama spoke in to the radio he'd taken from the wounded Afghan. This was a line they all learned in training and hoped they'd never have to use. Their call-sign, informing base they were in contact with the enemy, and that things were too hot to make a full report right then.

"I don't like the look of this Sir," said Corporal Dawes. "We're pinned down, but it looks like more men are coming from the village."

Jama looked down the road. He could see maybe ten to fifteen people gathering on the edge of the settlement. They were about eight hundred metres away but could cover that in a few minutes. They'd soon have trouble on two sides. He got back to the radio.

"Zero, this is one-eight Delta. We are about two kilometres from our drop-off point and we're on the road to Hotdog. We have a group of enemy about one hundred metres away in high ground. They have us pinned down." He paused. "It looks like another enemy group is gathering on the edge of Hotdog. We have one wounded ANA trooper. Need air support ASAP."

"Roger that one-eight. We'll have a chopper in the sky immediately. Hang in there!"

"One-eight Delta." He went off the air.

"We need more cover Sir," said the Corporal when the Afghans momentarily ceased firing.

"You're right. Especially if the crowd from the village come here." Jama looked around. "Just over there, about ten metres." He indicated an area to their right where they would get cover from their present attackers and also from the road.

"If you keep two men with you Sir, I move with two and the injured bloke. You try and keep their heads down while we shift, then you shift while we fire at them."

"Let's do it."

They split the group in two, letting the soldiers know what they were going to do. The party of three with the wounded Afghan prepared to go. Jama and his boys put their weapons up again, emptying a whole magazine each at the rocks. The Corporal and his team made it to the new cover.

Rolls reversed, Jama and the other two men sprinted for the new position. This time the Afghans were expecting the move, and bullets slammed in to the earth around them. A shard of rock that was kicked up by the rounds caught Jama in the face, but there were no other casualties.

"You're bleeding a bit Sir."

"I'll be fine. Let's ask what the situation is on our air support."

He took the radio and called base. A helicopter should be with them in about twelve minutes he was told. He looked at the men from the village. They were only about two hundred yards away now, and also taking cover and planning to start shooting. Rounds from both sides now.

BUMMPH! And not only rounds. That was a Rocket Propelled Grenade, or an RPG in military parlance. This was getting nasty.

"Split the party again, three to fire on the road party and three to the others!"

"How much ammo have we got left Sir?" the Corporal asked.

Good point thought Jama. They had a quick count. Each of them had about eighty rounds left, and the injured man still had a hundred and twenty. They divvied up his ration between them.

"So we have about one hundred each gents, so let's not be too wasteful in case the chopper doesn't show."

The attackers coming from the village were getting closer, moving from cover to cover. Another RPG round slammed in to the rocks just to the left of them. It was getting a little uncomfortable.

"They're too far off for our hand-grenades, but we could put down some smoke to better hide our positions," the Corporal said.

"Do it," said Jama. "But try not to obscure the attackers. We need to see them."

The Corporal directed the two Grenadiers. One hurled a smoke canister as far as he could towards the gunmen in the rocks, while the other man threw his canister to the right of sight line with the attackers on the road side.

"Maybe chuck a grenade in each direction too," said Jama. "Just to let 'them know we have more than these SA80s."

Though ineffective at the range they were at, the grenades made plenty of noise and helped to confuse the situation a bit. With the village group getting closer though, something needed to happen and fast. It was just then that they heard the sound of a helicopter, and then they spotted it, coming in low over the sand. It was an Apache gunship, flown by pilots of the Army Air Corps, and it was a wonderful sight to see.

They could almost hear the pilots assessing the situation as they buzzed over the top of the firefight, sweeping in to a long right hand turn and bringing them behind the group from the village. Then the gunner opened up with his mini-gun, pouring lead out of the sky on to the attackers. They had no chance, many of them dying or wounded immediately, the rest trying to put solid rock between them and the aircraft.

Jama and his group lay flat during this to ensure they were not hit by loose rounds.

The pilot broke his engagement with the village group and turned his attention to the men in the rocks. He released two Hellfire missiles at their position, a frightening prospect for the attackers. They started retreating, trying to get away from the beast in the sky.

"One-eight Delta, this is base. We have a second helicopter coming now for your casualty, then you should withdraw to your original drop-off point for extraction of the rest of you."

"One-eight Delta, roger that."

With the Afghans all on the run, the Apache took a high hover position to guard the casevac helicopter.

The action was over.


Back at base the OC wanted Jama for a de-brief.

"Your first time under fire Jama?" he asked.

"It was Sir. A bit scary, but there was just so much to think about. You don't have time to worry."

"You did fine son," the boss told him. "From your report and the verification from Corporal Dawes, you did a great job."

"He was good too Sir. He helped me get through it."

"He's a good man, well experienced. Well done Jama. Go and rest!"


Apart from the small patrols, the Grenadiers were also involved in large scale operations, clearing areas of land of the Taliban. The co-ordination that went in to the organization of these ops was immense. Everyone needed to know what the others were doing, especially when different units and nationalities were involved. Jama worked mainly with the Americans, but also with Danish soldiers and of course, more and more with the Afghan army.

On one operation, the Grenadiers worked in support of the marines of 42 Commando. The green berets had been dropped behind the Afghan lines by Chinook helicopter, the most reliable form of transport. The Grenadiers had closed up to them in Warrior armoured vehicles, squeezing the rebels between the two coalition forces.

One marine was wounded in the operation, and twenty-two terrorists were killed.


Back in Bastion there wasn't too much to do. You worked and then most of the troops did a lot of sport.

Jama used the gym most nights, and usually also made a five-mile run, but this depended on what the unit had done that day. If you had a long patrol, you often couldn't face more time on your feet.

The Grens formed a beach volleyball team and took on soldiers from other regiments. It was fun and helped to fill the empty spaces between working. Soon they were also being invited to Camp Leatherneck, the American base, taking on their teams. It was good for the fitness of the troops, and also meant that the various teams learnt to respect one another.

A lesson for life.


The six month tour was coming to an end, and soon the men would be back in London for another tour of ceremonial duties. That couldn't be further from what they were doing in Afghanistan. Jama thought about his highly polished drill boots back in the barracks in UK, the ceremonial sword that shone like silver, his leather Sam Brown belt gleaming in the sun. He compared this with the desert combats, desert boots and having sand in every orifice. No comparison.

But part of him was also ready to return.

For six months his men had been tested to the extreme. They had lost three colleagues to enemy fire, and two more had returned home early with wounds that would change their lives forever. One of them was at least getting his life back together and hoped to take part in the Paralympics in London.

They'd done their share, and it was time for a breather.

## TWENTY-TWO

Back in London the CO decided it was a perfect time to have a Regimental Dinner to re-unite the various parts of the Officers Mess. Not everyone had been in Afghanistan, and some who had been had spent their time attached to Brigade HQ.

He decided to let everyone have the first weekend at home with families, then set the following Friday as the day.

The Colonel enjoyed using these occasions as a chance to introduce the men to new topics, inviting guest speakers from all walks of life. On this occasion, through a contact in Whitehall, he managed to get the South African President-in-exile, Dumi Silongo, to come and talk about his country. He didn't advertise the speaker until the last moment, in other words not until after the meal and before the talk.

The meal was superb as usual, with a duck pate starter followed by a lime sorbet. The main, a rack of lamb with new baby potatoes and fresh asparagus. was followed by a dessert: a trio of ice cream with fresh country berries. Wines came from South African vineyards in honour of their guest, even though these were hard to come by nowadays.

With the port doing the second round of the table, the Colonel decided it was time to talk.

"Ladies, Gentlemen, brother Officers and invited guests," he started, looking pointedly at the senior female officer present. "I'm pleased to welcome you all back home following an excellent tour of Afghanistan. You all made me proud to be your boss."

A round of applause broke out from the junior officers.

"For those of you that do not know yet, that was my last stint of active service. Yes, this year the old man has to hang up his boots for the last time. It's time to start improving my golf and gardening skills."

A chorus of good-natured boos rang around the room.

"And now for the bit I enjoy the most – my mystery guest. Some of you may know him, but I don't think so. A clue – Jama, your job is to ensure he doesn't leave the Mess sober tonight." Everyone looked at Jama, but he just looked back, nonplussed.

"Ladies and Gentlemen, our guest tonight is the South African President, Dumi Silongo."

A round of subdued applause. Not many at the table had even heard of him.

Jama couldn't believe his eyes or ears. Here was his own President, and he hadn't even recognized him.

Dumi stood, looking at the officers assembled at the table, particularly the man they had named as Jama. Being a Zulu, he knew the name well.

"Thank you for your welcome," he started. "You should be proud of what you have done these last six months, representing your country at the highest possible level. This is not sport, this is life and death. You did very well from what the Colonel has told me."

He picked up his port and toasted the soldiers. "A toast to the leaders of tomorrow."

The officers returned the salute, still wondering what they could learn from this man's story.

"My country, the country I love, is a mess. My people are living in poverty. Medicine is almost non-existent. Brother kills brother, robs his fellow South Africans, rapes his sisters. We were the proudest nation in the whole African continent, but now we cannot even trade with the rest of the world, though we have the world's supply of minerals."

He looked down at his port.

"This is not a proud story, but it is a story that people must know. We had a great country, but I took it for granted, missed the signs and a young pretender came in to the ring and took my country to hell."

He sipped thoughtfully on the port.

"So what is the message. It is something you already know. Do not take your eye off the ball. Do not ignore the signs. Why do I say you know it? Because you just survived six months in Afghanistan. Six months when you never switched off. Now I'm saying you must do the same thing for the rest of your lives."

He paused, thinking. "I would be proud to have you men in my country as my army. You are loyal to the fellow officers, to your flag and to your Queen. You are all amazing role models for the next generations. I salute you all."

He sat took his glass again and raised it to the soldiers. They toasted him back and the Colonel stood up.

"The President of South Africa," he returned and all the officers joined him.

Jama felt immensely proud of his fellow countryman. He wasn't hiding from his demons but facing them full on.

With the meal over, the table started moving towards the bar and continuing celebrations. Jama walked over to the boss.

"Sir," he asked, "Can I have the honour of an introduction? I think my President needs to come and enjoy the rest of the evening."

"President, this is our very own South African, Jama Nomvula. He is a pleasure to work with and someone his country must be proud of. He will escort you for the rest of the evening."

"I look forward to every minute of it Colonel."

At the bar, Jama asked the President what he would like to drink.

"You must call me Dumi. I am a Zulu like yourself Jama, and Zulus are friendly people."

"Yes Mister Pres.... Dumi. But what can I get you?"

"A good stiff Scotch sounds great. Settles the nerves after being put in front of a bunch of people I've never met."

"Grab a seat. I'll be just a minute."

Jama returned with the drinks. He wasn't sure what he was meant to say to the President, but in his heart he knew this was possibly a turning point in his life. Though he loved England and the opportunities it had afforded him, he also knew his parents were still in Africa, as was his heart.

"Is it as bad as the papers say Sir?" he asked.

"My reports say worse. And it's Dumi, please."

"It's not easy to meet a President and just be on first name terms Sir."

"But you must. You are a hope for the future. You are a black man living in the UK and holding his own. You are accepted for your person, not for your colour. This is our hope for the next generation."

"I never really think about it. These are my friends. We fought together. We depend on one another. And besides, I was brought up in a mixed marriage. My father is a doctor from here, and mum is a Zulu nurse."

"People could learn a lot from you Jama."

An embarrassed silence. "So home is so bad? Do you see an end to it all?"

"To end it we need the mines to work. That makes the country money. That pays the police and army, then we have order. Then we can re-open hospitals, banks, shops. Then we can look at elections and democracy. But first we need money and stability."

"So our only hope is the mines?"

"Not really. We could go for stability first. But then we need someone to lead us out of this mess. We need someone to stand-up to the bullies who are running the place down. We need a Nelson Mandela, but he was a one and only."

"Can you not do it? You are still officially the President."

"If I go back to South Africa now I will be killed. The army and police that survive support Oliver Justice. They would kill me."

"But if you were protected? If you had your Zulu people with you?"

"They are not trained to fight a professional army, even a run down one. Spears and shields are not the same as guns and rifles, tanks and helicopters."

"I know you are right. You can be brave as hell and still die," said Jama.

"Enjoy the night son," Dumi said. "Nothing changes overnight. But keep in touch. We have frequent meetings with other exiles and I'd like you to attend one. I'll ask the boss so you don't get in any trouble."

"I'd be honoured Sir."

That night, Jama dreamed of returning to South Africa with a Company of Grenadiers and supporting President Dumi in his return to power. In the dream the mines were working again, mum was a Head Nurse and dad had become the Minister for Health.

Jama had become a highly successful General.

It was only a dream though, and largely forgotten in the morning.

Jama was in front of the boss again, and it was good news. He had received his promotion to Captain following his successful tour of Afghanistan. He was also being fast-tracked to Major, possibly as soon as the following year.

"I was also chatting to the President at the end of the evening yesterday," the CO told him. "He took a bit of a shine to you. Sees you as a positive find for South Africa's future."

"We had a good chat Sir, but the country is in a real state."

"He asked if you could be allowed to join some of his meetings with the other exiles, and more specifically with the cabinet-in-exile. I checked it out and we have no problem with that. Of course it's your choice at the end of the day."

"If it's OK Sir, I would love to attend at least one meeting. You know my parents are still there, so it might make communication with home a little simpler."

"Then attend the next meeting and see what you think," the CO replied. He wondered how long the regiment could keep this young man.

"Thanks Sir. I'll let you know how things go."

## TWENTY-THREE

Cathy had been back from Sudan for three weeks now and her feet were itching again. She didn't mind the mundane office work in London too much – her co-workers were good people, unlike the ones she remembered from the law firm in the north east – but she loved being there on the ground with day-to-day problems normal people never encountered in their whole lives.

She'd been in the job just over a year now and had spent nine of those twelve months out of the UK. It had been a life-changing experience. She'd even used her rudimentary law knowledge to help settle a dispute between a forwarding company and the charity, basically just frightening them off with her use of legal jargon.

Her rented flat in Jesmond was gone, and she shared a small, rented apartment in Southwick with Gladys Nxumalo, a twenty-three year old South African from Cape Town, who also worked with her when in the London office.

"Phil," she called to the other side of the office. "Nothing new in?"

Phil was used to her by now and didn't need to ask what she meant. "Nothing Cathy. Either all the wars have stopped, or people consider them too dangerous for us to go there."

"Has it ever been so quiet for so long?"

Another much used question from Cathy these days. "Never been quiet since you got here Cathy," he responded.

She decided to shut-up, getting her head down and logging shipments. But the itchy feet wouldn't go away.


Back at the flat Gladys was cooking something unusual.

"What the hell is that?" Cathy asked.

"This one is chicken and this is a tomato and herb sauce."

"And that one?"

"It's called pap."

"Pap?"

"Yep, pap. It's a ground-up sweet-corn mixed with water. We eat it a lot at home. Sort of a staple food for us."

Cathy looked at it. "Looks like it sounds – pap."

"Don't knock it till you've tried it!" Gladys countered.

"Alright Glad. Only teasing."

They'd shared the flat since Cathy came back from Sudan, and they got on well, both having the same wicked sense of humour. Each of them used their different backgrounds to find fault with the other, but really they enjoyed learning from their alternative cultures, and both understood no offence was intended.

Gladys had come from a poor family in Cape Town but managed to save her money and go to London for a holiday when South Africans could still easily get a two year tourist visa. Once there she got a job in a bar to extend the holiday fund, but then she met Debs one night. She was soon offered a full time position, and then, with the troubles in Africa, the government allowed her a visa extension until the crisis there was settled.

The rest – as they say – was history.

Over dinner they discussed the office, and Cathy joked about the food.

"Not too bad for pap."

"Better than some of the pap you've served me," said Gladys, having the last laugh.

"So what you doing tonight?"

"I'm going to a meeting of fellow South Africans. Our ex-President is speaking. I thought it would be good to catch-up on the gossip from home."

"I'm having a beer with Phil and Debs. Why don't you join us later?"

"I'll call you on the cell when I finish the get together. If you're still out, we'll join up."

Sharing the dishes – Cathy washing, Gladys drying and putting away – they prepared for their nights out.

Gladys didn't know what to expect from the evening, but she didn't expect what she got. She actually spoke to the president of South Africa. The meeting was attended by about a hundred expats, most missing family members and friends who were marooned in the new South Africa as surely as she was marooned in the UK. Some of the stories from home, emerging during the informal chatter after the main address, were horrific, but mostly it seemed people were getting on with life as best they could. The President still had many contacts there, and painted a gloomy picture of the rundown economy, but also explained that Western governments had expressed interest in getting the country back on an even keel when things were better.

A bigger shock for Gladys had been a hot young soldier there called Jama, a Zulu who really seemed to have the ear of the President, even calling him by his given name. She had spoken briefly to the man, and found him proud, but at the same time terribly humble. It was a tantalizing mix.

Things wound up at nine o'clock, and the gathering broke-up. Another was agreed for the following month.

As she was leaving the school hall used for the meeting, Gladys was surprised to see Jama still hanging around at the entrance. She smiled as she moved to pass him.

"Sorry," he stopped her, putting a hand lightly on her arm. "I don't mean to be forward, but would you like a drink with me?"

She looked around, checking he was speaking to her.

"You mean now?" she asked buying time.

He smiled shyly. "No time like the present."

"I was actually going to join some friends for a drink…"

"No problem," he said, a look of disappointment clouding his face for a second. "Maybe next time."

"If you'd let me finish, I was going to say you could come along if you like," she said, shocking herself. Well, it was out now.

"That would be great, but I don't want to get in the way."

"No, I think they'd like you. Hang on while I see where they are."

She tracked them down to a pub on the Thames about five minutes taxi ride away, so they jumped in a cab and went straight there. The place was crowded, but she soon spotted her friends and dragged Jama over. Introductions over, she explained that they'd met at the expats night. She also let them know that she'd met the President and that Jama was his friend.

Embarrassed, Jama tried to make light of it. "My boss introduced me to him at a Regimental dinner the other week, and because I'm a South African, I was asked to entertain him for the evening. It was a nothing event really."

"A Regimental dinner?" Cathy interrupted. "So you're in the military?"

"Yes, a Grenadier Guard."

"But from South Africa? Sounds a bit odd."

"Dad's from the UK, so I get dual citizenship. Lucky really with all the trouble back home."

He went to the bar and ordered a round for them all. Phil came across and joined him to help carry the beers. "Don't worry about Cathy," he told Jama. "She can be a bit abrupt, but she's a great person when you get to know her."

"No offence taken. I'm the intruder here tonight."

"Don't be silly. Glad invited you, and she's one of us. If she's happy with you, then so are the rest of us."

They returned with the drinks.

"From what Phil just said, should I assume you guys are just friends, or do you work together?"

"Both actually, said Debs getting her first words in. "We work for a NGO – basically a charity type organization – trying to help people in trouble spots across the world."

"Sounds like we're super heroes," Cathy chucked in.

"Maybe to some people you are," Jama said seriously. "Sorry. A bit heavy I guess, but I'm just back from Afghanistan and a little sensitive I guess."

"Don't apologize," Gladys chastised him. "Cathy likes a dig. It's not nasty, just her."

"No, I should apologize," said Cathy. "You've never met me and I'm giving you a hard time. Shake." She extended her hand and Jama took it.

"No problem," he said. "I think I had rougher days in the last six months. So what do you guys actually do?"

They spent the next hour exchanging experiences, the girls and Phil impressed with the situations Jama experienced, and Jama equally gob-smacked by the places and things the group had seen.

"Never judge a book by its cover," Cathy said cryptically at the end of the evening.

"What do you mean by that," asked Debs.

"I think I understand," said Jama. "You all look like normal everyday folk, yet you've done things that would scare a normal person half to death."

"And you too," added Cathy.


Over the next weeks, Gladys and Jama met as often as his duties would allow for drinks, dinner, cinema and anything else that bought them time alone together. They also met the rest of the group on occasions, but their relationship was developing and they needed space to get to know one another.

Within no time, the next expat meeting was looming up.

Two days before the meeting, Jama was contacted by President Dumi.

"I'd like you to say a few words at the meeting about your experiences in Afghanistan Jama," the President told him over the phone. "Nothing much, just what the army life has brought you. You won't be alone – I've got someone talking about their job in the National Health Service, and someone who works in the Royal Bank of Scotland. It's just to let the others know there are opportunities to make a life in England. What do you say?"

Jama hated the idea but knew that saying no to Dumi was a non-starter. "Just a short overview," he asked.

"Ten minutes max," was the reply.


The school hall was full to bursting for the next meeting, Dumi estimating the number attending to be around the 250-300 mark. News of the last meeting had spread from friend to friend, so many more stranded South Africans had decided to use the gathering as a chance to find out what was happening back at home.

Jama looked down on the crowd from his seat on the stage, wishing he'd had the bottle to say no to Dumi. Too late now.

Dumi gave an opening address and then spoke about the latest news that was filtering through from home. He then continued. "This week, I thought I would add an extra twist to the agenda by asking some fellow South Africans to say a few words about their lives here in the UK. I think it is a good way to illustrate that life can go on here. Work can be found. There are opportunities." He smiled. "If it wasn't for the weather, I'd consider staying here myself."

The crowd laughed good-naturedly, even though the quip was an old one.

"We'll start with Antje Jordaan, a nurse back home in Pretoria, and a nurse again here in the NHS in London." A middle aged woman stood and stepped up to the microphone, explaining briefly what she had needed to do in the UK to convert her South African nursing qualifications to something accepted in the UK.

Next up was a young girl who had managed to obtain a job as a junior manager in a local bank. Her ten minutes were soon up and she returned to her seat.

"Many thanks for that Michaela," Dumi said as the applause receded. "Now for the final speaker this week, a young fellow Zulu called Jama Nomvula, an officer in the British Army and just back from a tour of Afghanistan."

"Ladies and Gents, this is not something I usually do, so forgive me if I mess it up," he started. He fiddled with the mike a second, trying to focus his mind away from the audience. "I was in the SADF – our Defence Force for those here not familiar with it – but it was not well run. I was lucky enough to have dual nationality through my father, so I decided to try the army here. I joined as a private." He continued on for the next few minutes, taking them through his time in the Grenadiers, but not elaborating too much.

"And that's about it," he ended, hoping to escape to his seat. Dumi had other ideas.

"Jama, a second please. You mentioned that the SADF was not well run. With your skills now, could you improve it? Could you train our people to be good soldiers?"

"We train our soldiers everyday Sir," he answered.

"So you are not just a soldier, you are also a teacher and a leader."

Jama wanted the ground to swallow him up. "I didn't say that Mister President."

"Don't be embarrassed son, that is not my intention. I am merely pointing out how far you have progressed and how much of an asset you would be if we ever get our home back."

"Thank you Sir. It would be an honour to serve you back home," Jama answered, getting to his chair as quickly as possible, the crowd clapping for him all the way.

"I hope this idea of mine has served not one purpose, but two. The first intention was to show you all that you have a future here in the UK if you want it. My other goal was to show you we have great people here to rebuild our country one day. We have bankers, we have doctors and nurses, and we have fine, loyal soldiers to protect us. Our past looks bleak, but our future is still bright."

The crowd loved it. Clapping loudly.

"I think to finish this month's meeting, we should sing something together. A song we all know at least a part of." He smiled. The South African national anthem was a mix of lyrics in English, Zulu, Xhosa, Afrikaans and Sesotho. Every African knew at least their part.

Dumi started singing.

"Nkosi Sikelel' iAfrika…"

And the crowd joined in.

"Maluphakanyisw' uphondo lwayo,

Yizwa imithandazo yehtu,

Nkosi sikelela,

Thina lusapho lwayo.

Morena boloka setjhaba sa heso,

O fedise dintwa le matshwenyeho,

O se boloke, O se boloke sejhaba sa heso,

Setjhaba sa, South Afrika - South Afrika."

The volume swelled as the Afrikaan language came in.

"Uit die blou van onse hemel,

Uit die diepte van ons see,

Oor ons ewige gebergtes,

Waar die kranse antwoord gee,"

And everyone joined in the final verse.

"Sounds the call to come together,

And united we shall stand,

Let us live and strive for freedom,

In South Africa our land!"

Every eye in the house was wet, cheeks were flushed and everyone hugged their neighbours. This was a call for togetherness. This was a call for South Africans.

And Dumi hoped it was the call to return home.

# PART 3 – GOING HOME

# TWENTY-FOUR

Dumi was on a flight to Washington to meet with Hillary Clinton. He had won limited support already from David Cameron. He now needed the backing of the United States. They'd expressed interest verbally, but he needed nailed-down commitments, something he could sell to the expanding crowd of expats who were willing to lay down their lives to recapture their country.

After the meeting in London he was contacted by many of the attendees. The message was always along the same vein. How can we help? How can we get our home back?

There were also some messages that perturbed but didn't surprise him. Both the British and American governments had agents at his meetings, monitoring the discussions and mood of the crowd. Neither wanted surprises in the international arena.

He was sure he knew how his meetings in America would pan out: support for concessions, same as the UK. They would give support that didn't implicate them if things went wrong, and he would give them preferential terms in mining operations in the new South Africa. He smiled to himself, as it was a small price to pay. They had already held mining concessions before the troubles, so they were in effect paying to get back what they already owned.

A number of specialist groups had formed after the expat meeting: Antje Jordaan had started a team of medical professionals, and they were compiling a list of all South African doctors, nurses and midwifes working in the UK. They would contact all of them and find out their views on a return to the Rainbow Nation.

Michaela Pretorius – the girl from the banking sector – had been replaced by a more senior financial figure, a man called Pieter de Klerk who had worked in the Johannesburg stock exchange before the troubles. Michaela was still in the finance team, becoming Pieter's Personal Assistant. They were in the process of contacting financial institutions and sounding out borrowing terms should South Africa again become a stable economy.

And then there was the military wing, under Jama. This was the critical group. Without regaining control of the country, the other groups could plan solutions for the rest of their lives.

Dumi could see that Jama was a natural leader, even though the boy was uncomfortable with the role. People warmed to him. He was brave but played down his exploits. He shied away from discussions regarding Afghanistan and Northern Ireland, but Dumi knew from his CO that he had been an exceptional soldier in both of those theatres. Dumi was certain he was the right man to lead the revolt against Oliver Justice and his Generals.

As the Airbus 380 began its descent in to the heat of America, Dumi dozed. His eyes closed, he dreamt about the warm African sun kissing his face.

He longed for home.

It was seven o'clock in the evening and Jama was sitting in his room at the barracks preparing a list of equipment he would recommend for any action against the Oliver Justice regime. He still thought that the idea of taking back South Africa was just a pipe dream. Here they were eight thousand miles from home, with no weapons, no transport, no supplies and not even a plan. And the enemy had been in control for over a year already, so they should be well established.

There were positives though.

Dumi's intelligence network told them that the army and police had largely disbanded, with both troops and police officers deserting to their homes when salaries remained unpaid. The majority who had stayed were thugs, enjoying the authority they had with no-one to control them.

And as Jama had said himself, the SADF had not been so professional when he had been with them, and now they were even less so.

A problem was that it was not clear how many soldiers remained available to the regime. Or what weaponry they had, and if it was being correctly maintained. Jama wondered if they had ever had a day at the ranges since the fall of government or completed any training. He doubted both.

This meant the soldiers would be rusty. And if they were living it up as he was hearing, probably very unfit.

He put his lists away in folders to present to Dumi on his return from the States. As he did so, a map of Gauteng fell to the floor. He picked it up, studying it for the hundredth time. And something clicked.

He had a plan.

Antje was interviewing all of the health professionals that she had listed and then contacted. Not all of them wished to leave the UK, but the interested ones came forward and agreed to discuss their wishes. The next interview was with a Capetonian girl called Gladys Nxumalo.

"Hi Gladys," Antje greeted her as she entered the room.

"Hi. I hope you didn't mind me asking to join your team. I'm not really a qualified nurse, so to speak."

Antje frowned. She had enough interviews to get through without time wasters.

"Maybe you should explain?"

"I have a lot of medical experience from my job, but no formal qualifications."

"What is your job?"

"I'm an aid worker. We often run immunization programs and carry out minor first aid on the kids in the camps."

"Camps? Where have you been working?"

"Last time I was away, I was in Northern Kenya, close to the Somali border. I was also a few months in the Darfur region of Sudan, and I spent a few weeks in Ethiopia."

"Then don't be sorry for applying Gladys. We're going to need people like you with bags of practical experience. At least we know you won't faint the first time things go bad."

"Thanks Antje. I won't let you down."


Later that evening, Jama and Gladys met in their local bar.

Sitting next to an open fire, Jama was sipping on a pint of Stella, while Gladys had a Bacardi Breezer. They were comparing notes from their days activities.

"I can't wait for Dumi to get back," said Jama. "I think I know how we can get in to the country without attracting too much attention."

"That's great."

"I'll not go in to detail until I can bounce the idea of him, but if he can get us some support off the Brits, it could work."

Just then, Cathy walked in the door, wearing a large Paddington the Bear coat to ward off the cold. She saw them in the corner and headed over, a little worried that they would not want her intruding.

"Hi guys. How's it going? Do you mind me joining you?" She looked from one to the other with a serious expression on her face. "Be honest. If you want some peace, say so!"

"No way!" Jama replied. "Join us. What can I get you?"

He was soon at the bar, buying a round for them all.

On return to the table, the girls were deep in conversation.

"I was just telling Cathy about my days," Gladys informed him. "I sort of lied to Antje when I told her I was a medical person, but when I told her about the things we all do when we're in the refugee camps, she said she was pleased I had lied. In fact, she thinks we need plenty of people with that hands-on experience."

"She's right," Jama said. "Treating a cut in perfect hospital conditions is quite different from stitching someone up in a tent."

"You really are planning on going back to South Africa, aren't you?" Cathy asked.

"It's hard to describe Cathy, but it is our birth place." Jama pursed his lips, thinking of the right words. "UK has been great to both of us, but our families and our homes are in South Africa. If we can go back and make a difference…"

"I think I'll miss you both."

"We'll miss you too, but if our country can be repaired, then you can come and visit us."

"Thanks, but not the same. We're close, especially Glad and me."

Gladys leaned over and gave her a big hug. Jama said he had to go to the loo to escape the moment. He took his time and washed his face to remove any signs of his own emotions.

Returning to the table, he was pleased to see that the two women were all smiles. They were good friends and he felt at least partly responsible for the planned move to Africa. He was the military mind behind it, so in some small way, a part of the big plan.

"Another round girls?"

"Great idea," said Gladys. "Then we'll tell you our plan."

He went to the bar, wondering what the two of them had dreamed up. Luckily the pub wasn't too busy, so he didn't have to wait too long to find out.

"So," he said on return. "What's the story?"

"Cathy's coming with us."


As the Airbus A380 entered its descent phase in to London Heathrow, Dumi really felt tired out. His brain seemed to be working at half speed, a combination of the jet-lag and the lightning speed pace of meetings he had held in his three days in Washington. He had met a lot of government figures, including Obama, but also had spent time with some senior military personnel, getting a feeling for how much the US was willing to physically support his cause. In the end it seemed they would support him, but not with bodies on the ground.

Before Dumi had left, he recalled that Jama had identified about 200 ex-soldiers, police, or other military South Africans in the London area. He wondered if this was enough to overthrow Oliver Justice and his band of thugs.

The aircrew had now been asked to take their seats, so he guessed they'd be on the tarmac in the next ten minutes. He shut his sore eyes and tried for one last power-nap.


He slept again on the Heathrow Express into central London, thinking that perhaps he was getting too old for all of this travelling. Up and down the globe from Africa to the UK was no big problem, but once he started travelling east or west the time changes hit him badly. Jet-lag was a reality, especially as you got older.

Jama had said he should take a taxi from the airport for security reasons, but the Express was far faster. It was also always full of people, so Jama had relented, agreeing to meet him at Paddington Station on arrival.

As the train rolled in to Paddington, Dumi reflected on where things were. He had lost his country, and that was a stark reality. For over a year he had sat around feeling mainly sorry for himself and his people, but that was actually not helping either them or him. Taking a positive action made him feel better, and there was light at the end of the tunnel. He believed that the country could be put back on track. What he wasn't sure about though, was whether he was still the right man to lead it.


Jama was openly happy at the sight of Dumi, a white toothy grin on his face.

"Hey tourist," he called to attract Dumi's attention. "How was the States?"

Dumi looked across the platform, through a sea of faces and cases and moved to Jama dragging his trolley case.

"Let me take that."

"Thanks Jama. I'm worn out."

"Soon have you home."

They walked out of the mainline station and up to the taxi rank. The queue was short and they were soon on their way through the city.

"So how did it go?" Jama asked.

Dumi was thoughtful for a minute, looking at the passing buildings, then directly at Jama. "Good, I would say. We will get support from the US, the same as we will get assistance from the UK. Money and resources, but no people on the ground. No troops. How do you feel about that?"

Jama grinned. "Perfect. I have had some great ideas while you were away."

"For example?"

"Later," the younger man replied. "I need you fully awake for this one. So first a good sleep Mister President, and then we meet for discussions."

"I concede to your superior knowledge – and youth."

"Good. We have dinner together at seven."


At seven they met at the Al Fawer Lebanese Restaurant in Baker Street. It was a favourite of Dumi, so Jama had booked it earlier in the week, ordering a quiet corner table where they could talk privately.

Ordering a tabbouleh salad, some hummus dip and rice stuffed vine leaves, with a side plate of flat breads, they sipped a glass of dry white wine.

"So what is the secret plan?" asked Dumi.

Jama looked around the room, wondering if his choice of venue had been right. A few other tables were occupied, but no-one was within a few metres of them, and everyone seemed caught up in their own private discussions. It was safe.

"My plan depends on how much support we are able to get from the British. I suppose it would be equally viable if the Americans were to support us, but I know the capabilities of the military here, so my plan is based on their resources."

"They will not give us troops Jama," Dumi cautioned.

"I do not need troops. I do need pilots and planes to get us in though."

Dumi was quiet for a moment, studying the vine leaves carefully. "Where do you want the planes to go to?"

"There is an airfield close to Pretoria called Lanseria. I'm sure you know it. It has been used for commercial flights for the last few years."

"I know it, but it has few facilities and is probably out of service for the last year or so."

"That's what I hope. Then we can land there and get ourselves in order before we head for the Union Buildings."

"What about vehicles?"

"Again, this is where we need some help, but not too much. I believe there are plenty of vehicles around, but not much fuel. We take diesel with us and we can then commandeer vehicles as we require them." He smiled. "The alternative is a thirty-five mile route march."

"We could confirm most of this with my sources in country," said Dumi.

"I wouldn't. Some of them may be corrupt, then the plan is badly compromised."

"You're right, but how else do we check."

"The US has great satellite imagery. Get them to check with both camera and infra-red facilities. That should also let us know if there are people in the area."

"I think they'd agree to that."

"Way in would be to use Hercules C130 type aircraft. We could squeeze at least fifty troops in to one of them, plus some ancillary equipment and the fuel. Do you think the Brits would agree to that? I'd like four, giving us 200 men on the ground."

"They may not agree to that. It would mean exposing at least twelve of their aircrew."

"Do they want to sort out the mines?"

"I'll meet someone tomorrow and see what the reaction is. You could be right."

The waiter arrived at the table with some lamb kebbehs and fresh vegetables. "Is there something wrong?" he asked, looking at the untouched starters.

"No, not at all," said Dumi quickly. "We were just too busy chatting but leave the kebbehs here too. We promise to start now."

The waiter placed the new food on the already crowded table and withdrew.

"Let's eat and enjoy. It gives us a chance to ponder on these things. I then need to have a meeting or two tomorrow."

"What do you think?" asked Jama.

"I think it is dangerous." Dumi looked at his young friend. "But possible."


Oliver Justice had put on about fifteen kilos since he'd 'come to power.' He looked dreadful, but often couldn't really see how he looked as he was close to unconscious from the booze and the drugs. His 'brothers' around him were no better off, and he knew of three senior military officers who had choked on their own vomit whilst under the influence. Occasionally, when he awakened from one of the marathon drinking sessions that had become a way of life, he knew he had to change.

When he had the next drink, he simply forgot this.

His butler was in his bedroom, clearing up his clothing when he woke up. The girl who had crawled drunk in to bed with him the previous night was gone, and so was his Gucci watch that had come from one of the malls in Centurion. He was sure he'd find another one, so he wasn't worried about that. More worrying was he couldn't remember if he'd had sex or not.

He reached for a jug of water on the bedside cabinet and swigged directly from it.

"Ugghh!" he belched. "Can you get me a Bloody Mary? Need to settle my stomach."

"Yes Sir," said the butler, barely hiding his look of disdain.

Leaving the bedroom and walking along the corridor towards the kitchens, he found an army general comatose on an overstuffed leather sofa. His uniform jacket was on the floor next to him, and the knot of his tie was down at the base of his sternum. A pair of purple ladies underwear were perched on his head where someone had placed them.

"What does the bastard want now?" asked the cook, showing no respect for his employer.

"A Bloody Mary."

"I'll do a special for him," the cook said, and removed a five litre plastic container of industrial alcohol from the fridge. Pouring a half beaker of this, he added some tomato juice and a very liberal measure of Worcester sauce. "There. He'll never know what hit him."

"You must be careful Busi," the butler cautioned the man. "If they find out, they will kill you."

"The last time he was sober enough to tell what he was drinking was when we had mines that made money. The prick."

The butler left with the 'very' Bloody Mary and wished his old boss was back. President Dumi had been a stickler, but he was always fair.

Those days seemed a century away now.


"I met with a number of people today Jama," Dumi said. "Their answers surprised me a little, but in a positive way."

He paused for effect, but Jama was in no mood for that. "So do they support us, or not?"

"That was the surprise," said the President, refusing to be rushed. "They support us."

Jama's eyes lit up and a smile split his face. "You mean we get the aircraft?"

"We get the aircraft, but in a sort of roundabout way."

"OK, stop the teasing and fill in the gaps."

"With pleasure Sir."


It was unbelievable that Dumi could have achieved so much in only twenty-four hours, Jama thought. OK, it wasn't as straightforward as he might of liked, but they had their ride in, they would receive weapons but not as modern as he had expected, and they even had a few vehicles thrown in for good measure, though how reliable the vehicles were was also questionable.

The Americans had also agreed to donate some funding which would be needed in the early part of the operation and would divert spy satellites over both Pretoria and Lanseria over the next weeks.

Initially the only people going in would be the military wing of their team. They had to establish a safe base and try and remove the opposition from Pretoria. The medical group would follow, then eventually the administration people, but by then it was hoped at least some commercial air traffic would be serving the country.

The plan was to take Pretoria back in only three weeks, but this was known to only a very select number of people, possibly only a total of ten in the whole of the UK. In those weeks, Jama had to get the men familiar with their equipment and break them down in to smaller teams. The structure could not be too complex, as time was against them.

To manage what was needed, he had a duty to perform that couldn't be put off any longer.


Marching in to the CO's office, Jama felt like a Grenadier Guardsman for the first time in weeks. All of the secret plotting had been alien to him: he planned his tactics with fellow officers, bouncing ideas off one another to ensure their plans were perfect. Then he fine-tuned them with experienced non-commissioned officers who knew what was possible in reality.

Lately he'd been burning the midnight oil all alone.

Halting in front of the Colonel's desk, he waited while the CO signed off a letter.

"You needed to see me Jama?" the CO asked. "Grab a seat."

Jama sat stiffly in front of his boss, wondering where to start. He decided to take the bull by the horns. "Sir, I wish to resign my commission."

The CO frowned, looking intently at Jama. He saw before him a great young soldier who was truly struggling with his soul. "Are you sure you wish to do that Jama?"

Biting the inside of his lower lip to avoid a tear, Jama formed his answer carefully. He had thought it through many times in practice, but actually doing it was far harder than thinking it. "Sir, I love the Regiment, but I also love my country, and South Africa needs me more than you do. Sorry Sir, I'm not being derogatory, but you know the political situation back home."

"You might be shocked that this is no surprise to me. I have been in constant contact with your President, and I was told by him how things were going. He is very proud of you. So am I, but I'll be sorry to see you go. You had a big future with us." He smiled. "And probably a bigger one without us."

"Thank you Sir." The tears were very close now.

"You will always be a Grenadier Jama Nomvula, and I'm proud to have served alongside you. Now you must go where your heart is taking you and free your homeland. Good luck!"

As Jama got up to leave, the CO added one more thing. "Always remember our motto. 'Evil be to he who thinks evil.' I believe your Mister Justice will get his comeuppance soon."


As a final favour, the CO also granted Jama the use of one of the training halls in the barracks, where he could assemble and have his men practice on their new weapons. The boss had even managed to get his hands on fifty of the SLR rifles, the pre-runner to the present SA80. It was a heavy weapon to carry by comparison and had a kick like a mule. It also really stopped things dead.

Many of his troops had used such rifles during their time in the SADF, both in peace time and the old bush wars, though then they had called it a FN, a weapon from Belgium manufacturer Fabrique Nationale d'Herstal. The SLR was merely a derivative made for the Commonwealth countries.

This was to be their weapon in South Africa, but just when and where they were to receive the weapons was not entirely clear at the moment. Dumi was still being a little secretive on some issues and Jama was happy to keep it that way. The less people knew, the less chance of letting something serious slip.

He had also obtained permission to use the camp's assault course and he broke the men into teams of ten and had them timed around. The teams were carefully comprised of old and young, so some would struggle and some would be expected to assist them. In the time available, it was his best idea for team building.

Radio sets were to be old Clansman installations, dragged out of some bunker in the middle of nowhere and dusted down for training. They sufficed.

Most of the training was done in the evenings at first, as many of the men were still holding down full time jobs. In the final week, all had to stop work though, and training took place all day for three consecutive days.

At the end of the final day, Jama addressed the men. Dumi watched from the rear of the stage, knowing this was not his show.

"Gentlemen, I can now let you know the time for training is over, and the time to free our country of the thugs that are running it has come. I know we have barely scratched the surface as far as preparation goes, and I know this can hurt us later, but I believe we are more ready than the people we are going up against." He picked up a glass of water, sipping to relieve his dry throat. "We are fighting for our homes and families. They are fighting to continue their wasted lives, sucking our land dry. We cannot allow this to continue."

He glanced at his notes. "We'll be moving to Kenya in small groups over the next two days. You'll all be given tickets as you leave this meeting, and hotel details on arrival. We can all get visas then. Once there I'll brief you on phase two."

He looked around the room, surprised to see every person there looking his way. "You know I was a Grenadier Guards officer, junior to many of you during your service. I am not here to order you around. I am here to win our country back, so please accept any inexperience on my part."

"You're fine for us Jama," someone yelled from the back of the hall.

"We're with you all the way."

A round of applause broke out and Jama waited for silence, his eyes down to hide his emotions.

"When I resigned from the Grenadiers a few weeks back, my CO told me to remember the Regiment's motto. 'Evil be to he who thinks evil,' is how it goes, and my boss wished the evil on to a certain Oliver Justice." A grunt of general approval from the audience. "I'd like to close on another British Regiment's motto, the Special Air Service. 'Who dares wins.' And we are going to dare?"


That night Jama and Gladys spent an emotional night together. Cathy made herself scarce and they dined in the flat, having a bottle of wine with the dinner. Neither was sure when they would next meet and the tension was reflected in their lovemaking afterwards.

Later as Gladys slept, Jama silently left the flat. It was already four in the morning. He was in the first group to leave, so he went to the barracks for the last time and packed his bags.

Taking a taxi to his grandparents', he left the majority of his belongings with them, telling them he was going on a short holiday, then left for Heathrow.

His flight had six of his team on, but all sat separately and did not acknowledge each other.

Strength in numbers would come later.

## TWENTY-FIVE

Jama arrived in Nairobi at almost ten o'clock that evening and bought a visa at the immigration desk. He saw his fellow South Africans scattered along the length of the queue and waited for them to come through the Arrivals area. They split into two sets of three and grabbed a taxi per group to the nearby Moi Air Base, a military strip operated by Kenya Air Force, and not even shown on local maps. In the past it had been named RAF Eastleigh after the now civil airport north of Southampton. Its two and a half kilometre of runway would not take many civilian jets, but it would host a Hercules C130.

Once there, they began setting up a base in the corner of a hangar. They had toilets and showers, but not too much more. The rest of the men arriving that day, via various European and Middle Eastern carriers, would overnight in one of two hotels, the Jacaranda or the Panari. They had been told to have a quiet night then proceed to Moi at lunchtime the following day. By that time, most of day-two travel group should also be there, or thereabouts.

They were chaperoned around the base by a Kenyan Squadron Leader, who definitely doubted the cover story that they were British Army but had been paid enough not to ask too many questions by the British government.

The rest of the cover story was built around the whole expat team having been on exercise in the Kenyan Highlands, a semi-mountainous area in the west of the country. To save costs on their extraction, the RAF would be picking them up from Moi following a couple of days of Rest & Recuperation.

Anyone who recognized a South African accent wouldn't believe any of it, but they didn't intend being there long enough for anyone to really notice.

The six of them unpacked as much as they needed – a wash kit and a change of clothes – and set-up some camp beds and lightweight sleeping bags to get some rest. They were soon asleep after the day of travel.

In the morning, they set about some wooden packing cases that were waiting for them. They worked in pairs and counted the contents of each case, keeping out of sight of the locals.

After a couple of hours they had counted out one hundred and eighty SLR rifles, and twenty five General Purpose Machine Guns. (GPMGs). With the weapons was just over twenty thousand loose rounds of 7.62 mm ammunition, and about another fifteen thousand rounds in chain, the same calibre for both weapons.

Old British military combat clothing was boxed separately, two hundred sets of varying sizes that their people would need to mix and match once they got here. They already knew they had lost a couple of people to flu and injuries, so they expected one hundred and ninety two to arrive by the end of day two.

On the other side of the hangar were four open topped Land Rovers. They had seen better days but would do until they captured some better vehicles. The rear of each Rover was stuffed full of Jerry cans of fuel.

The rest of the boxes and plastic containers were full of rations and water, enough to keep them alive for about four days. By then they had to be self-sufficient.

The unpacking complete, they went back to lie on their camp beds and settled down to wait for the rest of the force. And the Hercules transporters.


The Hercs from the RAF could just make Lanseria from the Kenyan capital, so they had to be rigged with additional wing tanks to get them out of South African airspace after the drop. They had then been cleared to land in Gaborone in Botswana to take on fuel before they started the long journey home. The distance to the strip in South Africa was almost 1,800 miles and the flight would take about four hours depending on wind conditions.

The rest of the expats arrived during the afternoon of day two, and by six o'clock all but four were accounted for. After a few enquiries, it was found the four were on the same flight, and this had been delayed at Paris. They would be missing the trip.

By eight o'clock everyone had been kitted out in combat gear and all the spare clothing packed in the Rovers on top of the fuel. Weapons had been handed out and ammunition issued. Everyone had two days of rations, with the rest repacked on the Rovers. They wanted everything off the aircraft as quickly as humanly possible on landing, and the aircraft away to Botswana. They could repack once they settled down.

By nine o'clock, the nerves were jangling. The Hercules were due in any time now and had to be in the air again by ten o'clock. This meant a touchdown in the dark at Lanseria. Not great for the pilots, but nice for the soldiers.

US surveillance had shown no signs of humans out there, so they hoped to get in unopposed. No-one was counting their chickens on that one though, but an arrival in the middle of the night would afford them some advantage at least. Even good soldiers need to sleep, and the enemy were not rated as good.

At nine fifteen the drone of Alison gas turbine engines filled the air and one by one the four Hercules aircraft touched down on Moi airstrip. Turning at the end of the runway, they taxied towards the hangar that air traffic control directed them to. By nine thirty each had a Kenyan Air Force fuel bowser under their wings as the crews prepared for the next leg of the flight.

The four Rovers were driven up the rear ramps of each aircraft and fastened down. All loose gear was attached to the vehicles – anything else had to be carried. The plan was to have the birds on the ground for only ten minutes in Lanseria.

By nine fifty everyone was on board again and the engines were running. The noise from the sixteen engines was loud, but people inserted their personal stereo earphones and escaped from the real world. Some tried to doze off, knowing it might be some time before a proper rest would be possible once things got started.

At two minutes after ten the fourth aircraft lifted of the Kenyan soil and turned south. Climbing in to the cruise, there wasn't too much for the aircrew to do, and even less for their passengers.

They were on their way home and wondered and worried about what they would find there.

In a few short hours, they would know first-hand.


As the aircraft came close to the South African border, they dropped height to around one hundred feet, a tactic employed by the Israelis all those years back to get their troops in to Entebbe. It was assumed that no radar facilities would be functioning, but better safe than sorry, and it was the first bit of excitement for the pilots in hours.

One aircraft cruised forward at this height while the other three entered a holding pattern, allowing the leader to get 'eyes on' the airstrip. The troops in the back had been alerted to the manoeuvre, so all eyes were glued to porthole windows, looking for signs of life.

After a pass in each direction and absolutely no signs of danger, the leader called in the other three planes. Each took their turn to line up spaced one minute apart, then the leader followed the final Hercules. Reverse thrust was applied as soon as they touched the deck. They slowed to a stop, the rear ramp already lowered. Troops charged out and ran to the edges of the runway, assuming all around defensive positions. The Rovers were driven out and Jama gave a thumbs up to the Squadron Leader in the cockpit.

Radioing to the other aircraft, they all trundled back along the runway and turned in to the slight breeze to improve their lift abilities. Then one by one, they gated their throttles fully forward and accelerated down the length of the tarmac, slowly lifting in to the sky. With all four up, they turned north to Gaborone, Botswana.

Jama moved around checking his men. The drone of the aircraft faded, and he heard nothing except the chirp of crickets and other insects in the night air. It was two forty-five in the morning, and they had landed in South Africa unopposed.

Now they need to organize themselves quickly and get to Pretoria before daylight or risk a day in the airport. It all depended on whether they found vehicles here or not. The one hundred and eighty-eight soldiers were never going to get in to four Rovers.

They'd had their assistance from the USA and the UK, and now they were on their own.

Jama set the majority of the men to unloading most of the fuel from the Rovers to allow people to get inside them. They were storing it in a large aircraft hangar, but in the darkness it was difficult to see what was in there. Maglite torches split the blackness but did not illuminate large areas.

The force was now split in to four teams of around fifty each. One was designated to stay at the airfield and set up a base camp, while the other three would be used to take the Union Buildings in Pretoria. The old Clansmen radio sets would struggle with the range but, by placing an antenna on top of the hangar, they hoped it would suffice. Union Buildings, also being on a hill would help, but it was a part of their plan they had been unable to test to date.

With the Rovers relatively clear of cargo, five-man teams mounted them, all armed with their SLRs. They drove around the buildings at the airport looking for suitable vehicles to commandeer.

Jama and the HQ team leader decided to try and have a decent look into the hangar. Working their way back from the storage area, they found the building was split by a yellowed dividing wall, stretching all the way to the roof, about ten metres above their heads.

They worked along the length of the wall, searching for a door.

A yell came from Jacques end of the wall. "Got a door here Jama."

Jama moved towards the pool of light from his torch. A red fire door was in front of them.

"I'll open it, you cover me," said Jacques.

Moving to a position where he had the best view, Jama dropped to a kneeling position and shouldered his weapon. Jacques pushed the emergency release handle and dropped to the ground. Nothing happened. It really did seem that the place had been abandoned.

Jacques passed carefully through the door, rifle at the ready. It was even darker in here, and not a sound to be heard.

Jacques whistled. "Will you look at this," he said.

Turning, Jama saw the reason behind his comment. There in front of them were three almost new buses for passenger pick-up. Enough for about 150 troops.

"Looks like our fairy godmother is with us today," Jacques said.

"You're right there."

The buses were a Godsend. They were designed for ferrying passengers around the airport, not for cruising on public roads, and the troops soon discovered that they couldn't get more than forty miles an hour out of them, pedal to the metal. The good news was they only needed to travel the thirty-five miles to Pretoria, so the journey should only last an hour.

Jama called in the car search patrols, though one of those had already struck lucky and found two aircrew minibuses, so these were fuelled up and brought in to the central area. They now had three buses, two minibuses and four Land Rovers.

It was now four o'clock in the morning and Jama had a decision to take. One hour on the road to the city, meant arrival at five a.m. That was already daylight at this time of year, and that had its risks. There again, if the defending force was not expecting visitors, they may just be able to walk straight in.

Jama was also a great believer in luck. Preparation and planning was one side of the equation, but without a little luck, even the best laid plans could go to hell.

They had only lost four of their party due to flights so far. They had linked up with the RAF and arrived in Lanseria with no reception party. They had vehicles, weapons, ammo and food. How much more luck did they need today?

They were also tired, with very little sleep from the day and a half of travel. Jama made his choice: they would rest up during today, and that evening at midnight, make their move on Pretoria.

Sentries were put out, stags arranged and the men made themselves comfortable.

Jama hoped the choice wouldn't be the wrong one, but as the first sunlight started to appear on the eastern horizon, he was fairly certain he'd done the right thing.


The day passed uneventfully, men catching up on lost sleep, repacking equipment ready for whatever lay ahead, vehicles fuelled, checked and prepped as best they could be. The lookouts saw nothing of significance to report, and it looked as though the decision had been a good one.

Jama talked with all of the team who had ever been into the Union Buildings. He'd done this in the UK too, but he just wanted every snippet of information he could get. Any piece may be the one that saves a soldier's life.

Mid-afternoon, he too rested. Midnight was coming quick.

## TWENTY-SIX

At eleven-thirty that evening, everyone gathered for a final brief. They were fed and rested, their weapons were clean, magazines loaded. They were ready to go. Assembled in front of the hangar, they looked at their team leaders before them having a discussion with Jama. As it broke up, Jama climbed on the bonnet of one of the Rovers.

"OK guys, we go in an hour. We take the three buses with thirty-five riflemen in each. The two minibuses will each hold four GPMG operators and guns, so this leaves plenty of room for everybody. We'll also take two of the Land-rovers between me and three team leaders. They will carry spare fuel and ammo." He turned to the base camp team, off to the side of the main party. "This leaves seventy-odd men back here to secure our base. You'll have two Rovers for mobile patrols, and maybe you can find a few more suitable vehicles. You are just as important as the force going to town: we need a safe haven if things go wrong and we need the airstrip to bring in the medical and admin people later."

He put his rifle down at his feet on the bonnet. "Somewhere here will also be aviation fuel. From the intelligence we got, they had no electricity to pump it, but it should be here. See if you can do something to make it useful please."

He turned again to the men going to Pretoria. "We go in quiet if possible, same as we planned in the UK. We shoot only if necessary. These are fellow South Africans, just badly led astray. If they fight us they die. If they want to side with us, we'll judge them on their merits."

He climbed down off the bonnet, jumping the final foot.

"Oh, and one more thing," he said as the men just started to talk amongst themselves. "We mount up in ten minutes. Good luck!"

The ragtag army of expats saluted him.

It was the proudest day of his life.

At four minutes past twelve they drove through the gates of Lanseria, where the HQ Company had dug a trench that held two soldiers, one with the machine gun and the other armed with a rifle. They waved as the convoy passed.

Moving on the main roads towards Centurion, Jama could see that the roads had been neglected, with grass spreading towards the middle of the first lane of motorway and occasionally further. Potholes weren't as bad as he thought they might be, but then heavy traffic had ceased to use the roads, so less damage was being inflicted on them.

Entering the outskirts of Pretoria they saw their first fellow South Africans. They hung out on street corners, looking dirty and a little emaciated. They looked back at the convoy, not moving to impede it, but obviously wondering what it meant.

They passed the Voortrekker Monument and the Afrikaans bowed their heads, remembering the images in there of the Great Trek. They had been pursued the length of their country by the British, losing thousands of lives. How times changed. They now had the chance to win back their nation due to British help.

The housing became denser now, and they headed in the general direction of Hatfield and Arcadia. The Union Buildings were getting close now.

At the base of hill below the parliament, the buses pulled over and the troops climbed out and took up defensive positions. The minibuses and Rovers also emptied out. The buses were pulled next to each other, partially blocking the street, but taking a smaller area to make them easier to defend. The Rovers and minibuses parked in front of them, also close together. Two soldiers mounted the buses and positioned themselves at either end of the roof. Two more stayed on the ground with the Rovers in case a fast evacuation was needed.

The road climbed steeply in front of them and Jama knew from his briefings that the Union Buildings would be off to his left when they reached the top of the hill. The men took alternate sides of the street as they moved silently up it, spaced about five metres apart so as not to lose sight of one another.

Halfway up, they passed the German Embassy, its gates pulled down and the residence ransacked. To think this had once been a desirable area.

At the top of the rise, Jama dropped to his knees. The troops followed suit all the way down the hill. This was the last true cover before they came in view of the home of the government. Jama hoped that at one-thirty in the morning, no-one would be there to see them. He could see no-one.

Jama had a problem, and he knew it. None of the group with him had ever been in the hall, and it was vast. He needed to get in and capture Oliver Justice, otherwise risk him escaping and setting up a power-base elsewhere. He could storm the buildings, with a team left, right and centre, but this would have a higher chance of lives being lost. The problem was he had no other way to handle it that he could think of. He wished his old CO was here.

He called in the three Team Leaders, letting them know his thoughts. They agreed with his assessment but couldn't shed any more light on to the problem.

"OK," Jama told them. "I'm going to suggest a compromise, something I don't like, but that may work in this case." He looked from one to the other. "Not being insulting, but none of our boys here have stormed a house for some time, so going in slow might be a better, more structured exercise. So we go slow, and you take left, you right and you centre with me. Whoever finds Justice holds him until I get there."

"Makes sense," said the oldest man there. "What about if we come under fire?"

"You'll have to decide yourselves, but if possible, get in cover and one of the other teams will come to assist. Main thing is to let us know if you need help!"

"We'll definitely be doing that bro," said the youngest man of the three.

"Also let all teams know of any other relevant discoveries on the way in. They might save each other time."

"Jama, you're young but we're right with you," said the old guy. He put his hand forward and all four men clasped their hands together. "To all of us coming out of the other end."

"Amen to that."


The troops started moving out in single file, staying in the darkness of the wall on the right hand side of Fairview Avenue. Set back about thirty metres above them was the right wing of Union Buildings. To the left, Meintjieskop sloped downhill towards Pretoria, or more rightly nowadays, Tshwane.

The Buildings formed a semi-circular arc, the two wings forward of the centre and closest to the road. At the joining point, wide steps ran up to the structure. This was the only avenue of approach and it formed a natural ambush point. Jama hated it.

Rather than just start up the stairway, Jama decided to try and trigger any ambush first. He tapped the two men next to him and said, "You two with me. We dash to the other side. Now!"

They raced across the gap, mindful that bullets could fly towards them at any time.

Nothing but silence.

Jama waved his arm in a large arc to the men on the other side. One got up and started up the stairs slowly. One of the two who'd completed the dash with Jama started up the left side. Still no response from above.

The other guy with Jama started up the stairway, and another joined from the other side. A dozen more ran over and joined Jama, filtering in, so a line of bodies moved up both sides of the stairs. Because they were wider at the base than at the top, some cover was afforded on the way up by staying close to the wall. At the top they would lose this all together.

The man on the left top stair froze and waved the rest down. He passed a message down to the foot of the stairs, eventually reaching Jama. "He can hear voices but can't see the source."

Jama made a decision and crept up the stairs. He was further from the wall than the front man and felt very vulnerable. He lay as flat as possible and listened.

Voices, indistinct, but voices. "Wait here," he whispered and crawled forward. Ten yards further on and behind a large bush, he felt a little safer. Controlling his breathing and trying to control the noise from his heart, he focused on the conversation ahead.

"Hoosat da pardy, bro," a very drunken South African voice asked. "Iz da free skirt?"

"Shut up brother, you're pissed," a man ordered. "We got a job to do, even if you don't care!"

"Fuck it bro, everybody pardy on!"

"Only you bloody amateurs. Now get out of here and sleep! I'll get you if I need you."

"Shit man!" The sound of a door closing, then silence. The sound of disco music came from deep in the house – the party the man referred to, thought Jama. But that meant the drunk was gone, leaving a real soldier behind. And without the distraction of the drunken soldier, he had more chance of hearing their approach.

Guessing the man was only about ten paces away, Jama knew he had to act decisively. He signalled to the two men on the top step, then burst forward, dived and rolled towards the soldier. The two behind him fired a round apiece at the general area above the sound source, and the man ducked. Jama was now an arm's length from him and grabbed his weapon as he tackled him hard. The soldier fell to the ground and Jama was on him.

"Quiet, or you die!"

The two soldiers from the steps had followed up and had the man covered. He looked terrified but dangerous, his eyes popping, but still trying to see if he could retake his weapon.

"Who are you?" he asked, the shock of the attack still coming through his voice as it attempted to come down an octave.

"I think I might be asking the questions," said Jama, his voice hard. "And I don't have time to wait for answers, so consider your replies carefully."

The man was looking beyond Jama now and watched as men poured up the steps and took positions in front of the house. His eyes seemed to become even larger, but his breathing was controlled. Jama sensed he was a professional soldier, unlike the man who had been sent inside.

"How many troops here?" he demanded.

"Depends what you call troops, I guess."

"OK, how many like your drunken brother inside, and how many like yourself?"

"He's not my brother. And why the hell should I tell you?"

He was brave, and Jama didn't have time. The shots would have alerted everyone except those in the party. Last chance. "Are you a South African?"

"Course I am."

"Then why do you support the drunk who's destroying our country, eh?"

"I don't support the Oliver Justice, man, he just pays best. Give me the old days. I was special forces here."

"If you want the old days, answer my questions and think about joining some real South African soldiers."

He could see the wheels racing in the man's head, saw his eyes counting the odds against, and knew that anyone keeping their cool so well under this amount of stress probably was what he claimed to be.

"We got about a hundred of the drunks looking for a drink and a piece of skirt, and about twenty soldiers," he told him. Then he added, "And I think your team looks preferable to the one in there." He nodded to the doors.

"I'll give you a chance," said Jama taking the man's weapon and handing it to one of his troops. "You get us to Justice, and you join the Liberation Team." The title came from nowhere, but he decided it sounded good.

"Do I get my gun back?"

"Only when we feel we can trust you. You have to prove that first."


The two shots had alerted the troops in the house, but when no others followed, many wondered if they had been accidental discharges from the drunks in the security group. Some of the drunks then fired off rounds anyway, just because it gave them an excuse to do so, but they were harmless as they had no idea where things were happening.

The bigger problem was the professionals in there: they would now be at the ready, just in case.

The captured soldier led them to the left of the building, explaining that the main entrance was the most heavily manned. He also told them that the party is where Oliver Justice would be, drinking hard and deciding who the lucky woman or women would be that night.

Jama was concerned that he was assisting a little too easily, but as they had no other way of knowing the best way in, he thought he had to trust the man. Hedging his bets he sent a party of thirty men around the other wing of the house though, giving him a two-pronged attack. It also made sense to put the main defensive force at the main entrance, so he had to concede that the man was probably telling the truth.

As they moved along the left wing, the disco music grew in volume, another indicator that they were going the right way.

They advanced slowly, moving shadow to shadow.

The captured man was growing more confident as they advanced, making Jama more concerned about his thinking. Suddenly he bolted, yelling at the top of his voice.

"Fire! Fire! Fire!"

A second passed then five or six weapons opened up on the advancing force.

"Down!" yelled Jama. "Fire at will!"

The escaping man went down, probably hit by fire from his own troops. It was utter chaos out there now, with bullets flying in both directions and screams from the unlucky people who had strayed in to their path. Both sides were taking casualties, and in the dark it was hard to see who was coming off worst.

Spread over the path and lawn, the Liberation soldiers were without any cover.

"Left of me fire at will to hold them down. Right of me, we charge them. Go!"

They jumped and ran, Jama leading. The man closest to him went down, blood pouring out of a shoulder wound, cursing noisily. Bullets were still pouring in to the enemy position though, so return fire was becoming more subdued.

Then they were on them and rifles were really the wrong weapon for a close-in battle.

Jama smashed the butt of his weapon in to the head of one of the defenders, then felt something nick his combat jacket. He felt blood run down his right side, but then saw another defender coming at him from the left. Ignoring the wound, he shot a round at the man, lifting him off his feet and hurling him in to the building wall. He screamed like an injured animal, his stomach bleeding, and entrails escaping from the exit wound in his back.

Jama felt inside of his jacket, releasing he'd only been winged by the bullet.

Sheer weight of numbers won the day, and the ten defenders were overcome. By now though, everyone had to know that something bad was afoot, so Justice would probably be on the move.

Throwing caution to the wind, Jama stormed on in to the house, his men following. He headed towards the sound of music, hoping at least this part had been true.

"We must stop Oliver Justice escaping," he yelled to his radio operator. "Relay that to all of our people."

They had reached the door from where the music came, and the lead man paused. This could easily be a trap.

Slamming the door open, everyone out of line of the entranceway, they were ready for the worst.

The music was mind-blowingly loud, but it was still a shock that no-one had heard all the shooting. In front of them people were dancing, kissing, drinking and totally oblivious to the massacre that had just taken place in the garden.

They stormed in, pushing people to their knees and moving them up to the walls.

There was no Oliver Justice.


Hennie van Rensburg was as Afrikaan as they came and had no real love for Oliver Justice, but against that he was a highly professional soldier and performed his work as best he possibly could. And his task right now was to protect the stand-in President.

He had heard the shooting because he had been outside of the party, not being comfortable with all of the drunks in the room. Not that he didn't drink, he just didn't believe in being inebriated while he was on duty. As one of the members of the South African Special Forces group attached to Union Buildings, he had reacted immediately to the sound of gunfire, collecting two of his colleagues and then grabbing the drunken Oliver Justice.

He now moved swiftly towards the back of the house and away from the shooting, followed by the three men. He heard the sound of the disco music stop and knew he had not been long ahead of the attackers.

Taking a last wood-trimmed corridor, he entered an office that he knew had a door to the garden. As he came through the door he noticed movement in the yard. "Down!" he hissed sharply. One of his colleagues pulled Justice down and they lay there in the dark. Both he and colleagues were armed with MP5 machine pistols, but even in the moment he had glanced the people outside, he could tell that three men were not enough to take them on. He could only hope they carried on.

After a minute, he crawled forward to the house outer wall. He raised himself slowly, peeking over the window ledge, his head between the wall and the curtain. No movement outside. It looked as if they'd gone past.

The key was in the outer door, so he unlocked it silently. He opened the door inwards, careful not to make any noise, and looked out again. Nothing.

On the other side of the garden was a tall wall, but he knew from his frequent searches of the property that there was a gate there. And he had been careful to get hold of a copy of the key for the padlock, just in case of moments like this.

"Search the rooms! Don't forget any attic spaces!" In his heart, Jama guessed that Justice was probably out of the house, but as no-one had seen him, he had to check the property. If he'd made it outside he was gone anyway.

He'd lost five men and had three with wounds, two serious, the other nothing too much to worry about. Plus of course his own scrape. The opposition had eight dead and nine with injuries. All in all, things hadn't gone too badly, but he wished that they had captured Oliver Justice. As it was it appeared he had lived to fight another day.

His men came back to him over the next ten minutes or so. No sign of the man. Some of his troops had also gone, but only from the Special Forces. The other men had no more wish to fight and had surrendered. For them the fun was over.

Jama had the radio boffins set-up a Clansman antenna on the roof, and he contacted the force at Lanseria, briefing them on the situation. They had nothing really to report, except that they had found fuel storage tanks as had been reported and were now working on restoring power to pump the fuel out and make it usable. With the fuel they could also run generators and this would allow them to get in contact with the other expats in the UK.

There was still a long way to go, but the Union Buildings were theirs and they had an airport to bring in material and reinforcements.

It was a start.


Hennie led his two Special Forces colleagues and Oliver Justice quickly downhill from Meintjieskop, trying to put as much distance as possible between his group and the attackers. He didn't expect them to follow, but he also didn't know if they had other groups patrolling the city, so a certain amount of care was required.

Heading in to Hatfield area of Pretoria, he wondered what his next course of action should be. He had probably just saved his leader's life, but was the man still now a leader? He had no base now and almost no following. Hennie and the Specials had stayed there out of a sense of duty, but the others had remained there for the benefits and lifestyle they received. With the buildings in the hands of others, those luxuries were no longer available.

Hennie knew he had a decision to make.


With the battle for the Union Buildings over, Jama cleared out Justice's hangers-on, telling them to get back home to their families. He didn't want to kill people for the sake of it, and he didn't need to be lumbered with prisoners. He also thought it would be a good way to get word out on the street that things were changing, something he and Dumi had discussed during their months together in London.

With his men divided into shifts, the majority now had a chance to get some much needed rest. The adrenalin of the night was exiting their bodies and a heavy weariness was setting in.

Jama knew that they had to somehow get the television and radio stations running again, and to get the message to all of South Africa that the country was free again. That meant he had to get power, and that was a problem without accessing coal stocks and restarting the power stations.

The plan was first to get more access to fuel as his people at Lanseria had done, then run-up generators to create local power. This would be fine for radio transmission, and hopefully the noise would suck the crowds towards it. He would then use the same method as Oliver Justice had done – stand at the top of the hill before the seat of power and let the folk of Pretoria know Dumi was coming back.

How things went from that point in time depended on how the people reacted. If he could get them back to work, then Dumi could plan a way out of this mess with the international mining companies, and then South Africa would climb back to its feet again.

Or that's what they hoped.

He fell asleep in the gardens of Union Buildings, exhausted, but still planning the next move.


Hennie holed up in a boarded-up property on the edge of Hatfield. The four men were tired after the rush to escape, and Justice was also suffering the after-effects of the drink. The first light of dawn was in the night sky, so they agreed a roster and took turns sleeping. At nine o'clock, all of them had had a couple of hours. Justice was still out of it.

The three Special Forces men went in to the next room.

"Time to decide what to do," Hennie told them.

"We owe him nothing now," a muscular black man nicknamed Uzi said. "We saved him and now he's got nothing to offer us."

The third man remained silent, reserving his judgment for the time being.

"You're right Uzi. He's actually let the country down. Look at the state of things," Hennie said. "We can choose to drop him right now, or even hand him in to the new guys, whoever they are."

"Might be a good idea. Before they come looking for us."

The silent one, Hamilton, spoke up. "There's another option," he told them. "We stick with him and help him raise a force to take his position back."

"We don't even know who we're up against man," Uzi whispered. "Could be suicide. And for what?"

"I guess we hold all the cards right now. By himself, he's nothing. With us, he has a chance. We're in a great place to negotiate from."

"You're right Hennie. When he wakes up, we offer to assist. But he has to name the reward if we pull it off."

Uzi extended his left arm, hand open and down. Hennie slapped his left hand down on to it, Hamilton following suit. Next Uzi's right, Hennie and Hamilton slamming their own on top.

"Together," they chanted.

A pact had been made.


Jama woke as the light increased, smelling sweat and gun smoke from his clothing. A shower and clean clothes would be a blessing, but he couldn't imagine either thing happening in the immediate future. He rolled over, wincing as his injured side stretched and a little blood seeped out. He decided to find a bathroom and have a look at it, grabbing at least a rudimentary wash whilst at it.

On the way inside he ran in to Klaas, one of the Team Leaders.

"I'm going to clean up a bit," he told him. "Could you get one of the teams to secure our perimeter? Another should search the building in daylight and see just what we have here."

"OK, I'll get the other two teams on to that. What about my lads?"

"Do you fancy a run in to the city? See if the garages have any fuel in their tanks?"

"Could do. Just a drive round in the Rovers?"

"Yeah, sounds good. Have the vehicles been brought up here?"

"All in Fairview."

"Give me ten minutes and I'll come downtown with you. Will be good to see how it looks."

"I'll get the wagons ready to roll. We can comfortably get eight in each, and I'll mount a GPMG on each one too. Don't really expect to meet any serious firepower down there."

"Maybe get a couple of loud-hailers if you can find some. We can advertise our presence and try and get some of the locals together to see how things are."

"I'll see what we can rustle up in the next few minutes. Maybe delay our departure another ten minutes. Means you can clean up a bit better."

"Appreciated Klaas. Be there soon."

"No problem boss."


The first thing Oliver Justice noted when he woke up was that he wasn't in the Presidential bed with some woman or another. The second thing was that he had a hangover the size of a house, his brain aching to a point where it didn't want to function at all. He rolled over on the concrete floor, his body stiff as a board.

He opened his eyes, screwing them together against the harsh light from a window that had no glass. A large wooden board sat next to it.

"We thought we'd open the window for you," said a voice.

He turned towards it, trying to focus on the body shape in front of him. His brain slowly moved up a gear and recognized the man as one of his defensive detail.

"I need a drink," he said. "Get the butler and get me a drink!"

"I think you can stop the ordering now," said the man. He rolled over a bottle of water. "Time for you to get back with the story."

"Where are we? How did we get here?"

"You've been kicked out of the government houses and we managed to get you to here before the bad guys stormed the disco. If it wasn't for us, you'd be locked up at the best, and dead at the worst."

"OK, thanks," Oliver said, giving a dismissive wave of his hand. "It was your job, you know."

"Your right there son," Hennie told him. "It was our job. But now you're out of a job, how you going to pay us?"

Oliver looked at him, sensing the hostility in his reply. Two other men stepped in to the room, both blacks, but not looking at all sympathetic, arms crossed over their broad chests. The larger of the two spoke up.

"We could help you get the job back," he said. "For a price."

"Sure, sure," Justice blurted out, in a bit of a panic now. "You get me back in and I can give you all the fun you want. Girls, booze, property…"

"Gold." the big guy demanded. "A tonne of the stuff between us, and safe passage of our choice out of the country."

Gold? thought Oliver. Was there any left? Now was not the time to voice that doubt.

"No problem brother," he quickly told them. "We have plenty of that."

"If you cross us son, it'll be the last thing you ever do," the white guy threatened.

"The very last," Uzi added.


Jama, Klaas and twelve soldiers headed towards the city in the two Land-rovers. Some people were on the streets, and they stared at them but did not run. They looked unkempt – torn and dirty clothes, hair not seen by a barber for months – and they hung out close to doorways of what Jama guessed would be their homes. Homes they'd probably grabbed after the initial rioting, with no electricity, no running water.

Most windows were empty of glass. Rubbish was everywhere, both in heaps and scattered around.

In the central square of Pretoria, the massive statue of Paul Kruger, one of the country's founding fathers, lay on its side, the supporting plinth empty. The Museum of Apartheid had no doors or windows, its artifacts lying in the street broken or burnt.

Jama hated to think of the condition of the interior of the Voortrekker Monument, its paintings and tapestries depicting the early years of the Afrikaans race up country.

"Stop the car!" he ordered when he saw a bunch of about twenty middle-aged people standing outside of a flat doorway. They all looked on nervously when he dismounted, on the verge of running in to the building.

"Don't run!" he called to them. "We're not here to give you trouble. We want to put things right."

Klaas stepped to his side, and he guessed the GPMG gunners were covering him.

"We are normal South Africans. We took back the Union Buildings last night. Oliver Justice is on the run," he told them.

"Why should we believe that?" asked an older black man at the front of the group. He had his arms in his pockets and hadn't backed off like the rest. He looked as if he was fed-up with running.

"Tomorrow I will hold a rally in the park outside the Buildings. We need to recruit workers for all types of work. We need people like yourselves."

The man frowned, looking doubtful. "So we go up there and then you grab our young girls and we never see them again, is that it?" He was angry, despite the odds against him. "Why should we trust you?"

"I can only give you my word," said Jama. "The rest is up to you. We want our country back as much as I'm sure you do."

Klaas spoke up. "He speaks the truth. Don't bring your daughters. Bring yourselves."

The man looked at the others. Some shook their heads, others did nothing.

"Who are you?" he demanded.

"A soldier, but not a thug. My name is Jama Nomvula."

# TWENTY-SEVEN

The first Boeing 737-400 passenger jet for two years was lining up on the approach to Lanseria Airport in Gauteng. Sitting on the jump-seat between the two pilots was Dumi Silongo, craning his neck to get a view of his beloved country, hardly daring to speak as he knew he would not hide the emotion in his voice. It seemed an endlessly long time since he had been home, and now a couple of hundred feet beneath him was Africa.

He watched the red earth of the country come closer and closer, saw the yellowed grass with black patches where uncontrolled burns had taken place, saw a glint off a lake that he thought must be in Rietvlei Game Park, a waited to taste the warm air.

The waiting was over. Jama had secured his country, started the rehabilitation process.

The previous day, the first rally had been attended in front of the Union Buildings. Only about two hundred people had attended, but it was a start. Three of the people had been electricians for the city before the crisis and had some ideas on how to get a minimal amount of street lighting working with generators. This would make the nights a little safer. A start.

Some of the women had been taken on to start the clean-up on the government house. This needed no skill, just a lot of patience.

They had found ten nurses in the group, and these would soon be complemented by the nurses from London. Including Gladys and Cathy in their aid-worker roles.

One doctor had been found, but he knew where others had been, and Jama had started a planned round-up of key people.

The soldiers had been directed by the locals to where they could find vast marquees, and these were going up in the park to house people in a secure area. Other ex-soldiers had volunteered to assist, and joined the security force, though in unarmed roles until they proved their worth. This would take a little time.

Jama had done well. Magnificently in fact.

The jet was floating just off the tarmac now, and Dumi gripped the seat in anticipation of the jolt of the landing. The pilot – a South African who had worked with British Airways – was perfect though, and the touchdown was fault free, like running down a slope on to a flat road at the bottom.

The plane ran up the runway, reverse thrust slowing it down to drivable speed, then the pilot turned off the runway and towards the hangar. The stewardesses, also volunteers from the London based Africans, unlocked the doors and waited for steps to arrive at the jet.

Dumi waited impatiently at the front of the cabin, smiling like a child to all the passengers waiting to go home.


Jama watched the jet taxi towards the hangar, his heart pounding. He had never felt like this about anyone before in his life, even in his schoolboy crush days, but he just couldn't wait to see Gladys.

The aircraft came to a stop close to him and the aircraft handlers his men had found and recruited put in the chocks at the front tyres. The pilot switched off the two engines and the cabin door swung outwards, latching on to its locking device as the jets wound down. Steps moved towards the opening and Jama could already see Dumi behind the stewardess.

Soon they would be properly on South African ground.


One hundred and sixty passengers disembarked from the aircraft. They were all expats from London, but this flight consisted of professional people that would be needed to build a new South Africa. Engineers, bankers, nurses, doctors, mining experts, port managers, transport planners – only a few of those selected by Dumi and his team as essential to try and put the country back on track.

The President led the way, to cheers from on board and from the troops on the ground. He went straight to Jama, giving him a three-staged African handshake, followed by a big emotional hug.

"You did well son," he murmured in his ear. "South Africa has a new hero."

After a moment he broke away, moving through the soldiers and shaking hands. He said a few words to every one of them, a little praise they so deserved.

Jama stood looking at the aircraft steps, watching the rest of the passengers climbing down them. Some he knew and they shook hands as they passed him. Some kissed the soil as they reached the foot of the steps. It was a great homecoming.

Just when he was beginning to think Gladys had missed the flight, the blond Cathy came through the cabin door. He waved, still wondering where his love was.

The next passenger stepped out, and then there she was. His smile split his face from ear-to-ear. His joy was reflected on Gladys's face as she came down the steps as fast as the crowd allowed.

Cathy gave Jama a quick hug as she reached the base of the steps two places before Gladys, then swiftly moved aside.

Gladys rushed the last steps and into Jama's arms, eyes tightly closed but a couple of tears still leaking down the sides of her face. "I missed you so bloody much," she told him. "Do not leave me like that ever again."

Cathy blushed a deep red and moved away from the couple towards the hangar.

"If I have my way, I never will," whispered Jama.


The only failing in the whole operation, was the escape of Oliver Justice, who had disappeared from the face of the earth. The President's people issued a reward for his hand-over and the troops had been asking locals whilst on patrol for over a week now. No-one owned up to seeing the man.

Hennie, Uzi and Hamilton were past masters of escape and evasion, and they used their skills to keep Justice out of the public eye.

First they got rid of the expensive clothes and jewellery the man constantly wore. Then they shaved his head and the goatee beard he'd taken to wearing. Over four days, they made their way to Johannesburg, where they knew they'd easily keep off the map for a while. From his youth, Uzi still had connections with the old criminal underground there. Growing up in Alexandra, you got to know some bad people.

With the help of some of Uzi's 'acquaintances' they found a reasonable house in the area of Kempton, close to the airport. Making deals with the thugs proved expensive, but agreements were reached on a basis of payment on delivery – deliver the position of power back to Justice and he would reward handsomely. As a deposit it cost Oliver Justice the rest of his jewellery.

Hennie knew some ex-forces friends in Kempton's old white suburbs, so they paid them a visit, asking them to join their force to overthrow the New Liberation Army, as Jama's group had been dubbed. They found five suitable characters and decided a force of eight should be enough to make the hit. They only needed to take out the new military man and the President, then the beast would be headless again. Too big would only draw attention, so eight was fixed as the total.

They also discussed the future of Oliver Justice once they received their gold.

There is no honour between thieves.


Dumi addressed the assembled masses on the lawns below the government dwellings, the tented covering a lot of the ground between Fairview and the main road below. The crowd was in the thousands and seemed to grow with each passing day.

"As you can see people, our camping ground is growing fast and we have more friends than enemies in Tshwane," he told them over the new PA system. "It is time for us to move on to bigger things. We will start a project tomorrow to clean up buildings close to here, and then we will move in families with kids. The rest of you will need to be patient a little longer here, but soon we will all live in buildings again."

Jama, standing to his side, couldn't believe the speed of improvement. People wanted to get back to normal.

"We also have a much bigger project in mind, but it will need you all to come forward and work with us. We want to get the electricity back on in the city." A cheer went up from the crowd. Years of fearing darkness made it loud.

"Who here ever worked in Pretoria West Power Station?" Dumi asked. A few arms went up. "Come forward those who did and come forward the rest of you that ever worked in other power stations."

"Report over here please," shouted one of the electrical engineers who had come in on the London flight.

"I have tied up a temporary deal with Botswana to send coal down by train to fuel the furnaces. This is an old place, so I hope it will be easy enough to get back on line, but at full throttle it will give us 180 MW of power."

Another cheer.

"We will control the darkness again, not the darkness controlling us."

Jama smiled to Gladys who had moved up next to him.

They were winning back South Africa, street by street.


The trains were paid for by the USA, a payment direct to the Botswana government. They agreed to pay for the first ten loads of coal as well, enough to keep things going for a month or so until Dumi had some of his own mines operational again. It was an ambitious plan, and Jama had to organise a security force of forty men to join each train from the crossing point at the South African border.

Meanwhile, what was left of the reserve stocks at the Pretoria West plant were made secure, and the new workforce were preparing for the big switch on. A small, tented town was set up in the grounds of the power station, using the same model as used in the city. Eventually they would route out any hooligans in the surrounding area and start allocating accommodation to the workers.

Having light and power would really change people's lives.

A sort of basic police force was starting to take shape, and a large barrack area was secured to train the men. It was rudimentary training, but at least it was the first steps to getting some law and order in to the Pretoria area.

More flights brought in the rest of the London expats who wished to return, and three weeks after the arrival of liberators, the first foreign nationals entered the country. These were mainly English and Americans from the large mining houses, and security was laid on to get them to the local gold and platinum mines to access the situation. They found equipment damaged, offices looted but the mines basically not so bad With no electricity, lifts to the deeper sections had not been operational. For a relatively small investment, everything could be put right. Or at least as right as was needed to start production.

This was just what Dumi needed to hear.

With his mines running, he could begin to bring in money from outside of South Africa, allowing the repair work to the country to begin in earnest. He could also pay the workers, allowing them to improve their standard of living and support their families. At present, he had no unions, no opposition party and no Youth League stirring up the masses. Whatever he did would be better than what the people had lived with for the last years.

He was only opening up the local area right now and the lanes to get material in and out through Botswana. He knew it was still a dreadfully long way to go to reach where they had already been, but once people saw the way Gauteng was improving he could consider branching in to the other provinces.

One day he would reach Zululand and his people would live normally again.

With the mines operational again, the commodity prices on minerals would drop to normal levels, a major boost for economies like Europe and North America. This would not be such a popular event with Australia, Russia, South America and some of the Far Eastern countries who had benefited the last years from the reduced supply but allowing the large Western economies to grow would free-up more money for investment, and some of this would come his way.

The country would grow again.


Jama saw things from a different angle. He wasn't a politician or an economist, he was a soldier, but he could see the people were happier now than when he had come back. They had more freedom – though a late night curfew was still in force to stop the troublesome elements from ruining what had been achieved – and they were now earning some money, giving them back their pride.

But that wasn't the only reason Jama was seeing the rosy side of life. Having Gladys there with him was amazing. As a professional soldier and an officer, he always believed he had control over his emotions, but now he knew that not to be true. Every time he saw her his stomach did cartwheels.

He wanted to make South Africa safe enough to start a new life together.

## TWENTY-EIGHT

As Dumi nursed a can of beer in the Union Buildings kitchen, he reflected on how far they had come in a few short weeks. The area they held was stable and secure, with the people doing normal jobs for at least some reward. This would improve as more of South Africa's industry started functioning again.

The areas around them were more or less secure and being cleaned up. They had control of Arcadia, Pretoria Central, Hatfield, Sunnyside and Brooklyn, and had secured the old Transnet rail facilities in Eloff Estate, allowing trains to call there with goods from Botswana. They had also reclaimed housing in the Proclamation Hill area close to the power station that was now providing light and heating to all of their safe areas.

Of course everything needed troops to keep it safe, and no doubt they had a long, long way to go, but the progress was vast.

Dumi knew they had to leave their safe zone though and start spreading the word to other cities. The main target had to be Johannesburg, the old centre for trade and still where the eyes of the world watched for improvement. Johannesburg was South Africa.

Jo'burg also had the major airport in the region, and though Lanseria was easily secured due to its limited size, it was also limited in what could land there because of its runway length. If he wanted to land machines like the Airbus 380 in Gauteng, then he needed Oliver Tambo to be re-opened. This meant not only taking the airport and securing it, but also the surrounding neighbourhoods covering a vast area.

He took another pull on his beer, enjoying the cold bitterness.

A knock at the door, and then Jama entered the room. The boy smiled, almost glowing in his happiness. Dumi wished he were a young man again.

"Like a beer?"

"Good idea. Feel like I've been out in the city forever."

"How are things out there?" asked Dumi, lifting another can out of the fridge.

"Getting better by the day," said Jama, settling down on an enormous worktop. They hadn't taken up the luxury of a full house staff yet, preferring to focus efforts on more important things, such as fixing the city. "Still some problem areas, but even the thugs don't bother us much. They've almost no ammunition left."

"I wish it could stay that way. Once trade starts up again, you'll able to buy anything."

Dumi sat on a long bench fixed on one of the walls. The two of them enjoyed another slug of the ale.

"Hypothetical question," said Dumi, breaking the silence. "How would you secure Johannesburg airport?"

Jama rolled his head back and pursed his lips, thinking. "A tough one. The place is massive."

"Your army is growing."

"Dumi, it's not just the size of the airport, it's also because it stands in the middle of a developed area. Kempton Park, Germiston, Boksburg, Benoni. How could you secure all of that? It would be like guerrilla warfare. House-to-house fighting. We have a growing army of half trained soldiers, not British Paratroopers."

They sat in silence for a minute, Jama looking in to space before sipping his beer again.

"There is another way," he said thoughtfully. "I did learn a few things with the Grenadiers"

"Go on."

"You know the SAS in UK. They are always associated with daring deeds and macho action, but a lot of their work isn't really like that." He paused, scratching his head. "When the odds are against all out action, they try and win over the locals, bring them onside. They call it 'hearts and minds.' They win the people over to stop the trouble."

"Could we do that?"

"Why not? It worked in Malaya, Burma, the Middle East, all over. Why not in South Africa?"

"How do we do it?"

"I think that's simple. We do the same as we did here: give them stability, safety and power. Then they'll show us the bad guys and we remove them."

"Let's make a plan."


The next day Jama took the two Land-rovers and a commandeered Range Rover towards Johannesburg. He had twenty troops with him, plus two civilian engineers who had experience in airports. The plan was to give O R Tambo International Airport a once-over before committing to using it. If it was badly damaged, they had neither the money nor the resources and know-how to fix it. Then the plan would have to change to another major airfield, such as Durban or Cape Town, but these would be hard to handle due to their distance from the Pretoria base.

They were driving down the R21 towards Johannesburg. The sun was blindingly warm today, the winter truly over. It felt a bit like going on a picnic.

The road-signs for Irene, Tembisa and Benoni were all behind them, and next town on the right-hand side would be Kempton Park. They could see the fence that bordered the runway off to their left, passing the old buildings that had housed DHL, TNT and other mail and goods-related courier businesses. They all looked deserted.

Jama loved the fact the roads were empty but for his convoy, but it still felt totally odd. This road had been infamous for road works and traffic jams, yet here they were alone on it.

They came off at the sign for the airport, the slip road winding around to the left. It was partially grassed-over at the edges, in some places quite badly. Jama wondered how much of the runway would be the same way.

They decided not to bother looking in the terminals. It was a given that they would be a mess. A large clean-up crew would be needed if they were to bring them back on line, plus they would need electric power. They passed the international and then the domestic parts of the long building, then carried on, following signs for Jones Road. Here was where most of the airport maintenance was controlled from, and here they hoped to be able to break on to the active side of the field.

They turned into the South African Airways staff compound and saw a barrier about a block ahead of them. There were signs for reception, training wing, electrics bay and other functions needed to run a major airport but headed straight to the gate.

Reaching it, they could see the red and white electric boom barrier was down, but that was no problem. A Rover would go through it with no difficulty. The harder obstacle to overcome was the steel-barred gate behind, which was secured with a large padlock. Jama, in the lead vehicle, made the decision.

"Full speed at it!" he told his driver.

The man smiled and gunned the vehicle forward. They hit the boom barrier at about thirty miles an hour, the pole sheering off at the hinge point and spinning away. They hit the bigger gate at around forty. The padlock clasp held, but the galvanized iron it was holding together failed and the gates sprang open, hit their backstops and swung forward to close again. Clang! By then the lead Rover was through though, so no damage done.

The second Rover approached the gate more slowly, pushing the swing barriers back. The Range Rover followed. Not being military, the drivers treated it with a little more care.

Jama's vehicle waited while the rest caught up, then they headed out onto the aircraft dispersal area. It was weird having no planes out there. All of them had at some time or another flown through this airport, and it was always busy.

O R Tambo has two main runways running roughly north-south and one cross runway that is not used. The most westerly of the runways is almost three miles long, allowing any type of aircraft to touch-down there, and putting it amongst the longest civilian airport runways in the world. The additional length is needed due the less dense air here – the airport is at an elevation of almost 1,700 metres.

They decided to start with the nearest runway, one because it was the longest and therefore would cover all of their initial needs and two because it was not lying adjacent to any domestic property that may be inhabited. They were playing cautious.

They turned right on the runway and drove to the far end. There the two military vehicles went to either edge of the tarmac, while the Range Rover with the two civilians ran along the centre. In position, they started slowly forward, stopping from time to time to let the engineers out to examine minor potholes and growths of grass.

An hour later they were at the northern end of the strip and dismounted to discuss their findings.

"It needs a bit of weeding, and the odd hole levelled," said the younger engineer. "But you could land an airforce aircraft there now, and with a bit of work, it would even accommodate an Airbus."

"Could we complete the repairs with what we have?"

"Of course. I'm sure we would find any materials we needed in the SAA compound back there. And we have people who've worked on building sites. With a bit of supervision, it would be no problem at all."

"Let's have a glance at the other one then."

They drove across to the eastern runway and completed the same inspection. The result was roughly the same, though being shorter it took a little less time. It was close to lunchtime now.

"We've made good time here," said Jama. "Why don't we have a quick look-see in the terminals?"

They decided to stay on the air-side of the terminal. It was easier to see people approaching over the dispersal.

Parking the Rovers fifty metres from one of the air-bridges, Jama left the three drivers with their vehicles. Each had his SLR with him. Jama, the two civilians and the other sixteen men walked across to the wheels of the passenger loading bridge and looked around. Half-way down the square box structure, some stairs led up to a door. They climbed up to it, only to find it locked.

"Break it down," Jama told one of the soldiers. He put his shoulder through it, knocking it open.

They moved through cautiously, listening for movement, voices, anything. There was nothing, so they went on.

"Feels like we just got off a plane," one of the soldiers quipped.

"Best we remember the gate number," said one of the engineers. "Might be useful when we come back."

Coming out of the tunnel, they followed the signs for baggage reclaim and exit. It was a fair walk. Coming to the empty immigration desks and unmanned X-ray machines was a strange feeling.

"Wish it was always this easy," said one of the soldiers, happy to break the deafening silence. "You can queue here for hours."

Through the Customs area, they were in the main terminal. It was like walking around in a cathedral. The hall was massive and deserted. The only noise seemed to be from their own shoes. No piped music, or hustle and bustle of travellers.

The mess was terrible to behold. Every shop window had been put out, and whatever had been on display was long gone, except for the naked mannequins. Food outlets had nothing, fridge doors stood wide open and bare of contents. There was evidence that people had lived there, with burn marks on the tiles where small fires had been lit, but it looked as though they had all left when the goods ran out.

"It's gonna take a shit-load of work to put this lot right," the soldier who thought he was a comedian joked. "Looks like a plague of bloody locusts came through!"

"It's bloody horrible," another said. "These people were like animals, not humans."

"That's what happens when there are no rules."

Having seen enough, Jama turned them around and headed back towards the vehicles, this time going through customs and immigration via departures, not arrivals to ensure this was also clear.

Back at the Rovers, they had a quick review to see if anything else could be gained from the visit.

"We achieved what we wanted to, but what about checking the fuel stores while we're here," said the older engineer. "We've been quite lucky with that in other places."

"Good idea. Where would that be?" asked Jama.

"Across there in the old days," the engineer said pointing.

"Let's go!"

They drove the short distance to where the engineer indicated and the two civilians went to work checking the fuel situation. Within ten minutes they were back.

"It's good news again," the young one said. "Looks like they took what was reachable, but the main store needed electrics for the pumps, so when that went off, the fuel was safe."

"It'll need testing for water content after standing so long," the older man cautioned. "But we can filter it and probably save most of it."

It was mid-afternoon by now and they still had a fifty-mile journey back to HQ. Jama decided they should get on the road and back in the safe area before dusk, so they again took to the R21 and headed for Pretoria.

The day had been highly successful.

Now they just had to win the people's hearts and minds.


In Kempton Park, Hennie and his associates sat in the walled garden of a two-storey villa that had once served as an exclusive guest house. In the corner a BBQ was burning – a braai in local dialect – and the men each had a beer in their hands. Alone in one corner of the garden was Oliver Justice, also with a bottle. He was excluded from the conversation.

"So how do you think we can get him back in the hot seat?" asked an Afrikaan man who had skin like burnt leather from too many hours in the sun. "And if we do, do you really think he can pay us?"

"He can pay us," answered Hennie. "This land's still got plenty to give up. But he's going to pay a lot more than what he thinks right now. We're gonna own him."

The men laughed.

They didn't care too much about the proximity of Justice. They'd found the best way to deal with the guy was to keep him drugged and drunk, and this was exactly what they'd done again. To them he was nothing more than a way to get a load of cash.

"So how do we get this money?" asked the leather-head again. "I heard he spent everything we had."

"We take out these new guys and put him back where he wants to be. He can still talk like hell, so he gets control of the crowds again and gets them back to work, then we take a ten percent cut of whatever the country earns."

"Ten percent? That's big cash Hennie!"

"And we only need to split it eight ways. We all end up loaded."

Uzi took a big slug of his beer. "But where do we spend the money? This place is screwed."

"We can head north, into Namibia or Tanzania, or even up to Europe. I heard the girls in Russia and the Ukraine look great and do anything for a few dollars."

They chinked bottles at that one, laughing heartily.

"So how do we take down the new guys?" This came from a small white guy called Ghys Van De Merwe. "I hear they're quite well organised."

"We have to be more organised. Remember, they won't be expecting us."

"And also remember that we don't actually have to run the place, just kill them. Then sonny boy here does the magic and we get out of the way!"

Van De Merwe walked across to the braai, to turn some sausages. The rest of the party relaxed in the sun, drinking their beer. After a few minutes, Hennie spoke. "Being serious for a minute, I think the easiest thing to do is take them out at one of their rallies. We've already seen that they like to get close to the people and that they have no real protection. We get in close and take them down, then bring in Justice as though he organised it all."

"We'd need to keep him off the drugs for a few days beforehand, especially if we want him to talk."

"We also need to decide on weapons, transport, who is doing what."

"Let's get in to some details tomorrow. Right now I need food."


Down in one of the giant marquees on the lawns, Cathy organized a group of young nurses to prepare an inoculation programme for the local children. Over three hundred in length, and none of them had taken any preventative medicine in the last two years. It had been decided to start with the common MMR vaccine, something that was carried out as a matter of course in Europe, almost totally eradicating diseases such as rubella amongst children. The vaccines had been funded by the World Health Organization and flown in to the country through the Lanseria corridor.

In the next marquee, Gladys was operating a simple clinic to try and re-establish the supply of ARVs to the local adults. AIDS had ravaged the population in the last two years since the drug supplies had dried up, and WHO also backed the program to try and get some control over the sickness again. It was all too common a sight to see groups of people in Sunday best burying another parent, grandparents called on to look after a family of homeless youngsters. Sometimes it was even worse, with a fourteen year old left to try and run a parentless family.

Now that people were again living in normal houses, the tented areas were also being used for administrative purposes: interviewing and recording people for the many job vacancies that needed filling.

One tent was a kitchen, preparing basic food for the poor. It always had a line of at least fifty waifs and strays.

Cathy was explaining to the ten young nurses that it wasn't just about giving the kids the injections, but also about trying to keep a record of who had been immunised. This meant they would know who was covered and who still needed a jab.

"But how will you know who is done?" one of the nurses, a skinny young girl with long braided hair, asked. "They do not carry ID. They do not even have birth certificates. Many don't have parents."

"I know it's not easy Precious, but we must try. Even a name and street ties them down a little," Cathy reasoned, knowing she was probably wasting her breath.

"We will try, but I am sure these kids have no clue about where they live. They probably lived in two or three places in the last couple of years."

"Do your best ladies, I know you will."

Gladys was having a similar, or possibly worse, problem with the ARVs. Everyone wanted them, believing the more they took, the better they would get, so going around and claiming twice was a simple cure.

"We only have ten thousand tablets right now," she told her team. "We need them to get to as many people as possible, not just a few who will take them all themselves or sell them on."

Cathy's girls were ready, each one seated on a chair with a supply of syringes and needles at hand. A smaller chair was next to theirs to allow the child to take a seat too.

"Are we ready?" she asked.

"As ready as we ever will be," Precious told her.

"Let's go!"

Across the lawn, Gladys was in the same position, watching horribly sick human beings limping in to receive the drugs that would hopefully give them a reasonable life for a few years longer.

At midday, both operations halted for lunch, and a sentry stood at each tent to ensure nothing was stolen.

The girls met at the kitchen tent, which also prepared food for the staff during the day.

"How's your MMR stuff going?" asked Gladys.

"We're giving the injections no problem," Cathy told her, "But we have really no good way to maintain a decent record of who we have put through. The kids have got no paperwork, often no parents, and live day-to-day."

"It's the same with the adults, except they don't want me to know who's who. A bit frustrating, to say the least."

"How's Jama?"

"He's very tied up with this new venture of Dumi's to get the Johannesburg airport up and running. Spent all day there yesterday."

"And that's just Johannesburg. One day we have to do the same with the rest of the country."

Gladys sat on the grass with a bowl of mealie and looked at the ground. Her hair was brushed back severely and fanned out stiffly behind her head. A couple of tears rolled from her left eye, then one dripped from her right.

"What's wrong?" asked Cathy, worried. "Are you and Jama OK?"

Gladys said nothing for a second, a quiet sob and sniffle the only sound. "I'm pregnant," she said. "I missed two periods now."

"But that's marvellous!" said Cathy, grabbing her friend around the shoulders and pulling her close. "What does Jama think? He must be thrilled!"

"He doesn't know," sobbed Gladys. "He doesn't need this pressure."

"Bollocks to that," Cathy exploded. "You need him and he's going to be over the moon, I can tell you. Come here!"

Gladys put her arms around Cathy and cried on her shoulder, her hormones everywhere. "Thank you," she whispered in to her ear.

"I think it's time you told Jama. We have another hour before the fun starts again, so let's have a walk up to the house. I think a certain President up there needs to know the new South Africa is having its first baby."


Up at the house Dumi, Jama and the four Team Leaders were having a brainstorming session with regards to 'Project Pegasus', the bringing on line of the O R Tambo Airport. Jama had just run through the summary of what they had found on the previous day's reconnaissance trip, and Dumi had already mentioned the 'hearts and minds' plan for winning over the locals in his introduction.

"So the runways are usable as they are?" asked Victor, a Xhosa from the Free State.

"A few holes filled and a bit of trimming back of the vegetation, and yes, we could land a modern jet there again," Jama answered.

"The terminals?" asked Klaas.

"Hell of a mess. Will take a lot of clean up, but structurally still sound. Can be used later."

"Did you experience any type of resistance? Were people hanging around the place?"

"Nothing, not a soul in sight. Looks like they stripped the place and got out of there."

Victor poured himself a coffee from a large flask on the table and offered the others a cup. Jama took one, but the rest were happy with water. The room had been partially refurbished, the woodwork re-varnished and the carpets cleaned. It wasn't perfect, but it looked a little more like the seat of government than it had when they arrived there.

"So how do we handle the local population?"

"That's the hearts and minds bit."

"Understood, but how? What do we have to offer?"

"Same as we did here, a mix of security and more comfortable living. We need to get another power station on line to give them electricity, then we try and get some work happening."

"What's the nearest power station?"

"That's where we are very lucky," said Dumi. "Kelvin Power Station is in Kempton Park, and at peak output can provide 600 MW. In its day it was churning out about twenty percent of all the power the city needed."

"And the other good news is it is coal powered," added Jama. "No special technologies needed to bring it on line."

"Can we get more coal from Botswana?"

"Now we have some mining people in from UK and the US, both countries are willing to advance more funds to get us up and running. Payback later."

There was a knock at the door. The butler popped his head in, looking to the President.

"Sorry Sir, I've a couple of the ladies insisting on coming in…"

Cathy came past him, followed by Gladys. The men looked at them, wondering what was going on. Cathy was red cheeked and Gladys was looking to her to take the lead.

"Sorry to burst in on you all like this gents, but I think Gladys and Jama need to have a chat."

Jama looked at Gladys, frowning as he tried to work out what was happening.

"Can I ask what is so important…" began Dumi, then shut up as Cathy gave him a withering look. "Let's pause the meeting for a second," he continued.

Gladys was close to tears again, and Jama moved forward. "What is it?"

"I'm pregnant Jama," she blurted out. "I'm so sorry."

Jama grabbed her, pulling her close and using the moment to get his bearings. "And I'm so proud," he said after a couple of seconds. A round of applause came from the assembled men.

"I guess this is time for a toast," said Dumi, nodding to the butler.

Two minutes later, things a little calmer, they all sipped a small cognac.

"To a brand new South African and hope for our future," Dumi saluted. They all raised their glasses and repeated the words. "For our future."

Gladys was smiling widely now.

"This will be my last drink for a while I suppose, so I better enjoy it."

"Meeting adjourned until the morning," Dumi decided. "Some people have more important things to talk about."

"I'll second that," Cathy added.


The morning meeting started swiftly as everyone had already had the chance to consider the options. They had commandeered another couple of open-topped Wrangler Jeeps from an abandoned showroom, so it was now possible to put out five small roving patrols. They opted for the same campaign as had worked so well in Pretoria – loudhailers on the patrols and putting together a low powered radio station to try and capture the wider audience. First sortie would go out the next morning, target areas Benoni, Germiston and Boksburg at the south of the airfield. Following day would concentrate on the industrial areas to the west and Kempton Park.

Running in parallel to this would be a clean-up campaign for part of the terminal. The main international arrivals area was a vast marble floored circular hall, able to house well in excess of a two thousand people. This was at a central point for the area. Here Dumi could address everyone once the word was out. It was planned the speech would take place in three days, and this would be the message from the patrols.

The only problem with the plan was raised by Jama: the terminal had multiple entrances and exits, so anyone wanting to cause trouble could do so easily. In the end they stuck with the plan as no-one knew a better location. At the end of the day, everywhere was at least a bit unsafe.

Jama planned to pay the terminal another visit with the clean-up crew to look at how to handle the security.

Power from the Kelvin Power Station would be the trade-off to win the people's support. Like in Pretoria, this would give them heat, light and night-time safety. For jobs they targeted the mining sector in the area, and also made a secondary plan to try and join up the two cities, Johannesburg and Pretoria. Between them was a lot of land, presently laid to waste, that could be used for agriculture. This represented more jobs for the lesser skilled locals. It would take time, but it would also result in a good food source.

With a clear direction in place, the men left the Union Buildings and went to their men to plan the necessary equipment needed to send out the patrols the following morning. Jama stayed with Dumi.

"Do you think we are biting off more than we can chew? Are we moving too fast?" he asked.

"Maybe," Dumi reflected. "But we need to move forward. While the people see improvement, they stay with us. If things stall, I think their support might do also."

"You could be right."

"We also need a good and safe South Africa for a certain baby that's on the way," Dumi smiled.

"That," said Jama, "I cannot argue with."

## TWENTY-NINE

Hennie was aware of the visit, to the airport, by the Liberation Army from sources in Boksburg who had premises overlooking the runway. It didn't take much imagination to work out that they intended switching their operation away from the Lanseria strip to the main O R Tambo airfield, and that this would mean an escalation in travel, in and out of the country. This was not a bad thing – he may also want to get out soon.

The group still had their MP5 machine pistols, but on top of this had an assortment of pistols and an AK47, none of which really suited the plan that Hennie had.

He had decided that he did not plan to take chances by going in close for the hit. Better to do something at a reasonably long range, giving him more chance to stay anonymous and escape. For this he needed a rifle, not necessarily a specialty snipers weapon, but at least something that had a good chance of a hit at around one to two hundred metres. In the chaos following a strike, this would give him enough time to disappear.

The location for the hit had been planned for Pretoria, but if operations were moving to his doorstep, then better to carry it out here. At present, he just wasn't sure exactly where.

Locating a rifle shouldn't prove too much of a problem. South African Defence Force armouries had all been raided in the aftermath of the take-over by Oliver Justice, so a good weapons black market was available.

With the step-up of activity now in his area, he decided that finding a decent weapon had to take a high priority. Things may move fast.


The mobile patrols, five in total, went out the following morning plus a bus-load of general workers to clean up the terminal. Making good time on the R21, two vehicles containing a total of twelve soldiers took the turn-off for Benoni, moving to the side of the town closest to the airport.

The other three cars and the bus continued on, passing the Kempton Park exit. The bus and one Jeep then peeled off for the terminal, the last two continuing on to Boksburg and Germinston. They again targeted the airfield side of the towns.

The Range Rover ignored the one-way systems and lead the bus to the international arrivals area, pulling up outside a burnt out Intercontinental Hotel. Here the five troops on the bus and the six in the Rover dismounted and started checking the area for problems. The forty-odd cleaners on the bus also climbed down and the smokers amongst them lit up.

Klaas was the cleaning party team leader, and took a couple of men into the terminal, sending two others up to the next level. Ten minutes later, all of them were back down at ground level, confirming no-one was around in the building. Klaas positioned his troops in positions where they could monitor possible approaches from others, checked they could all contact one another on the walkie-talkie sets they'd discovered in Pretoria, and went out to bring in the cleaning party.

"OK Ladies and Gents," he said. "We've got two days to clean-up this hall and the approaches up so the President can be proud to be back at O R Tambo. Let's do it!"


Hennie had just found himself a weapon he was happy with, an American Army 1967 Armalite M16 rifle. These weapons had seen service in Vietnam, Cambodia, the Gulf, Afghanistan and Korea, but by 2010 were being withdrawn for more modern alternatives. It was more than up to the job Hennie had planned for it.

He checked the action of the weapon and quickly stripped it down to its main components, checking the firing pin and the rifling of the barrel. All looked good, there were no signs of corrosion, but a good clean and oil would make it better.

Paying the dealer the going rate, Hennie placed the weapon back in its green canvas sack along with a hundred rounds of 5.56 mm ammo and headed for home.

He was getting closer to his fortune one step at a time.


The Boksburg mobile patrol was running along Slangkop Road, a residential street parallel to the eastern runway and about 300 metres from it. The low bungalow-style houses looked no different now than they had before the troubles began, but the cars on the drive hadn't moved in more than a year. A couple of people watched them pass.

They'd passed Emperors Palace on the way there, a large hotel and casino complex close to the airport that had always teemed with life, car-parks full. Now they only had the odd burnt-out wreck.

"We'll pull up along the road here before the open area and see if we can attract a few locals out with the loud-hailer," the Team Leader said. "It's pretty quiet."

They pulled over at the end of the road and dismounted the vehicles. The soldiers pulled out some cool-boxes and soon all had a sandwich and a bottle of water in hand. Weapons were slung across their backs or leant against the vehicles, but eyes remained alert and on the nearby houses. It was a pleasant twenty-five degrees but felt warmer now they'd lost the cooling effect of the vehicle speed.

Slowly, one at a time, then in small family groups, people emerged from the houses and moved nervously towards them. The soldiers stayed where they stood, but the Team Leader advanced a little way from the cars, towards the gathering crowd. He held a grey megaphone at the end of his arm, hanging it close to his thigh. He waited a moment more, then raised it to his lips.

"Hi folks," he started in a welcoming voice. "I guess you heard of us?"

"Maybe we have, but maybe you should tell us anyway," a shout from the crowd.

"OK. We are the Liberation Army, or that's what people are calling us. Basically we're a bunch of South Africans who ran off to UK when the trouble started, and now we've come back to try and make things right again."

The crowd was closer now, so he lowered the loudspeaker. The soldiers behind him still had an outward appearance of nonchalance, but inside they were judging distances to their weapons in case anything went awry here.

"You have President Dumi in your group?" one of the women called.

"Yes, we have the President. He wants the country to get back to normal. He wants you people to have work, food, electricity. I'm sure you want it too."

"And how's he hope to do all of that?" a white bearded black man asked, looking suspicious. "We got no electricity here, so how you gonna get some? And work? Well mister, that stopped a couple of years back."

"He did it in Pretoria, why do you think he cannot do it here?"

"Here's a bit far from Pretoria, but we heard he was making things normal there. He has an English general working with him, we heard. Sounds just like that bloody Oliver Justice again!"

"First thing I have to put right is we have no general. Our Jama Nomvula was a Captain in the English Army, but he's as South African as you and I."

Someone in the crowd started to say something, but it was not to the Team Leader but to one of the other onlookers. Whatever it was started a few of them arguing. Finally, a larger man amongst them stopped the chatter, taking control.

"You say that the President wants to give us work. Says we will get food. That he will give us back electricity. How can we believe that?"

"Come and hear it from the man himself," the Team Leader replied. "In two days he will make a presentation in the international arrivals area of the airport. He'll tell you in his own words what we will try and do for you. If you want to hear it, be there at twelve o'clock and bring others who are interested."

"We're interested, but we're also cynical. For the last years we've only been screwed around and cheated, so why would that all suddenly change?"

"It changed in Pretoria, why not here?"

Some crowd members looked at each other, doubt in their faces. You could sense they wanted to believe, but after so many let downs, it was hard.

"We might come along," said the big guy.

"You won't regret it."


The Benoni patrol was in a similar situation, parked up in a green grassland area of the Bonaero Park Estate, just off Carp Road. The low level housing around was typical of the area and obviously suitable for the airport – high-rise towers didn't help pilots.

They had attracted the attention of a sizeable gang of teenagers when they first arrived there, but the group had moved on when they realized that the soldiers had weapons. They estimated the size of the gang to be about forty strong. It gave them an indication of how things could probably get quite out of hand in the area at night. As in Pretoria, some street lights and a police or military presence would soon end that though.

A similar dialogue evolved between the patrol and a crowd of about fifty adults who were with them now. After getting the main message across, one of the soldiers asked the crowd about the gang of youths.

"They're a bunch of bastards," came the reply. "They roam around like a bunch of wild dogs and take what they can. If they get inside your place at night, God only help you. They are animals."

"They raped my sixteen year old daughter one night. She died the next day from the wounds she received."

The soldier was silent, half wishing he'd never asked. His Team Leader deflected the pressure from him.

"Come and see President Dumi," he told them. "Let him share your problems, then let him solve your problems. Between him and Jama, you will be safe."

"Who's this Jama?"

"He's the guy that will get you and all of us out of this mess. He's the future of South Africa."


It was four o'clock in the afternoon, and Klaas knew only about two hours of daylight were left in the sky. By six it would be dark.

"Let's call it a day," he told the workers. "Pack your things back on the bus and we head back to Pretoria."

The gang of tired workers trudged back towards the coach, the military pulling together in a protective ring to join them. Klaas looked around the terminal, content with the progress the workers had made. Smashed windows had been fully removed and the glass cleared up. Areas of wall had been repaired, painted and holes filled. Rubbish had been bagged and stored.

Another day and it would look fine. Just a shame they couldn't fit new windows, light them up and fill the shops with goods and people.

"You have to start somewhere," he reminded himself.

By the time he was outside the bus was full and the mobile team from Boksburg was waiting to escort them back to Pretoria.


Gladys and Jama finished early from their respective tasks and had a picnic tea in the gardens of the house. The plants were in flower all around them, with wonderful blues and purples and whites set off by the strong green of the lawns and trees. They sat on a blanket the butler had found for them and ate simple ham and mustard sandwiches, a little biltong and some fruit cake cooked that morning.

"Are you really OK with the baby?" Gladys asked for about the fifth time, though each time she phrased it differently.

Jama smiled at her. "Of course I'm OK. I'm having it with you, and you have changed my world. This is just going to change it a little more."

"I think a little might be understatement, Jama!"

"Don't panic Gladys. We can do it. We will do it. It will all be perfect."

"I wish I had your confidence. It's quite scary having a new life growing inside of you."

"You'll be a great mum. I've watched down in the clinics with the kids. They love you."

"And I love you Jama, so please take care."

"I'll be careful Gladys. I have two special people to come home to now." He kissed her on the top of her head. "And I love you too."


The next day the convoy left again from the Union Buildings at seven-thirty. It followed the usual route, one of the Jeeps sweeping about a mile ahead to ensure no surprises lay in store. By eight-thirty they were coming up to Kempton Park turning. The bus and soldiers with Klaas continued on to the airport buildings. The other four vehicles continued on, two going in to the airport side of Kempton, the other two going straight to the power station to give it a once over.

The two cars designated for the promotion of Dumi's talk the following day, headed along Pomona Road, then joined Pretoria Road through the residential area of Rhodesfield. Going along Gladiator Street, they then turned into York Street which ran parallel to the R21, with the airport spreading out on the other side of the motorway. Coming up to the Protea Hotel O R Tambo, they pulled into the car-park to have a look around.

Four troops climbed out of the Jeep and eight exited the Rover. Stretching after the hour-and-a-bit on the road, a few relieved themselves by the building. Others reached for water bottles.

"Before we start our job to spread the word, let's see if we can get on top of the hotel. Should give us a good view of the area. Might help."

The team leader took five men with him, leaving six with the transport.

The hotel had been trashed inside and with no electricity the lifts were out. The stairs were a long haul, but it would give them a great view of the airport and Kempton Park. At the top of the stairs the door was locked, but a couple of hefty boots later and they were on the roof. The team halved again, three to the airport side and three to have a look over the city.

The view all the way to Johannesburg was fair, but not great. Over Kempton business district it allowed them to see that people were about, but not in great numbers. It made them wonder if the sound of the cars was scaring people off the streets. With no other ambient noise, this was a possibility.

On the other side of the building, the runway could be seen behind other administrative buildings. Only the higher parts of the terminal were visible, the lower parts hidden by multi-level car-parks and the newish City Lodge.

They were about to turn and leave when one of the soldiers exclaimed, "Isn't that someone on top of the City Lodge?"

The Team Leader took out a pair of binoculars, and sure enough picked out a man on the far side of the hotel roof. He was unaware of the troops watching him and was totally absorbed in watching something below him through his own set of bins.

"Get on the radio to the Terminal Team! Let them know they are under observation. Probably nothing more than an inquisitive local, but better safe than sorry."

The radio man made the transmission. Even from the top of the Protea it was obvious that this caused a reaction on the ground, as the watcher suddenly stood and scanned around him. After a few seconds he saw the men on the roof of the hotel on the far side of the motorway. Giving them a cheeky wave, he headed for the roof exit and was gone.

"Bastard!" a soldier swore. "We'll get him next time."


Jama was with the group for the power station but was informed of the transmission.

"Looks like we are attracting a bit of attention," he said. "Tell Klaas to keep an eye out. Not everyone wants things to get back to normal."

They were at the gates of the power station and as usual they were locked. By now the drivers didn't need to be told what to do, and just yelled a warning to hang on as the Land-rover smashed through the barrier.

The party consisted of eleven soldiers and one engineer spread between the two vehicles. The Jeep headed directly towards the buildings with the engineer, while Jama and the team in the Land-rover, started a recce around the edge of the facility. The fence had been breached in a few places, but there was no signs of fresh activity or new foot marks. It was another one of those places where not too much could be sold other than coal, but even this wasn't the best for home fires. Power stations burn steam coal, otherwise known as thermal coal, and this is designed to burn hot and fast to superheat water to steam in order to drive the plants turbines.

Jama was also checking the areas beyond the plant, thinking of safe housing for the workers. Things he once never noticed were now a part of his everyday decision-making process.

He saw a small housing complex just beyond the wire. It had only one road in, so it would be fairly easy to limit access. Better, as it backed on to the plant, he could extend the fence-line around it and make all traffic pass through the plant.

Completing the outer circuit, they headed over to have a look at the coal reserve stockpiles. Based on what he'd learned from the Pretoria plant, he thought this also looked to be okay, so it was time to join the experts.

Parking next to the Jeep, Jama went straight in to the plant and headed towards the voices. The technical man was inspecting the turbines, using his knowledge to assess their serviceability as best he could.

"Doesn't look too bad," he told the assembled troops. "Will take a couple of weeks to run things up and test them, and then we see how the wiring is."

"Good news. I think we should all head for the airport now and see how the terminal's coming on for tomorrow's speech," Jama told them. "Not much more we can do here for now."

They climbed on board their vehicles and headed over towards the airport, pausing at the gate to secure it with a new chain and padlock.

They arrived shortly after the team from Kempton Park, and Jama took a quick report from the Team Leader, mainly asking about the man they had spotted on top of the City Lodge. With the distance between them, there wasn't too much to say, other than he had been spying on the terminal using field glasses and had taken off when spotted.

"Probably nothing," the soldier summarised.

They strolled into the terminal and Jama was impressed by the work that had been completed. The marble floors shone, and the walls were clean and windows boarded up. A slightly raised dais was on the far side of the hall, just about where the international passengers would have first entered the country. Dumi would look good up there.

"We'll leave a small team of men here overnight to ensure no-one undoes all of the good work," said Jama. I want eight to stay but ask for volunteers please."

The manual labourers were quietly getting back onto the bus, ready for the trip home. Jama climbed the steps after them and stood up on the driver's seat. "You should all be proud of yourselves," he told them. "One day the whole country will look that good again, and it'll all be down to the likes of you and your families. Well done!"

As he climbed down, a cheer went up for him. "Three cheers to Jama. Hip hip hooray, hip hip..." He climbed out of the bus, slightly embarrassed. Someone had their mouth to the long, narrow window below the bus roof.

"You've made us proud to be Africans again Jama."

Jama turned, smiling politely at the man and waving a hand. He returned to his men.

"Did we get eight OK?" he asked.

"More than eight offered, and I'll stay with them," said Klaas. "We'll rig up a radio on the roof, so if we have problems, we get you."

"Perfect Klaas. Take care. I'll be here around eight tomorrow, and Dumi and the rest can follow later in the morning. See you then."

"Safe trip Jama."


It hadn't been hard for Hennie to learn about the President's planned visit to the airport the following morning. His own people had telegraphed it with their frequent visits to the area, then with the clean-up crews at the terminal, and finally by telling local people about it in all the surrounding towns.

For Hennie it sounded like a gift from God, but he had to prepare his people quickly.

The hardest part was to get Oliver Justice into a state where he could address the crowd once President Dumi was out of the way. They had changed his drugs to keep him high but coherent, but it was going to be a test as to whether he could still hold the attention of a crowd.

Tomorrow they would find out.

## THIRTY

The sun came up at around four thirty that morning, a beautiful big burning orb rising through a pale blue cloudless sky, the sort you never see in Europe. Jama was already awake and full of nervous energy, standing at the window and watching the sunrise. Gladys was still fast asleep in the bed. Since her pregnancy was announced, Dumi had insisted that they both stay in the main buildings of the house.

His mind was buzzing – he was still in shock that he was a father, but he tried to put that far from the front of his mind right now, trying to focus on the events planned for today. If this worked, then they had really taken the next step, and the rest of South Africa would hear about it. Hopefully, they would all want to follow. First Pretoria, then Johannesburg. It could be the catalyst needed to lift the nation.

Part of his brain also worried a little about the man who had watched the preparations at the terminal. Could be anyone, but why the overconfident wave at his exit?

He had decided to bring both buses today, trying to put at least a hundred soldiers on the ground. He had heard nothing from Klaas and his men overnight but couldn't wait to speak to them on the radio to confirm everything was well.

He picked up a bottle of water from the window ledge and took a swig, holding the fluid in his mouth and contemplating the day.


Hennie was also watching the same sunrise from his porch at the ex-guesthouse in Kempton Park. Like Jama, he also contemplated the day ahead. Unlike Jama, he was having his doubts about the plans he had in mind.

He had grown to hate Oliver Justice. Back in Pretoria he had served him as he was the Head of State, or as near as they had to one since Dumi fled their country. He hadn't liked him even then, with his wild parties and lack of discipline, and the way he had allowed the whole country to descend into a lawless wasteland. But by then, he had nowhere to go, so he stuck with it.

On the night that Jama and his boys had raided the Union Buildings, Hennie had considered handing Justice over and joining the new guard. Greed had stopped him as much as loyalty. He had seen a chance to get rich on the back of Oliver Justice, so he had made his choice.

Living with the man for the last weeks had made him detest him even more though. Justice was weak. He was arrogant. He was a lazy pig. And his indiscipline was unforgiveable: drugs and booze and women were all that his world was about. Africa was just a place where he lived.

He ran his fingers through his thinning hair, wondering if it was too late to swap sides.

Just then Uzi walked out, the big black man wrapped only in a towel. "Morning Hennie. Howzit going?"

"Good big man. You?"

"Ready to make my fortune."

You make your bed, then you have to lay in it, thought Hennie. Oh well.


Klaas was at the radio operator's side when Jama called, so he took the mike.

"Morning Jama. You're up early? Hope you weren't too worried about us. We had a ball."

"So all's well? No surprise visitors in the middle of the night?"

"Everything's fine." Klaas replied.

"See you in an hour or so."

Jama signed off.


Oliver Justice was rudely awakened from his alcoholic slumber by Uzi, trying to roll away from the man and attempting to push away his hands. He protested lamely. "Gerroff, tired… stop…."

Uzi didn't stop though and poured a glass of cold water on to the man's head.

"Shit man!" Oliver stormed. "Wha' you doin'? Fuck!"

"Get up you piece of shit!" Uzi ordered. "It's your big day. You gonna be the big man again."

He turned and left the room, leaving the ex-ANC Youth Leader to pull himself together. Somewhere in his drug-mushed mind he remembered the white man Hennie explaining to him that they were getting rid of Dumi today, and then that he would talk again to the masses. It was his chance to be someone again.

He rolled to his left and plonked his feet on the tiled floor. His head throbbed, but the thought that this was his day to return motivated his already massive ego.

Walking unsteadily towards the bathroom, he remembered his nights of pleasure in the Union Buildings. If that was coming back his way, it was worth all the pain right now.

He stood under the shower head and turned on the cold tap.

Jama arrived at the terminal in the convoy with the first busload of troops just after eight o'clock. The second coach load would arrive with Dumi nearer to lunchtime. Hopefully the crowd of locals would also be there by then, otherwise this whole thing would be a bit of a flop.

Klaas met him as he came in to the Arrivals area and gave him a quick report on the situation.

Looking around, Jama decided on the safest way to control the crowd. First off, he needed to offer them only a single point of entry, and this would be from the main doors on the roadway opposite the old hotel. This meant closing down the upper levels of the terminal, and also the passage connecting the arrivals meeting point from the domestic arrivals and also the link towards the Gautrain. With a hundred men in the place, this should be doable, but he had also brought a good supply of chains and padlocks to secure doors as needed.

He called a meeting of the team leaders and let them know his plan. They then were all allocated parts to execute and went off to organise their people.

By nine-thirty, the terminal was locked up and under control.


Hennie was hit by his first problem of the day about the same time, but it wasn't a major headache. One of his men had been injured the night before in a brawl, but with his latest plan he could easily live with this.

The rest were assembled at the house, Justice in the garden with a large bottle of water, thinking through his speech.

"So," said Hennie. "The operation is basically in three parts, so I'll cover each in turn. One is the hit on Dumi, the second is the introduction of Justice to the crowd post-hit, and the third is a diversionary action. So we will be splitting into three groups."

"How does Max being missing affect things?" asked Uzi.

"He was on the hit with me, but I will now operate alone. No problem, and maybe it makes it easier to get in and out unnoticed."

"OK."

"The other six of you will spilt in to two groups. One gets Justice close to the edge of the crowd ready for Dumi going down, the other three of you will be organising distractions for the soldiers out there."

He spent the next thirty minutes going through the details. The men knew most of it already as they had discussed options over the last weeks, but now everyone knew their roles.

It was time to join everyone on the exodus to O R Tambo.


Ten-twenty-five, and Jama was surprised to see that already about a hundred people were standing or sitting around in the terminal. It looked like some sort of social occasion and there was a bit of a carnival atmosphere about the place. People who hadn't seen one another for possibly two years were chatting and slapping backs. Hugs and handshakes everywhere. Dumi would love it.

They looked poor, but they didn't seem to mind this. They were just happy to be together again.

Troops were out on the roads approaching the buildings, steering the people towards the controlled entry point. The people were compliant, not arguing with the authority the troops were asserting, actually welcoming the re-introduction of law and order.

By eleven o'clock, the hall had around five hundred black, white and coloured South Africans chatting together. The security provided by the troops seemed to loosen tongues, and the party atmosphere intensified as the crowd grew.

Jama had worried about confrontations between the different groups, but to this point there was no evidence of it. He prayed silently that it would remain that way.

At eleven-thirty, the arrivals area was almost full and people were still coming.

Jama called the second bus convoy on the radio, learning that they were about twenty minutes out. Things were going to time.


The three men with Oliver Justice – led by Uzi – were almost at the terminal. They had made it past the soldiers positioned on the approach roads with no questions asked. The three only carried pistols, but even this had been a risk as they didn't know that security would be so lax. With no screening equipment, organising searches of over a thousand people was always going to be impossible.

Justice had a woolly hat pulled down over his ears, a fleece jacket masking his shape. Dark glasses added to his anonymity. They did want him to be recognised until the right moment, and then he should take to the stage, minus his disguise.

As they entered the doorway of the Arrivals, Uzi was shocked to see so many of his countrymen in one place. Gatherings like this hadn't happened for years.

The three men tasked with causing the distractions, when called for by Hennie, avoided the busy international end of the airport and instead made their way through the endless multistorey parking garages to the domestic side. Here they found the main entry doors chained up, stopping all access. They informed Hennie of this by walkie-talkie.

"Make your way quickly around to the airside of the building. You'll probably need to climb a fence or two, but they won't expect people entering from here. I'll do the same."

They went past the domestic entranceways and came to some buildings that once served the customs and police. Several windows were smashed, so they climbed through. They were more than a kilometre from the international side now, so no soldiers were here to challenge them.

Once in the offices, it was quite easy to work their way back to the domestic arrivals, where they planned to set-up their side shows.


Hennie had been through Jo'burg many times over the years on military business, so he had a good idea of the layout of the place. A lot of it was relatively new from the 2010 World Cup preparations, but once you'd been through a couple of times it was fairly easy to navigate.

He knew that the main road side would likely be better patrolled than the aircraft side, so he broke in there by the old DHL offices on Voortrekker Road. Despite expecting to meet no opposition on this side, he still moved forward warily, moving cover to cover. Carrying a metre long green canvas sack would certainly draw a little attention.

When he reached the first aircraft parking bay, he used the same air-bridge style entry as Jama and his troops had, but on entering the terminal, found a route up from the arrivals level to the higher levels. He guessed the address would be given on the ground floor, so this was an area to be avoided.

He was in the departures business lounges now, and two levels above the arrivals zone. To get to the entrance he had overlooked from the City Lodge roof, he needed to come down one level and go through the Immigration and Customs stands for what would normally be passengers exiting South Africa. He didn't expect anyone to be there to explain to him that he was going the wrong way.

When he reached the X-ray machines, he guessed he would be visible to anyone on the departure level, so he approached them carefully, using the machines and their conveyors as cover. Crouching behind his last line of cover, he peeked up ahead. It was just as well he did. Three soldiers were just outside of the glass outer boundary of the search area, but luckily all were looking over the balcony at the crowd below in the arrivals area.

He looked for a way past them. It was a little too early to use his team to cause a commotion. He needed this later to get out.

Looking around, he saw a door marked 'Staff Only' leading into an office suite. Once it would have been busy with uniformed officers, but now it was just a ransacked space. On the far wall he saw a green and white sign. 'Emergency Exit.' He smiled and made his way in this direction. Pushing a quick release handle on the door there, he opened it silently. Spiral stairs ran downwards.

And upwards. He took the latter.


The second bus and its convoy of lighter vehicles arrived. Dumi got out of the Range Rover and was met by Jama at his door.

"Hi Mister President. It's going to be a job getting you across the room to the dais."

"What have you done boy? There must be thousands here! I might get stage fright."

"No fear of that from a politician," Jama jibed.

"You're probably right."

"I'd prefer it if the crowd don't see you Dumi. It might start a riot." Jama looked around him, also not expecting the numbers he was witnessing. "I'm going to make a tunnel of troops to the stand. Please wait in the car and keep a low profile."

Crossing to the bus with the new group of soldiers, Jama grabbed the only team leader he could see.

"Temba, grab those men from the bus and form a double line through the centre of the crowd to the dais. We need to get the President there."

"Roger that Jama."


Hennie carefully opened the door at the top of the stairs and looked out. No-one there and just another office suite. He crossed the room and peered around the door in to a hallway. Clear. He moved in a direction of the gathering – he knew the direction was right because of the rumble of voices coming from there.

At the end of the hallway he found himself beside three doors. Opening the one ahead of him, he discovered a galvanized stairway leading down to more or less where he had seen the three soldiers earlier. The noise from below was even louder now, and from here he could see the platform that he assumed would be used by the President. Perfect position, only a little too exposed.

Quietly closing the door again, he tried the door on the right. Another office, but no view and nothing of any use to him. Crossing to the final door, he stepped into an office. But not just any office. It had a wall-long window starting at waist height, with reflective tape on the outside of it. He could see out, but no-one could see in. Even better as he could still see the platform below.

Now he just had to wait.


Temba led two files of men in the central doors of the arrivals and towards the crowd.

"Excuse me gents," he called through a loud-hailer that had been left in the Rovers since the town visits. "Give my men a bit of room please!"

The crowd backed away without protest, guessing the meaning of this disturbance to their get-together. The place went quiet for a few seconds, then the volume increased again as people started telling each other that things were about to happen. That 'he' was coming.

The soldiers filed through the gap in an endless double line. When they reached the dais, they turned towards one another and linked arms. Now there was a solid wall of troops from the entry doors to the dais. Between the troops was a gap of roughly two metres.

The noise from the crowd was rising in expectation.

"DUMI! DUMI! DUMI!"


"Sounds like it's almost time," Jama told Dumi. He looked towards the door and saw Temba returning with four soldiers.

"Look Jama, I'm shaking."

Jama looked at the President, surprised he still had any nerves after all the years of public gatherings he'd hosted. "You'll be fine," he told him.

Temba was at the car now.

"We go through the tunnel Sir, me at the front and you in the middle of my four lads. They'll stay at the base of the dais steps to stop anyone getting ideas about coming up to see you."

"Well done soldier." He saluted Temba, who smiled from ear-to-ear. "Let's get this show on the road."

"I'll take the rear," said Jama, following.

The crowd roared at the sight of the soldiers and Dumi coming their way. Hennie knew it was time, and again felt a twinge of guilt. These people were trying to rebuild a country destroyed by the coward he was assisting. He thought he should maybe just walk away from this, to leave them all.

The greed kicked in again.

He hurriedly unstrapped the canvas bag and removed the Armalite. It had been cleaned and oiled again that morning and was in tremendous condition. He had a two twenty round magazines and pushed one on to the rifle, slapping its base to make sure it was fully engaged. He pulled out the cocking handle and pulled it back, chambering a round. The range to the dais was about fifty metres, so this was not even target practice. This was a cinch.

Dumi couldn't believe his ears. Support hadn't been as good as this when he was elected. Maybe it was the acoustics of the terminal, but the noise was unbelievable. People were trying to touch him, and he could see the soldiers struggling to hold their human wall in place.

Jama's eyes were everywhere on the crowd, looking for any sort of threat. He didn't see any though, only a crowd of ecstatic people.

They reached the dais and moved Dumi to the three stairs up to his notes and the microphone. The roaring continued as he adjusted his papers. He tapped the mike. Smiled at the people. Tapped again. Slowly the noise reduced.

Jama smiled.

Hennie found that the window was formed in two halves and could be slid sideways to allow air to enter the office. He moved the right hand pane about an inch and a half to the left, giving him a clear view down on the hall through the gap.

Dumi was moving over the hall below him, but with so many people around him, he may hit the wrong person and then they would go to the ground, forming a human shield around the man who was so obviously still a hero with South Africans. He had to wait and be patient, but time was on his side, and once on the platform, his target would likely be alone. Then he could take the shot.

He looked along the rifles sights, getting comfortable.

It was almost time.

Dumi tapped the mike again. The noise was a murmur compared to thirty seconds before.

"So you haven't forgotten me?" he asked, a smile as wide as his face. The crowd laughed, then cheered.

"I haven't forgotten you either," Dumi said. "But I have missed you. For two long years."

The crowd's noise rose in agreement. They had missed him too.

"Well I'm back, and I want South Africa back. Not back for me. No. Back to the way it was, except better." He looked down on them, serious now. "I let you all down. I missed the pain that you were going through, because I was too caught up in political decisions, too busy entertaining people from far off countries. I missed what was happening with my own people. I have to hope you can forgive me for this."

Everyone was shouting at once, so none of it really made any sense. Occasionally Jama picked out the odd phrase, but the basic message seemed to be that nothing mattered, only that the President was home.

And then a sharp crack swallowed the crowd noise.


Hennie knew it was time. The speech didn't even enter his ears, his whole focus was on his breathing, the line of the weapon on the target, the gentle squeeze of the trigger, not pulling the shot…


Dumi was smashed off his feet, falling where he stood, becoming a crumpled and folded body. Blood poured from a wound in his back, coming out in unsustainable quantities. So swift. He didn't even scream out.

The crowd was still loud, but now it was sounds of panic. Somewhere on the far side of the hall someone was shouting.

Jama ran towards Dumi, shouting for help. He got there and Dumi saw him, but blood was escaping his lips and he was having difficulty getting air. He lay on his side and Jama saw a small blood stain high on the right side of his chest, but worse he could see blood puddles behind his back.

"Get me a medic!" he yelled.

A soldier was next to him with a field first-aid kit. Between them they tried to plug the hole in Dumi's back, to block the small wound in his chest.

"He needs fluids. Get a drip on him!"

A saline solution was attached to the microphone stand and an intravenous drip set on his forearm. He'd lost consciousness.

Another medic had arrived with an oxygen bottle and they strapped a mask on the President.

At the back of the hall, Uzi had released Justice to the crowd. "Do your stuff," he told him, shoving him forward.

Oliver Justice had never been lost for words in his life, but for a few moments he had no idea what to say. He looked at the crowd, some frozen to where they stood, some trying to get out and others trying to get to the aid of their President.

"Do it!" Uzi hollered in his ear and passing him a megaphone.

Justice raised it to his lips, licking them to try and get some moisture to talk. "Brothers," he began. "Stay calm! Relax! We have to stay calm."

"Who the fuck are you?" yelled a man close by. "They just shot the fucking President."

Oliver realized that he was still covered up. No-one knew who he was. He pulled of the hat, threw the glasses to one side and unzipped the fleece.

"I'm Oliver Justice, your true friend and President. I stayed while he ran. I was here all the time."

The crowd had gone silent, watching and listening. Uzi suddenly thought this was not going as expected. He looked at the other two mercenaries and they backed away, blending in to the crowd.

"Let's make the country great again," Oliver continued.

The crowd weren't cheering though, and he couldn't think why not. They seemed to be glaring at him.

"Come on people, we don't need foreign investors, we don't need jobs for whites, we need each other."

The crowd suddenly came out of their trance. As a single unit they charged him, knocking him to the floor. He was punched, kicked, trampled, crushed. Within thirty-five seconds he was dead.

That was African justice. Justice for Justice, as the papers would report.

From above, Hennie could also see things were not going to plan. It was time to get out.

"Set alight to the domestic end," he called to the other group. "Then get the hell out of here. If this bunch get you, you're dead."

He made his way through the offices and back towards the aircraft dispersal, hoping it was still a safe way out of the terminal.

He was wishing he'd followed his instincts that morning and changed sides. It had been a good time to quit.

Too late now, he turned to his survival instincts and headed for Kempton Park.

He needed somewhere to lay low for a while. A good while.


Jama got Dumi in to the back of a Land-rover that had been turned in to a bed. Oxygen and drips were rigged and the two medics stayed with him.

"Get him to Pretoria as quickly as you can. I'll call ahead and our doctors will be waiting. It has to be quick. He has to survive."

The vehicle was off, an escort car running with it.

Jama looked at the men around him, all looking expectantly to him for direction.

"Get your men together and secure the area. Take patrols through the terminal. If anyone looks threatening, shoot them. They will not think twice about shooting you."

He stopped, thinking a little more clearly now. "Sorry. There will be confused people out there. They shouldn't die. But if you are threatened, use all the force you need to." He pulled in a big lungful of air, then slowly let it out. "I need to calm the crowd."

As his men set about their tasks, Jama pushed through the crowd, stepping over the pulverized body of Oliver Justice. He glanced at it for a moment, sickened. He reached the platform, and like a robot, climbed up to the mike.

"Ladies. Gentlemen. South Africans." The last address caught their attention.

"What we witnessed here today was sick. Shocking. A man who loved this country more than any other person here today was gunned down for trying to put it right again. We cannot let this go on." He stopped, noticing that the whole crowd had turned their eyes on him, listening. "President Dumi Silongo is a good man, and if he dies I will hunt down his killer and do the same to him as he did to my friend."

The silence was intense. Not a sound from anyone.

A quiet woman's voice from the front of the crowd spoke. "Who are you?" she asked, not in a rude way, just inquisitive. "I don't think we know you."

"I am Jama Nomvula, a Zulu boy who is lucky enough to be considered a friend of Dumisani Silongo. And that's a privilege I don't want to lose. Ever."

"What do we do now?" asked the woman.

Jama thought for a full minute. No-one spoke. No-one left the hall. Everyone was waiting for the answer of Jama Nomvula.

"We continue with his work young lady," said Jama. "It's what he would want, and if God wills, it is what will keep him alive for us."


Jama realized that the fires in the domestic terminal were only a diversionary tactic and swiftly had them extinguished. He had the information from Pretoria that Dumi had arrived there and that the round had passed straight through him, leaving massive damage to his right lung and upper stomach. It was still very much touch and go.

His men were preparing to leave, but the crowd still hung around. It was early afternoon, and he felt he still had a duty to them. He went back to the fateful arrivals area and fired up the PA system.

"People," he said. "You must go home today, but first I must let you know that your President is still alive." A cheer went up at this. "He is not well, and it will take some days to see if he will make it, so please pray for him this night."

"Let's pray together for him now."

Jama hadn't expected this, and was not really a religious man, but he led the congregated people in the Lord's Prayer.

"Amen," they all finished.

After a respectful silence, Jama spoke into the microphone again.

"I'd like you all to come back tomorrow, not to hear speeches though. We need workers. We want to open the Kelvin Power Station to give you all electricity again, but we need people who can help us, ex-workers. Can you assist us?"

He glanced around the room, noticing the odd hand in the air. Good.

"We also need miners. We need our country to produce minerals. We need teachers, nurses, doctors, engineers. We found them in Pretoria, and I'm sure we can find them here. Will you all be here tomorrow? Will you all enrol in to a better Africa?"

A silence at first, then a murmur of voices as they realized he had finished. It grew louder, then an old man stepped forward.

"I speak on the behalf of my people from Kempton. We will be here."

"And I will speak for Benoni. We will spread the word, and we will be here."

"Boksburg will not let you down," said an Afrikaner. "We will be there for the mining."

"Thank you, all South Africans," Jama said. "Your spirit will keep Dumi with us to see his dream."

## EPILOGUE – EVER ONWARDS – 2 months later
## THIRTY-ONE

The sun came up like normal over Gauteng, bathing the province in a soft yellow light. The jacaranda trees hung with beautiful purple flowers, ivy climbed the walls of the Union Building gardens, a gecko sunned itself on the sundial.

Jama rolled silently out of bed, carefully placing the sheet over Gladys. There was no need for quilts now the temperatures were up, and even through the linen he could see the beginnings of a swollen belly. The doctors said she was almost twenty-two weeks pregnant now, so more than half way there. She had insisted on not being told whether it was a boy or a girl, and really Jama didn't care. It was theirs.

Pulling on a pair of cargo shorts, he let himself quietly out of the bedroom and in to the garden. It was slightly chilly, and he half wished he'd put on a shirt, but another part of him wanted to savour the African sun.

Moving to the front of the house he marvelled again at the view over Pretoria, or Tshwane as it was more commonly called by the natives. The park just fell away in front of him, and at this time of year every colour of flower lit the place up.

He heard a sound behind him, and turned to find Dumi sitting in his wheelchair, a tartan blanket wrapped around his shoulders, looking at the same view.

"It's great to be back," Dumi said, not adjusting his view, just knowing it was Jama there.

"How did we ever survive in the UK? All that cold and rain."

They stood in a companionable silence for a while, loving the scenery before them.

"What do you have planned for today?" asked Dumi. Though he took little part in activities since the shooting, his interest in developments never dulled.

"We should switch on the Kelvin Power Station this morning. Supply half of Johannesburg with electricity."

"Who's pulling the switch? It should be a big affair?"

"You, Dumi."

Now Dumi looked at him, a tear in his old eyes.

"And you're making a speech."

"Are you trying to kill me young man?"

"I leave that to other people," Jama joked. "Do you want to do it?"

"Try and stop me."

"Be ready at ten. You're travelling with Gladys and me."

At eight o'clock Jama and his Team Leaders gathered for the morning planning meeting. They had the get together every day except Sunday and ran through the day's events and progress on longer term projects.

"Did Dumi accept the challenge today?" asked Klaas.

"Is he healthy enough to do it?" Temba enquired.

"Try and stop him," Jama told them. "But we need to take special care of him. He's still a little fragile. Taking away his right lung was a massive trauma for him, but he will survive and he will get better than he is."

"I had a security team take the plant to pieces last night," Klaas told them. "Nothing found, but today we have to be on our toes."

"I don't envisage any problems," Jama said. "You saw what happened to Oliver Justice. The people are in no mood for anyone who tries to prevent our country moving forward."

"We will also put a screen of soldiers closer to him this time," Temba said. "Klaas has selected his best people for the job."

"They all think they're in the American Secret Service now as well."

After a run through other business, the meeting broke up.

"At the wagons for nine-forty-five," said Jama as they went their ways. "Dumi will be with Gladys, Cathy and me in the Range Rover."

Twelve o'clock at the power station. In the two months since the shooting, the engineers and former workers at the plant had given it a complete clean-up and service, and trial runs on the steam turbines had gone well. Today was more or less a formality. A PR exercise, but it meant more to the local community than all of the backstage work that had been running during the last weeks.

As envisaged by Jama, the fence line had been extended and a small group of workers' houses now formed a part of the grounds. Security was maintained mainly be local labour under the command of people who had been with the Liberation Army from the beginning.

Jama was considering dropping the title of 'Liberation Army' and going back to the old South African Defence Force. Though it had some bad memories attached to it, it also demonstrated that the country was returning to days more normal.

Once there they debussed out of sight of the main entrance. Dumi was loaded in to his wheelchair wearing a dark blue suit, white shirt and red tie. He looked proud as punch. Jama was similarly dressed, while Gladys wore a shiny red dress that highlighted her bump. Cathy wore a white dress, and Jama noticed she was developing a suntan, something a little unusual on a girl from Ireland. South Africa seemed to like her.

On the far side of the office block, they could hear the crowd. Klaas estimated that five thousand people were out there, waiting for the electricity to be turned on.

"How do you feel Dumi?" he asked.

"Electric Klaas, electric," he joked. They all laughed and went inside for a coffee.


At twelve-fifteen they left their coffees and waters and went out to a raised platform in front of the reception building. Local community leaders were already sitting on the stand in plastic chairs. They had all agreed to wear African dress, as had their wives, so the whole area was awash with bright colours and big hats.

Jama pushed Dumi up a ramp and along the front row of dignitaries, letting him pause to shake hands and exchange a few words.

He turned and allowed himself his first look at the crowd. All the way to the gates of the plant and in each direction to the fence line were faces looking his way. A shiver went through him. He felt sorry for Dumi, who had avoided looking out there at all. He must have known how it was though, because the noise volume was intense, even with the open sky above them. Five thousand happy people.

It was time. They had waited long enough. Jama nodded to Dumi and they moved the last steps to the microphone stand.

Jama bent down to the sponge ball on the end of the device. "Ladies and Gentlemen, The President of South Africa, Dumisani Silongo."

The cheer almost raised the height of the sky, it was so loud. They could all feel the sound pressure on the podium. Never had any of them – including Dumi – ever felt anything so strong. It was the power of a people that were truly happy for the first time in many years. A people who knew they had a future.

Dumi looked at Jama, his eyes wide. Jama nodded. He turned his gaze back to the crowd, sucking in their energy, waiting for them to fade. He had to wait a full three minutes, then at last the noise levels dropped.

"Brothers and Sisters," he began. "You can see that reports of my injuries have been exaggerated. I am not quite dead yet."

Laughter broke out. Loud and happy laughter.

Dumi thought a few seconds. "I only learned of this engagement this morning, so I am more shocked than you to be here." A few titters. "Because of this, I have not prepared any kind of speech for you. But I can tell you, I have two bits of good news, and only one piece of bad news."

The crowd quieted again.

"I'll start with a piece of good news. From tonight you will all be able to go home and turn on a light in your homes. You will be able to boil a kettle and cook a meal for your family without a fire. You will have light and security."

The crowd roared in to life again, cheering and clapping.

"But don't thank me for this. I've been on my sick bed for the last months. I did not change one thing here." He looked to Jama. "For this you must thank this young man and his great team."

A chant of Jama, Jama. went up, but Dumi stopped it after about twenty seconds.

"So the first good news was good. I believe the second good news is better."

He let them hang, still a great performer.

"But first the bad news."

Total silence. You could have heard a pin drop. It was almost impossible to believe a group so large could be so quiet.

"From today my friends, I am standing down as President of South Africa." An audible gasp came from the crowd. The people on the podium looked at Dumi, then at Jama, but the look on Jama's face said he had known as much about the announcement as the rest of them.

"I am now an old man," Dumi continued. "The shooting has made me older. I cannot travel well, and a President who cannot travel is not much use when his country needs support from a world still eyeing us nervously. You need new energy, but whoever brings this, I will still be around to support them with my experience. Please accept my apologies, but I would be irresponsible to try and do anything else."

The crowd remained silent, trying to come to terms with getting Dumi back and then losing him again in such a short space of time. Dumi knew what they were thinking.

"I've already said it, but I will repeat myself. I will be going nowhere. I am here for South Africa, I am here for you. I will never be Nelson Mandela, but I can try and copy his lessons. He also stepped down when he felt it was right, but he never left the people. I am here until I die, I promise you all that."

He looked at a quiet crowd, feeling their uncertainty about the future. They had grown hopes and dreams due to his return, and now they felt let down.

One of the local leaders voiced the thoughts of the thousands of people there.

"And what is the other good news Dumi?"

Dumi tried to think if the right words, but he was unprepared for this. He knew it was time to stand down and had often thought about how to do it in the middle of the night. Actually doing it was another story.

"The other good news is that life goes on. I stand down, someone will stand-up. You will all elect someone. South Africa will have a democracy again. You will choose the new leader of our country."

The same voice came from the dignitaries. "Who would you choose Dumi?"

Dumi looked at the man, then back at the crowd. "That's the easiest question I have been asked all day." He smiled. "My vote goes to Jama Nomvula."

Once again, the crowd went wild.

## THIRTY-TWO

Five months later and Jama was again standing on the lawn of the Union Buildings. A major difference now was he had a one month old baby in his arms, his son, Freedom Dumi Nomvula, coming in to the world at a healthy eight pounds. Sitting on sun-chairs were his wife Gladys and her best friend, Cathy. Both had their skirts rolled up as high as was decent, enjoying the sunshine.

Leaning on the low wall at the top of the stairs from Fairview was the former President of South Africa, Dumi, the source of the child's middle name. He was a very proud Godfather.

"The place has come a long way Jama," he said, turning, with the help of a crutch, to face the other three people. "Basically the whole of Gauteng is powered up and living normally, plus this side of North West Province, a little of Limpopo and the top end of the Free State. You just have to push a bit harder down towards Durban and then I can go home."

"You can go home when you want now Dumi, and you know it. Problem is you're too comfortable here now."

"You're right. The alliances we formed with the Zulu power-brokers mean movement down there is pretty simple. And it works for them too. We have most of the jobs up here, so we can offer them some employment."

"And you being a local hero here means you actually don't want to go home."

"He doesn't want to go home because of his Godson!" Gladys added.

"There's that too…" Dumi conceded.

They all laughed. Klaas walked in to the garden from the house.

"We just completed the opening of the old Eland Platinum Mine out by Brits in North West. Will be producing platinum metals by the end of the month. Another income stream for South Africa."

"That's great news Klaas. Another one on line."

Cathy jumped out of her chair and went to him, treating him to a kiss and a hug. "Well done."

Gladys smiled. They'd been seeing one another for about four months now, and she couldn't remember Cathy ever spending that long with anyone. Maybe it was the 'Freedom effect.'

"Where's the next target?" Dumi asked.

"Temba is working on a power station in the Free State right now, but I think the next one up might be the coal mining complex at Waterberg, Limpopo. That's a major project, because then we can reduce our dependence on the Botswana supply." Klaas beamed at Cathy, giving her a private little squeeze.

The butler came out on to the grass, looking at Klaas. "Can I get you a drink Sir?" he asked.

"A large coke would be great."

"Does anyone else need something?"

Teas and coffees were ordered.

The butler looked at Jama.

"And for you Mister President?"

**Please leave a review!**
I love the feeling of finishing a book, completing a tale. For me it gives both negative and positive emotions: on the one hand, I can look forward to starting the next story, to dreaming up a whole new set of characters, new scenarios, trying to make all my new ideas sound believable.

The negative part comes because once you finish the fantasy side of writing, you need to take up the technical side – corrections, tidying the manuscript, cover design, book description, etc.

That's the hard bit.

I hope that you enjoyed South Africa – Our Land!, and also hope you can find time to give me some feedback by way of a review. Your words influence my books, so please let me know what you want to read, what you enjoyed. Good, honest opinions are worth gold!

Thanks for reading and please try the next one!

Gordon Clark

Next, a short excerpt from *Future Virus*...

# Future Virus

# PROLOGUE:
# China Crisis

**Wuhan, China**
**1st June 2019**

The laboratory was on the edge of the city, set in an area of green belt, tall bushes obscuring it from the main road. It had its own armed security force, a silver metal fence and a manned gatehouse. It didn't leave much for the Russian protection detail to do, the only possible threat being the hosts own security people, and if they turned on them, then they were beaten anyway. Four well trained men in charcoal coloured suits armed with an outdated Makarov PM revolver each was never going to be a real deterrent to the small army that the lab seemed to employ. Or were they actually Chinese military? It wasn't that easy to tell.

The whole trip was a bit of a joke really, quite a change from gathering intelligence on the Syrian border or monitoring extremist groups in Chechnya. The Chinese handled everything; the security team were just along for the hell of it they had decided, but on paper at least they were there to provide security for the three scientists and two politicians that made up the Russian party.

Right now they were sat in a small kitchen trying hard to get a decent cup of coffee from their hosts, the herbal teas that were on offer not at all to their taste. It would only need a bottle of vodka to make it feel like they were on holiday. Perhaps a beach too.

The politicians and eggheads were in a meeting room next door, discussing whatever people like them discussed. Some sort of trade deal was one rumour, something to help the Russian oil companies overcome the American sanctions another. At the end of the day, their wards were happy and in safe hands, and for the four security men that was all that mattered. Their job was done.

At breaks in the meeting – lunch, dinner, coffee, smokes – the four of them would join the rest of the group, standing on the edge of the gathering, eyes alert, hands hovering close to jackets that hid their weapons, trying hard to look like they were actually working and dangerous. In truth they just looked like something out of an American movie, totally unnecessary and over the top. But it was a job, and somebody had to do it.

They were called through now for another of the official coffee breaks, one man standing next to his Chinese equivalent on the main door, the other three spread around the room, all shadowed by the stern faced company security people. It was a bit of a game, seeing who could look the hardest, who had the best thousand yard stare.

Snippets of conversation were overheard and exchanged later when they were alone, the men bored of having nothing really to do.

"He was asking about the wet market," one of the team recounted afterwards. "What the fuck is a 'wet market' anyway?"

No-one had an answer to this. They would eventually. But even then, it wouldn't make any sense to them. Wouldn't make any sense for months to come.


The next day they were collected from their hotel's reception, the place really top-notch, classy, far better than any of the four had seen before. Travelling with politicians did have its perks it seemed.

They took a small bus, just the nine Russians, one host come tour guide who explained where they were passing in the city, offering figures like total population, factory outputs, number of hospitals in the province, airport numbers, etcetera. Bloody boring stuff, even for the scientists, but the political animals wolfed it all down, always questioning whatever fact was being offered.

To their front and rear was a police escort, behind the rear car another small bus. It looked like it contained the Chinese security team, meaning another day of them protecting their wards but also being protected themselves. Seemed like a waste of time being there, but the food and drinks in the hotel bar had helped make the trip worthwhile.

They pulled up outside of a large building, more security people already there waiting for their arrival. The Russian security troop noted that there seemed to be no locals around, as if the place had been cleared out for the visit. That just made their job much easier. Even less hassle.

The bus doors opened, and a dreadful smell invaded the interior. It was a smell they all knew well: death, the smell of blood, the dead and decaying. Possibly not human though.

They were offered face masks, and gladly put them on. It nullified the smell a little, made things slightly more bearable.

The company host led them into the building, and now they had the beginnings of an understanding into what a 'wet market' was. Even in the outer stalls they couldn't miss the dead and live animals, chickens, ducks, geese, fish.

Inside it got even more interesting.

Hanging from the ceiling were snakes – pythons was the decision in later discussion – at least three metres in length, some longer. A little Chinese man walked past with a full pig on his back. Small birds filled baskets, still alive, frightened, making one hell of a racket. Fish and frogs, dogs and bats... the place was simply unbelievable, unimaginable. Some freshly killed, some still alive, some being slaughtered there and now.

They rounded another corner and everything they'd seen previously seemed to fade into insignificance. In a cage in front of them were two bears. Bears! What the fuck!

The politicians looked like they were going to be sick, but the scientists were studying the gruesome goods as if they were all just part of a lab experiment. The four security men did what soldiers do best and made some sort of sick joke about it. From experience, they all knew it was the best way to get bad stuff out of your head.

After half an hour of wandering around the place the politicians insisted that they'd seen enough. The scientists wanted to check a few more details but were overruled.

The hosts had set-up a final meeting at the hotel, a finger buffet available on the side, this to go with cold drinks and coffees.

For some reason, the buffet went largely untouched.

The following day they flew out of Wuhan for Moscow. The trip had finished with a large dinner party, the alcohol had flowed, everything free.

The security men would quickly forget the wet market experience. At least for the next six months.

# BOOK 1:
# Virus

**Natural Born Leaders**

**20th March 2026**

Nikolai Ignatov stared blankly out of the window of the large, unlit building, seeing nothing in the driving snow, but aware that he would also be seeing nothing of note if the view was clear. It had been a long time since there had been anything worth looking at: to see people strolling below on pavements, rushing to their jobs, sightseeing, stopping to have a coffee in the curb side cafes. Beautiful women in their summer best or winter woollies. Cars, buses, trams, bicycles. All gone.

Now he knew it would be deserted, even if he could see through the blanket of white.

He couldn't believe what the world had come to. It had been a sort of social experiment, a way to flex the country's scientific muscle without actually admitting to it. 'A scare tactic' they had labelled it, something to make a mark, to ensure that the world didn't mess with them. Posturing on international borders was a thing of the past they'd decided, military exercises costing millions and only resulting in their opponents doing the same thing, neither side really wanting to take the next step, to press the button to a certain Armageddon. Yet where were they now?

He was so pleased that the rest of the world didn't know the truth. It wasn't his own fault, but it was still his country. Not Russia alone, admittedly, but still the main driver.

He looked back to his computer screen; it was a place he had been forced to spend most of his time for social interaction in the last six years. Face-to-face meetings were rare nowadays, and when they happened it was only with trusted and tested colleagues. Sex was the same, just a 'select' bunch of ladies – for that read prostitutes – who had been screened for their health, and not just for the usual STI type symptoms or for HIV of the past, but the full on check to ensure they had had no possible traces of the latest horrors, the virus. He probably met a 'real' person only a couple of days of a week, and only when it was deemed essential.

On the screen were the latest worldwide mortality figures, not at all accurate nowadays as so many countries had no way to gather them, and the communications links between the countries were unreliable at the best. Politics had always consisted of a lot of lies, he reflected, but these days it was worse. No-one wanted to admit to the horrid mess that their countries had become. Many didn't even know how bad or good it was out there. There were no media stations, no investigative reporters, no news channels. All that was long gone.

So instead of good statistics, the screen now showed him the figures that their scientists had extrapolated from data that was getting more out-of-date and less meaningful as every month went by. But it was all he had.

**INFECTIONS WORLDWIDE: 4.8 billion (62%)**

**DEATHS WORLDWIDE: 1.44 billion**

**INFECTIONS RUSSIA: 95 million (65%)**

**DEATHS RUSSIA (approx.): 38 million**

**All figures based on known statistics since 2020 outbreak.**


Despite the immensity of the figures on the screen, Nikolai barely blinked, never mind gasped. They were there daily, updates always available. He often wondered if they were far worse than those circulated, or if there was actually any chance of them really improving, something that was shown again in today's statistics, the same as they had been for the previous five months. If it was improving, then why was he not seeing it? Why were other world leaders not reporting it, not forecasting a return to the 'old' normality?

He still had some contacts out there in the big world, a place he had often travelled to before the series of country closedowns that had rocked the world. They had also led to the misreporting that had them where they all were now. The cover-up to preserve your nation. Not to admit to the total collapse of state control, of law and order. Something that was also true here at home.

He considered calling his opposite number in the United Kingdom, someone he at least trusted to tell him 'How It Is' as the man would have phrased it. He had no trust in most of his country's old allies. They had been allies of convenience, not because of respect, only necessity. For gaining a real opinion they were worth nothing.

He clicked on his contacts. Little had changed in the computer world since the virus had taken over the planet, no-one had the time or a place to work on such petty things, and the ones that did operate in that sector were mainly hackers, exploiting the aging of firewalls and IT systems, robbing companies of funds and facilities, stealing secrets that ended up having no worth. You simply didn't have a market out there to sell your ill-gotten gains to.

Humans were really such scavengers, only looking out to live. Dog eat dog. Every man for himself. A thousand other clichés.

Boris Johnson, the Prime Minister who had tried so hard to pull the UK through the virus in the early years, had eventually lost his job when he had lost his life two years back. How was still unclear, some saying he himself caught a new strain of the bug, others that the thugs roaming the land had killed him when his guard was dropped. He guessed the facts would come out one day, but when... At least things were clear with Putin: he'd taken all he needed and headed out to a dacha he'd had built far away from civilisation. No doubt he was shooting bear and eating deer even now. Him and his cronies.

The replacement in the UK was a young man, a doctor and scientist called Dominic Wild, a political maverick who would never have strayed into the political arena if life had continued in the old way. He was in his late thirties, average height, weight, appearance, not someone who you would expect to rise-up to lead a country, even in such times as this. The difference between him and 'Joe Normal' was that people trusted him, believed his calm words, hoped that he was the 'New Jesus' to take them out of this mess. He still had limited use of a nationwide radio system to get his message to the masses – they still called it the British Broadcasting Corporation, the BBC, many saying it was the modern-day BBC World Service – and people tuned into his occasional broadcasts religiously. He gave them hope in extremely troubled times, usually on a weekly basis.

It wasn't the first time that Nikolai had reached for him, but this time he wasn't just looking to compare figures or try to see where things were headed in that corner of a segregated Europe. This time he thought it was time to make something happen. And to make it happen, he needed support that other people would believe in.

He clicked on the contact name, heard the system's hands-free speaker click in, and smiled that the Norton protection software he still used was a pre-virus version. No updates, and not too much security he surmised. Probably hacked and recorded. Never mind.

The connection whirred a little, the system simulating the telephone sounds of a previous era. He knew this was unnecessary but chose to leave the noise on. It brought back memories of better times, times when the world was normal.

"Nikolai?" a voice responded from the other end of the connection. The man sounded as though he'd just woken up, but the response had been fast.

"And how is my comrade from the other side of the civilized world?" the Russian asked jokingly. "Can you recommend a good fish and chip shop in Moscow?"

He heard the sounds of a bed creaking, movement. He imagined the Englishman propping himself up, shaking his head clear to prepare himself for the exchange. It was only six in the morning in the UK, so perhaps it was a little unfair to expect a fully switched-on response.

"A bit bloody early," the Brit complained. "Had a long day yesterday, a late night. Give me a second."

The bed groaned again, the sound of padding feet on a wooden floor, a bottle opening. The phone handset was lifted, the voice returning.

"What's up then my Marxist mate?" Dominic was awake now, his educated brain in full swing again. Somehow, he knew that this call wasn't just the usual exchange of views when the Russian needed a little leg-up. "Can't be trivial, not at this hour."

Nikolai Ignatov paused a second or two before committing. This was a big step, not just a run-of-the-mill political decision, though there weren't too many of those happening nowadays. This was a possible game changer. He inhaled slowly, released his breath thoughtfully. Finally, he spoke.

"I think it time to initiate our plan."


Dominic quietly put the phone down into its cradle, his wife still snoring gently on her side of the bed. 'Girly snores' she'd call them. Over the years he'd discovered that she could sleep through anything, quite unlike his own resting patterns. He guessed this was from his junior doctoring days, sleeping wherever and whenever the opportunity presented itself, jumping fully awake at the drop of a pin.

He left the bedroom, pulling the door to and opening the fridge, looking at the limited items it held. It hadn't been full for years now. He took a swig of cold water, decided to wait for food until Trish was up and about.

It was almost spring outside, but still too dark to see far. At least it wasn't raining.

He sat down in an old leather chair that he'd hung on to since he'd first qualified as a doctor, the brown hide still beautiful to look at, but soft and worn to the contours of his frame. It was his favourite thinking place.

He reflected on the conversation with Nik. Both abbreviated the others name, both enjoyed poking friendly fun at each other. Nikolai had been a soldier prior to the crisis. He was a down-to-earth sort of man, someone you trusted. Considering the high amount of trust between the two men it was odd that the two leaders had never met. It was a sign of the times: no-one travelled much, and certainly not to other countries. Not for years. And definitely not just to meet and say hello, to cement a relationship. Perhaps one day…

Was that all about to change? he asked himself silently. 'Initiating the plan' meant that someone had to travel. Someone had to take the first step, risk the visit to the rest of the silent world. It would be a brave man, a man who quite possibly wouldn't make it back.

And he would have to make the decision as to who that person was. He would probably be signing the unfortunate man's death sentence.

It was a sobering thought, even at just after six in the morning.

He decided it was time for a coffee, something that he lived for, though the quality of the stuff nowadays was far lower than before the collapse. Trish could make her own when she eventually woke-up. He needed something to get him fully awake and thinking straight now.

It was time to work.

Printed in Great Britain
by Amazon